THE GREAT PASSAGE

Miura, Shion, 1976-
The great passage : a
novel /
2017.
33305239339736
mi 07/18/17

...E GREAT PASSAGE

a novel

Shion Miura

translated by Juliet Winters Carpenter

This is a work of fiction. Names, characters, organizations, places, events, and incidents are either products of the author's imagination or are used fictitiously. Any resemblance to actual persons, living or dead, or actual events is purely coincidental.

Text copyright © 2011 Shion Miura
Translation copyright © 2017 Juliet Winters Carpenter
All rights reserved.

No part of this book may be reproduced, or stored in a retrieval system, or transmitted in any form or by any means, electronic, mechanical, photocopying, recording, or otherwise, without express written permission of the publisher.

First published as 舟を編む *(Fune o amu)* by Kobunsha Co., Ltd. in Japan in 2011. This English edition published by arrangement with Kobunsha Co., Ltd. Tokyo through Tuttle Mori Agency, Inc., Tokyo. Translated from Japanese by Juliet Winters Carpenter. First published in English by AmazonCrossing in 2017.

Published by AmazonCrossing, Seattle

www.apub.com

Amazon, the Amazon logo, and AmazonCrossing are trademarks of Amazon.com, Inc., or its affiliates.

ISBN-13: 9781477823071
ISBN-10: 1477823077

Cover design by Adil Dara

Printed in the United States of America

CHAPTER 1

Kohei Araki had devoted his entire life—his entire working life—to dictionaries.

Words fascinated him, always had.

He had learned early on that *dog* contained other meanings besides the four-legged animal. Once when his father had taken him to the movies, a blood-spattered gangster, betrayed and dying on screen, spat out the words "Damn that dog!" So an enemy spy was a *dog*. The gang boss, upon receiving word of the gangster's demise, jumped up and shouted, "What are you all standing around here for? Polish your daggers! Don't let him die a dog's death!" So the word could also mean "pointless."

Dogs were faithful partners—trustworthy, intelligent, endearing—yet *dog* could also refer to a traitor or a condition of meaninglessness. How strange! In his child's mind he tried to work out how this could be. Faithfulness to the point of servility, devotion going pathetically unrewarded—all the more pathetic as it increased in intensity. Perhaps such canine traits were responsible for the negative associations attached to the word.

Despite his precocious interest in words, Kohei Araki's first real encounter with a dictionary came later. His working-class parents, busy stocking their hardware store and waiting on customers, had been little inclined to buy him a dictionary or urge him to study. Their educational philosophy was "If a boy is healthy and stays out of trouble, that's good enough." Araki, for his part, had been less interested in studying than in playing outdoors with his friends. The lone dictionary in his elementary school classroom had failed to impress him. It was simply there, an object whose spine occasionally entered his field of vision.

Everything changed with his first dictionary, the *Iwanami Japanese Dictionary*, a present from his uncle to celebrate the start of junior high. From the moment he took the book in his hands, he was hooked. The pleasure of opening up a dictionary of his own and leafing through it was indescribable. The entrancing shiny cover, the closely printed lines on every page, the feel of the thin paper. Most of all, he liked the concise definitions.

One night, as he and his younger brother were romping in the living room, their father had scolded them: "Keep your voices down!" As an experiment Araki had looked up the word *koe* (voice). This was the definition:

> *koe* (noun) 1. sounds people and animals make using a special organ in the throat. 2. a sound resembling vocal utterance. 3. the approach of a season or a time of life.

Examples of the word's usage were also listed. Some were familiar, like *koe o ageru* (to raise one's voice) or *mushi no koe* (the cry of an insect). Others would never have occurred to him: to sense the approach of autumn was to "hear the voice of autumn," to be nearing one's forties was to "hear the voice of forty." The idea was novel to him, but he realized it was true: *koe* could definitely convey "the approach of a season or a time of life." Just like *dog*, the word contained a range of meanings. Reading the dictionary could awaken you to new meanings of commonly used words, meanings of surprising breadth and depth.

Still, that bit about "a special organ in the throat" was cryptic. Forgetting his father's scolding, forgetting even his kid brother clamoring for attention, Araki looked up *tokushu* and *kikan*, the words for "special" and "organ."

> *tokushu* (adj.) 1. qualitatively different from the ordinary; having a particular nature. 2. (philosophy) that which is individual, as opposed to universal.

> *kikan* (noun) a constituent part of an organism that has a fixed morphology and carries out a certain physiological function.

It wasn't all that helpful; it was rather confusing, actually. Since he knew that the "special organ in the throat" could only be the vocal cords, Araki dropped the matter. But anyone ignorant of vocal cords would be left in the dark as to what the "special organ in the throat" might be.

Far from dampening Araki's interest, the discovery that his dictionary wasn't perfect only fanned his ardor. If some definitions weren't quite successful, he liked the way they at least made a good effort. The dictionary's very flaws made the exertions and enthusiasm of its compilers real to his imagination. The vast array of words—entry words, definitions, examples—was cold and impersonal at a glance, yet the book as a whole was the result of people puzzling over their choices. What patience they must have, what deep attachment to words!

Araki began saving up his allowance for trips to the used bookstore. When a new edition of a dictionary came out, a copy of the earlier edition could usually be purchased on the cheap. Little by little he collected a variety of dictionaries from different publishers and compared them. Some were tattered and worn. Others had annotations and underlining in red. Old dictionaries bore signs of the linguistic struggles of compiler and user alike.

Araki dreamed of becoming a philologist or a scholar of the Japanese language and getting his name on a dictionary. The summer before his senior year in high school he asked his father to send him to college.

"Huh? You want to study Japanese? What are you talking about? You already speak Japanese. What do you need to go to college for?"

"No, that's not the point."

"Never mind. How about helping out around the store? Your mother's back pain is getting worse."

He couldn't get through to his father, but his uncle, the one who'd given him the *Iwanami Japanese Dictionary*, pled his case for him. A crewman on a whaling boat, this uncle had learned to appreciate dictionaries on long sea voyages. Within the family he was known as an eccentric. On a rare visit with Araki's parents, he had interceded on the young man's behalf: "He's a pretty smart kid. Why not go ahead and send him to college?" Araki's father had listened and ultimately agreed.

Araki studied furiously and managed to pass the difficult college entrance examination. Over the next four years it became clear to him that he lacked the makings of a scholar, but his desire to compile a dictionary stayed strong.

In his senior year, Shogakukan began to put out its *Great Dictionary of Japanese*. It was a massive achievement, a twenty-volume behemoth over a decade in the making, with some 450,000 entries by as many as 3,000 contributors. Such a marvel was far beyond the means of a penniless student. As he surveyed the tomes on the college library shelf, Araki trembled at the thought of the passion and time involved in creating them. There in the dusty library stacks, the dictionary seemed to emit a light as pure as the beams of the moon.

The name Kohei Araki might never lend scholarly cachet to the cover of a dictionary, but another path remained open to him: he could serve as an editor. His mind fastened on the idea. What else but dictionaries could he pour his passion and time into without the least regret? He applied himself to job hunting and was hired by a prominent publishing house, Gembu Books.

"From then on, for thirty-seven years, all I've done is make dictionaries."

"Really? That long?"

"Easily. It's been more than thirty years since I first met you, you know. Back then you were a little, shall we say, shaggier." Araki cast his eyes on the bald pate of Professor Matsumoto, who was sitting across from him.

Professor Matsumoto laid down the pencil he was using to write on a file card and laughed, his thin body shaking like a crane. "You've gathered quite a bit of hoarfrost on top yourself."

Their orders arrived—soba noodles, accompanied by a pungent dipping sauce. It was lunchtime, and businessmen and women on their breaks crowded the shop. The two men were quiet for a while, concentrating on their meals. As he ate, Professor Matsumoto, always on the lookout for unusual vocabulary or usage, kept an ear cocked to the stream of words coming from the television on the wall. As usual, Araki kept his eyes fixed on the professor's hands, knowing that when the professor became engrossed in word collecting he was apt to reach for a mouthful of noodles with his pencil or to attempt to scribble with a chopstick.

When they had finished eating, they sipped cold barley tea and relaxed.

Araki said, "What was your first dictionary, may I ask?"

"One I inherited from my grandfather, Fumihiko Otsuki's pioneering *Sea of Words*. When I found out Otsuki compiled the whole thing himself, overcoming a slew of challenges, child as I was it made a great impression on me."

"I'm sure it did, but I'm just as sure you must have tried looking up a few dirty words."

"Certainly not."

"Oh, no?" Araki said. "As I mentioned, my first was the *Iwanami Japanese Dictionary*, the one I got when I entered junior high school. I went thumbing through it, looking up every indecent word I could think of."

"But that dictionary is extremely refined and proper. I can only imagine how disappointed you must have been."

"I was. For *chinchin*, the only meanings listed were 'sit up and beg'—the dog's trick—and 'the sound of a kettle boiling.' Not a word about peckers . . . You do realize you're admitting you looked them up, too?"

Professor Matsumoto chuckled.

The lunch hour was almost over. The noodle joint was nearly empty now, and the proprietress came over and refilled their glasses.

"You know," said Araki, "I've had the privilege of working with you for a long time now, but we've never traded memories about dictionaries like this."

"We certainly have made a lot of them together," said Professor Matsumoto. "No sooner would we finish one than we'd start right in on revisions and amendments. There was never time to chat. First *Gembu Dictionary of Modern Japanese*, then *Gembu Student's Dictionary of Japanese*, then *Wordmaster*. Ah, what memories!"

"I deeply regret that I can't be of any more assistance on our latest project." Araki placed both hands on the tabletop and lowered his head until it nearly touched the surface.

Professor Matsumoto, who was bundling up his file cards, seemed to deflate. For once his shoulders slumped. "Then you weren't able to postpone your retirement?"

"The rules are the rules," said Araki.

"You could stay on part-time."

"I intend to come into the office when I can, but my wife isn't well. So far I've spent our marriage up to my ears in dictionaries and never done anything for her. I'd like to spend my retirement at her side."

"I see." Professor Matsumoto let his head drop momentarily to his chest, then said in a clear show of bravado, "Yes, that's what you should do. It's your turn to be there for her."

If I sap his motivation, thought Araki, *what kind of an editor does that make me?* He leaned forward. "Before I retire, I'm determined to find someone to replace me. Someone who can offer you all the assistance you need, take charge of the editorial department, and carry our plan forward. Someone young and promising."

"Editing a dictionary isn't like editing any other book or magazine," the professor pointed out. "It's a peculiar world. You need extreme patience, a capacity for endless minutiae, a love of words bordering on obsession, and a broad enough outlook to stay sane. What makes you think there are any young people like that nowadays?"

"There's got to be someone. If I can't find the right person among our company's five hundred employees, I'll go headhunting. Promise me that you'll continue to give Gembu Books the benefit of your wisdom in the coming years."

Professor Matsumoto nodded and said quietly, "I'm blessed to have been able to make dictionaries with you, Araki. No matter how hard you try to find a successor, I know I'll never encounter another editor of your caliber."

Moved, Araki bit his lip to keep from emitting a small sob. He had spent more than three decades alongside Professor Matsumoto, immersed in books and galleys, and now that shared time seemed like a beautiful dream. "Thank you, sir."

It tore at Araki to have to leave just as they'd completed plans for a new dictionary. Dictionaries were in his blood and had been his lifelong passion; he now felt the stirrings of a new, related mission. The affection, loneliness, and anxiety he read on Professor Matsumoto's face inspired him. Until now he'd assumed his role before retiring was to shepherd the plans for the new dictionary to completion, but he'd been wrong. *My task is to find someone who loves dictionaries as much as I do—no, more.* He would do it for the professor's sake. For the sake of all those who used or were learning to use Japanese. And most of all, for the sake of that hallowed book-to-be, the dictionary itself.

Araki went back to the office keen to carry out his last great task.

He swiftly contacted the company's other editorial divisions to inquire if they had any likely candidates, but the results were discouraging. All anyone seemed interested in was a quick profit. The economic slump meant that every department had its back to the wall. The responses he got were all similar. If he needed help with a magazine where advertisers were sure to flock, say, or with a book with relatively inexpensive content, sure—they would welcome these projects—but they had no one to spare for dictionary work. Araki grew frustrated. *Dictionaries are well respected, and they're immune to market fluctuations. Isn't there anyone with the balls to aim high and think long-term?*

"Forget it." Nishioka appeared from between the bookcases and responded to the thoughts Araki had muttered aloud. "Dictionaries cost a vast amount of money and take an enormous amount of time to produce. People have always preferred to make a quick buck, and they always will." He went over to his desk and sat down.

Nishioka was right. The Dictionary Editorial Department of Gembu Books had been hit hard by the recession, forced to slash its budget and staff. The plan for the new dictionary had been stalled and was still awaiting approval.

Araki flipped through *Wide Garden of Words* and *Great Forest of Words*, both of which he kept on his desk, checking the difference between *vast* and *enormous*. He clucked his tongue as he searched. "Don't make it sound like this has nothing to do with you, Nishioka.

If you did your job right, I wouldn't have all this trouble, and you know it."

"Yes, boss. I apologize."

"You're just not cut out to be a lexicographer. When you're out picking up manuscripts, your footwork is nice and fast, but that's about it."

"Now, don't be mean." Without getting up, Nishioka kicked the floor and rolled his chair over. "My footwork just brought in a nice juicy piece of news, I'll have you know."

"What is it?"

"There's somebody who's perfectly cut out to be a lexicographer."

"Where?" Araki sprang to his feet.

Nishioka gave a teasing smile. Then, dramatically lowering his voice even though no one else was around, he whispered, "Sales department. Twenty-seven years old, same as me."

"Good grief!" Araki said, whacking Nishioka on the top of the head. "Are you telling me you were both hired in the same year? Why didn't you say anything sooner?"

"That's the thanks I get?" Nishioka rubbed his crown ruefully and rolled his chair back to his desk. "As a matter of fact, we weren't hired at the same time. This somebody went to grad school. Been here just going on three years."

"Sales, eh?"

"Dashing over there right now won't do any good. Everybody's probably making the rounds."

But Araki was already out the door.

The Dictionary Editorial Department was on the second floor of the annex, an old high-ceilinged wooden building with floorboards that had darkened to the color of toffee. Araki's footsteps rang out in the dim corridor. He raced down the stairs, pushed open the double doors, and was suddenly blinded by the early-summer sun. Squinting, he made out the eight-story main building next door and headed for the entrance.

He stepped inside the offices of the sales department, to the rear on the first floor, then pulled up short. Damn it, he'd forgotten to ask one crucial bit of information—his potential successor's name. He didn't even know if it was a he or a she.

He calmed himself at the doorway, looking around with a nonchalant air. Fortunately, the sales staff had not all taken off on rounds. Six or seven people were sitting at desks, either facing computers or talking on the phone. *Which one is a twenty-seven-year-old with a graduate degree who's been here going on three years? This'll be awkward; they all look about thirty. God knows which one I'm after. What's wrong with the sales department, anyway? Somebody ought to make these people get off their butts and go out to bookstores. All except the one I want, that is.*

As Araki stood lost in thought, the employee sitting nearest to him came up and asked, "Are you looking for someone, sir?" She tried to lead him back toward the entrance, apparently mistaking him for an outsider who'd wandered in without first stopping at reception. Despite Araki's thirty-seven years next door in the annex, many veteran employees at Gembu had never laid eyes on him.

"Ah, no, that is . . ." He tried to explain the nature of his errand and stumbled over his words. His eyes were drawn to a young man in a corner of the room.

The young man was standing with his back turned, facing a row of shelves along the wall. He was tall and thin, with hair that was awfully unkempt for someone in sales. He'd taken off his suit coat and rolled up his sleeves, getting ready to rearrange the shelves. Araki watched as he took boxes, large and small, and whisked them around from one shelf to another until they fit together snugly in apple-pie order. His movements were deft, like those of someone assembling a complicated jigsaw puzzle in the blink of an eye.

Araki held back a low cry of exultation. Such dexterity was crucial for anyone involved in compiling a dictionary. In the final stages of editing, the number of pages was fixed and immutable, as any change would affect the printing and price. Fitting the contents into the allotted number of pages meant making swift decisions in a short time—eliminating illustrative quotations, however reluctantly, or condensing definitions. Exactly the sort of puzzle-solving knack that the young man had just displayed.

This was the one! The very one suited to becoming the next head of the Dictionary Editorial Department!

"Tell me something." Unable to contain his excitement, Araki turned to the woman standing beside him. "That young man over there—what's he like?"

"What do you mean?" She sounded wary.

"I'm Kohei Araki, from the Dictionary Editorial Department. What can you tell me about him? He's twenty-seven and this is his third year here after grad school, is that right?"

"I think so, but you'd better ask him. He's *majime*."

Majime, eh? Serious, diligent. Araki nodded in satisfaction. This was very good. Lexicography was slow and steady work—exactly the sort of work that required someone *majime* at the helm.

The woman turned toward the man, who was now double-checking his handiwork, and called, "Majime! You have a visitor."

He'd told her he was from the Dictionary Editorial Department, not a visitor—didn't she get it? Araki was peeved, but persuaded himself that she may have used the word in the simple sense of a "caller," without any nuance of "outsider." More worrisome was the fact that she'd actually called the fellow Majime. Just how serious would a person have to be to earn such a nickname? This wasn't a schoolyard where kids scattered after school let out, or a police department overrun with detectives in jeans. It was a dignified publishing company. Yet here was somebody whose very nickname was Majime. He must be megaserious. *Proceed with caution,* Araki told himself as he eyed his prospect with greater intensity.

In response to the woman's summons, the man looked back. He was wearing silver-framed glasses. And yet his nickname wasn't Megane (Specs) but Majime. As Araki braced himself, the bespectacled young man came over slowly, seemingly ill at ease in his lanky frame.

"Yes? I'm Majime."

Whoa. Did the guy pride himself on his seriousness, or what? Araki was taken aback but managed to recover without betraying his shock. He felt his eagerness to recruit this man rapidly melting away. To brazenly declare oneself Majime showed a total lack of *majime*. Somewhere inside he was making light of the virtue of diligence; he probably had no idea of its true importance. In any case, this was not somebody to whom he could entrust the making of dictionaries.

As Araki stood silently glaring, the young man seemed baffled. He ran a hand through his hair, messing it up still more. Then, apparently hitting on an idea, he pulled out a card case from his shirt pocket. With a slight bow, he held a business card out in both hands. His movements were slow and clumsy.

Araki felt let down, indignant. Didn't this greenhorn know better than to hand out his card to strangers? Besides, they worked for the same company! Keeping his irritation under wraps, he glanced down at the card in the young man's hands. The nails at the tips of his long fingers were round edged and neatly trimmed. The business card bore this inscription:

Mitsuya Majime
Sales Department
Gembu Books, Inc.

The characters for Majime were not what Araki had assumed them to be. The meaning was not "diligent" but "horse dealer."

"Mitsuya Majime . . ."

"Yes, that's right. I am Majime." He smiled. "You must have gotten the wrong idea from the sound of my name."

"I beg your pardon." Hastily, Araki retrieved one of his own business cards from his back pocket. "I'm Araki, from the Dictionary Editorial Department."

Majime politely studied the business card. Behind the silver frames his eyes were clear and calm. The cut of his shirt was a bit out of fashion. He didn't seem to pay much attention to his personal appearance, but his skin was taut. He was still young—young enough to have decades ahead of him to devote to dictionaries. Araki felt a twinge of jealousy but did not, of course, let on.

"That's a very unusual surname. Where are you from?"

"Tokyo, but my parents are from Wakayama. Apparently *majime* was the word for 'wholesale dealer' there."

"Ah—as in a person who controls horses, supplies them to travelers." Araki searched his pockets, but unfortunately he hadn't brought his notebook. He scribbled a note on the back of Majime's business card.

MAJIME—"WHOLESALE DEALER"
NOT IN WGW OR GFW. MUST CHECK GDJL.

Though not as dedicated as Professor Matsumoto, Araki had a habit of recording unfamiliar words on the spot. Afterward he would check the index cards in the office. If there wasn't an index card for the word he'd written down, he would track down the source (if possible, the earliest recorded occurrence) and add another card to the growing collection. The office contained a vast number of index cards. In compiling a dictionary, deciding which of the words listed on these cards to include took careful consideration. Electronic data was playing an increasingly prominent role, but the card stacks were the department's heart and soul. Long before the movement to divide workplaces into smoking and nonsmoking areas, smoking had been strictly forbidden in the room where the card stacks were stored.

The sight of Araki suddenly jotting down a memorandum on the back of his business card seemed not to surprise or upset Majime in the least. "People are always asking me about the origin of my name," he said, "but nobody's ever written it down before." He peered with calm interest at what Araki had written.

That's right, you're here to recruit this fellow. Distracted by the man's unusual family name, for a second Araki had forgotten his purpose in coming. He tucked the card and pen in his breast pocket and cleared his throat. "If someone asked you to define the word *migi*, 'right,' what would you say?"

"'Right' as in the direction, or 'right' as in politics?"

"The former."

"Let me think." He tilted his head pensively, swinging his long hair. "Defining it as 'the hand used to hold a pen or chopsticks' would ignore all the left-handed people in the world. 'The side of the body that doesn't contain the heart' wouldn't work, either, since a few people do have their heart on the right side. Maybe something like this would be the safest: 'when facing north, the side of the body that is to the east.'"

"Okay. Then how would you explain *shima*?"

"'Stripes' . . . 'island' . . . the place name . . . the suffix in words like *yokoshima*"—evil—"and *sakashima*"—upside down—"'conjecture,' as in the four-character phrase *shima okusoku*"—conjecture and surmise—". . . the four devils of Buddhism . . ."

As Majime reeled off possible candidates, Araki hastily cut him short. "*Shima* as in 'island.'"

"All right. Something like 'a body of land surrounded by water'? No, that wouldn't do. Enoshima is connected by a bridge with the mainland. In which case . . ." Majime muttered to himself with his head still pensively tilted to one side, seemingly oblivious to Araki as he considered the meaning of the word. "Maybe something like 'a comparatively small body of land surrounded or set off by water.' But wait, that's no good, either. It doesn't include the sense of 'gangster territory.' Then how about 'land set apart from its surroundings'?"

He was the genuine article. Araki looked on with admiration. It had only taken seconds for Majime to work out the underlying meaning of *shima*. Back when he'd put the same question to Nishioka, the results had been dismal. Nishioka had never considered any possible meaning but "island," and his answer had been "something sticking up from the sea." Appalled, Araki had yelled, "Idiot! Then the back of a whale and a drowned man are *shima*, are they?" Nishioka had looked flustered and then laughed foolishly. "Oops. You're right. Gee, that's a tough one. What should I say, then?"

Majime stood, nodding intently to himself, and then swiveled toward the bookcases. "Let me go look it up."

"Never mind." Araki grabbed him by the arm. Looking him straight in the eye, he said, "Majime, I want you to give all you've got to Daitokai!"

"Daitokai?" said Majime. "Okay." The next moment he let out a kind of yodel. Everyone turned and stared. Araki was perplexed, but as Majime went on singing it dawned on him. This was the hit song "Daitokai"—"The Big City"—by Crystal King! Sung totally off-key.

Quickly he yanked Majime out into the corridor, midwarble. "No, no, that's not it. Forget it."

"No?" Majime broke off, looking disconsolate. "Sorry about that. I'm not really up on the latest songs."

Where the hell did he get the idea he'd been asked to sing? The fellow's thought processes were mystifying. Araki decided to tell him what he'd come for.

"Listen to me. *Daitokai—The Great Passage*—is the name of a new dictionary, one that's still in the planning stage. The title is written with the characters for 'crossing the ocean.' And I want to entrust the job to you."

"A dictionary?" Majime's eyes and mouth went round with astonishment. He stood frozen.

Like a pigeon hit by a peashooter, mused Araki. This was exactly the look of thunderstruck astonishment the phrase referred to. Yes, and just the other day he'd read that in a row of chanters for certain scenes in *bunraku*, the traditional puppet theater, the last one is called a *mamegui* (pea-eater), supposedly because of the way he moves his mouth while trying to keep up, as if munching on peas. *I wonder if any dictionaries carry that word. I'll have to check it out and then decide whether or not to include it in* The Great Passage . . .

The two men stood silent, each absorbed in his private rumination, while others passed by them with strange looks.

At last Majime unfroze. "Actually—I'm sorry. Today I'm scheduled to make the rounds of Shibuya bookstores, starting at one thirty."

"I see." It was already one fifteen. He couldn't possibly make it to Shibuya on time. Would he be all right?

Majime checked his watch, then scrambled back to his desk with that same ungainly gait, grabbed his suit coat and a black briefcase, and was back. "I'm really sorry," he said again with a bow, managing to muss his long hair still more. Then he dashed off, twice tripping over his own feet on the way.

Watching Majime go, Araki wondered again if he would be all right—in more senses than one. Majime seemed to be under the impression that he'd been asked to work on the dictionary just for today. Why would he think such a thing? Shaking his head, Araki got into the elevator to sound out the head of the sales department.

After patient negotiations, official permission was finally granted for the making of a new dictionary to be entitled *The Great Passage*. At the same time, Majime was transferred out of sales to join the dictionary editorial staff, bringing with him a small cardboard box packed with his things. There were two months remaining until Araki's retirement. Seeing Majime standing in the office doorway, Araki breathed a sigh of relief. This was cutting it close, but he had pulled it off.

No negotiations had been necessary to pry Majime from the sales team. The department head had been delighted—"Majime? Yeah, we've got someone by that name. Seriously? You'll take him?" The personnel manager was merely mystified: "Who?"

Araki felt he understood why. When he'd first approached Majime, the young man's reaction had been off-the-wall. He must never have expected anyone to take him seriously. He'd languished in such obscurity that if Araki hadn't asked for him by name, his immediate superiors never would have taken note of his existence.

Araki also sensed just why Majime's profile had been so low. Beyond the admitted oddity of his ways—who else would burst into a loud, off-key rendition of a popular song on company time?—he was a square peg in a round hole. The firm had failed to assess him properly, breaking its own rule—"the right person in the right place." His strengths were many: an uncanny feeling for words; a conscientiousness that had led him to marshal every scrap of knowledge he possessed to answer Araki's questions. Conscientiousness that went overboard, which was what made him such an odd fish—and would make him a great lexicographer.

Responding to Araki's body language, Nishioka got up and greeted Majime cheerily. "Welcome to the Dictionary Editorial Department!" He snatched the cardboard box from Majime's hands and led him inside the office. "We're shorthanded right now, so there are plenty of desks to choose from. How about this one?"

Majime glanced around the room with its rows of tall bookcases as he proceeded to the desk beside Nishioka's. "Sure," he said, nodding meekly.

"So, Majime," said Nishioka. "Got a girlfriend?"

Nishioka had the notion that talking about girls was a good way to break the ice. From his desk, at a remove from theirs, Araki silently observed Majime's reaction.

"No."

"Then let's organize a mixer. I'll set it up. Let me have your cell number and address."

"I don't have a cell phone. I returned the company one I was using before."

"How come?" Nishioka looked as shocked as if he'd seen a walking mummy. "Don't you want a girlfriend?"

"I don't know. Never really thought about it. Whether I want a girlfriend or a cell phone, either one."

Nishioka shot Araki a pleading look.

Stifling a laugh, Araki managed to smooth things over and maintain his dignity. "Majime, there's a welcome party for you tonight. We reserved a table at Seven Treasures Garden for six o'clock. Nishioka, go get Mrs. Sasaki."

At Seven Treasures Garden, Professor Matsumoto was already seated at a round red table, drinking Shaoxing wine. Once a week he allowed himself to enjoy a drink, or two or three. Even while drinking, he was never without his cards and pencil.

Araki sat down and began the introductions. "Masashi Nishioka here, you already know. Next to him is Mrs. Kaoru Sasaki. She mostly keeps track of the index cards and classifies them for us."

As her name was spoken, Mrs. Sasaki, a woman in her early forties, nodded without changing her expression. What she lacked in warmth she made up for in efficiency, Araki thought. She was an indispensable member of the team. At first she'd been a part-time employee, but now, her children nearly grown, she was a full-time contract employee.

What would Professor Matsumoto think of Majime? Araki was tense. The professor greeted him with a light, unreadable smile.

Majime bowed his head awkwardly to each person in turn.

Someone proposed a toast, and then the food started to arrive.

With his usual tact, Nishioka first served Professor Matsumoto from the array of appetizers, making sure to skip the preserved duck eggs, which he knew the professor disliked. Ah, but what about the all-important Majime? Araki glanced toward him in time to see him pour beer into Mrs. Sasaki's glass with such exuberance that the froth overflowed. *Nice try. You almost had it.* Araki was beginning to feel as if he'd taken on a kindergartener. Mrs. Sasaki seemed to share the impression. Still impassive, she was tolerantly filling Majime's glass in return.

"What's your hobby, Majime?" Nishioka boldly asked, searching for a friendly overture.

A bit of wood ear mushroom was sticking out of a corner of Majime's mouth. He swallowed it and considered the question before answering. "If I had to pick something, I guess it would be watching people get on the escalator."

Silence descended on the table.

"Is it interesting?" Mrs. Sasaki asked evenly.

"Yes, it is." Majime leaned forward slightly. "After I step off the train onto the platform, I make a point of walking slowly. People rush past me to get on the escalator, but there's never any struggle or confusion. You'd think somebody was controlling them, the way they line up in two rows and get on the escalator. Not only that. The people on the left stand still and are carried up, while the ones on the right walk. They divide up neatly, even at rush hour. It's beautiful."

"Sorry, boss, but isn't he kind of a weirdo?" Nishioka whispered in Araki's ear.

Ignoring this, Araki looked over Nishioka's head and locked eyes with Professor Matsumoto, who nodded comprehendingly. They both understood what it was that Majime sought to convey. People swarming onto the train platform, lining up at the escalator as if controlled by a puppet master, and then whisked neatly upward—just as vast numbers of sprawling words were codified and connected, ending up arranged in orderly fashion on the pages of a dictionary. Majime's perception of beauty and joy in that process marked him beyond all doubt as a born lexicographer.

"Do you know why we decided to call our new dictionary *The Great Passage*?" Araki asked, unable to contain himself.

Majime was nibbling peanuts one at a time, squirrel-like. Mrs. Sasaki tapped a finger lightly on the table to draw his attention. Only then did he realize that the question had been addressed to him. Flustered, he shook his head.

"A dictionary is a ship that crosses the sea of words," said Araki, with a sense that he was laying bare his innermost soul. "People travel on it and gather the small points of light floating on the dark surface of the waves. They do this in order to tell someone their thoughts accurately, using the best possible words. Without dictionaries, all any of us could do is linger before the vastness of the deep."

"We need to build a ship suitable for an ocean crossing," Professor Matsumoto said quietly. "With that thought in mind, Araki and I decided on this title."

It's in your hands now. As if he had heard these unspoken words, Majime lowered his hands to the table and straightened his back. His eyes were shining. "How many entries will there be? What will set *The Great Passage* apart from other dictionaries? I want to hear all about it."

Professor Matsumoto put down his chopsticks and picked up his pencil. Mrs. Sasaki took out a notebook from her briefcase and laid it open.

Araki said, "Okay, here goes," and opened his mouth to relate his conception of the new dictionary.

"Wait!" interrupted Nishioka. "There's something else we need to do first. This calls for another toast." With one hand he refilled Professor Matsumoto's glass with Shaoxing wine, and with the other he gave the lazy Susan a spin so that the beer traveled around the table and everyone had something to drink.

"Allow me to do the honors." Nishioka held his glass high. "May there be smooth sailing ahead for the Dictionary Editorial Department! *Kampai!*"

"Kampai!" everyone echoed.

Laughter broke out. Majime cheerfully clinked glasses with Professor Matsumoto.

Make it a good stout ship, Araki thought, closing his eyes. *One that many people can travel on safely for a long time. One that will be a comforting partner throughout their journey, even on days of crushing loneliness.*

I know you people can do it.

CHAPTER 2

"I'm back," Mitsuya Majime announced to his empty room upon his return.

He set down his heavy briefcase and opened the wood-frame window, humming a line from a popular song: "Under the window, the River Kanda." Except that in his case it wasn't the River Kanda but a narrow canal. He sang anyway, out of habit. The Ferris wheel in Korakuen Amusement Park loomed high in the evening sky.

He felt worn out.

Leaving the light off, he sprawled on the floor in the middle of the six-mat room. It had been nearly three months now since his transfer, but he still wasn't used to his new job. The hours were nine to six, with none of the usual obligatory drinking with colleagues afterward. It should have been many times easier to handle than his old job in sales, yet he was always worn out.

Today he'd taken the long way home, transferring on the subway line even though it was an easy walk from Gembu to his lodging house. He'd wanted to watch passengers ride the escalator, but the sight hadn't cheered him the way he'd hoped. He'd been a little ahead of the evening rush hour, so the passengers were mostly old people and housewives. Perhaps unused to station escalators, they had fumbled and ridden in chaotic fashion, with none of the orderly beauty he craved.

All at once he felt a heavy warmth on his stomach. He lifted his head and checked. Yes, it was the cat, Tora. Whenever he came home and opened the window, Tora dropped in to say hello.

There was nothing on hand to eat, and Majime didn't have the energy to go out shopping. He could make do with instant ramen noodles, but what about Tora?

"Dried sardines okay with you?" he asked, stroking the cat's head. Tora purred and flicked his bobtail, striking Majime on the chest. The pressure of the cat's weight was uncomfortable. Tora was getting tubby.

Majime had been living in this lodging house for nearly ten years. A college freshman in the beginning, he was now pushing thirty. Tora, once a bedraggled kitten mewing piteously in the rain, had grown into this oversized specimen of a ginger tabby. Only the two-story wooden building in this quiet residential neighborhood was unchanged. Maybe it had already been so old when he'd moved in that it couldn't look any older.

With Tora still curled up on him, he reached up and pulled the long cord hanging from the fluorescent light overhead. He called it his "lazycord." There was a small gold bell attached to the tip, and he tapped it to rouse Tora's interest. When the big cat finally jumped off him, he stood up.

Looking around the brightened interior, Majime sighed. The first-floor room was pretty drab. All his clothes and everyday items were shelved in the built-in closet, behind sliding doors. A small writing desk and wall-to-wall bookshelves were the only other pieces of furniture in the room. Still more books lay piled—or spilled—on the tatami mats.

In fact, this was only part of Majime's collection; his books occupied the entire downstairs floor.

Nowadays nobody wanted to live in a lodging house. Like maple leaves leaving a branch, the other lodgers had gradually drifted away, leaving only him. He'd been quick to take advantage of the opportunity, moving books first into the room next door, then the one two doors down. Finally his landlady, Také, had vacated her first-floor room by the stairs to live on the second floor. She was a good-hearted soul and readily accepted the new arrangement. "Those floor-to-ceiling bookshelves of yours are like extra pillars. This way I don't have to worry about earthquakes."

The weight of the "pillars" threatened to push the lodging house off its foundation, but neither of them worried about such details. She never raised the rent, and Majime was so absentminded that he went right on paying for the one room without stopping to think that his rent didn't cover the extra space he had appropriated.

And so he and his books occupied the downstairs, and she had the upstairs to herself.

What if the interior of a room mirrors the interior of its inhabitant? he wondered. That would make him someone who stored up words but couldn't put them to use, a dry-as-dust bore.

He took out a pack of Nupporo Number One, soy sauce flavor, from the cupboard. A nearby discount shop sold this instant ramen by the case at a bargain price, but it seemed suspiciously fake. The instructions were full of obvious mistakes: "Five hundred liters of water will reach the boiling point." "You should break noodles after throwing them in." "Enjoy eggs, green onion, ham, and so forth." Five hundred liters of water seemed altogether too much, but Majime liked the earnest tone of the instructions, and lately he'd been eating a lot of Nupporo Number One.

With the packet of noodles in hand, he opened the ill-fitting door and headed to the communal kitchen, with Tora padding behind him. With every step, the wooden floor creaked like the hull of a ship.

As he was hunting on the shelf below the sink for Tora's dried sardines, a voice called from upstairs. "Mitsu, is that you?"

"Yes, I'm back," he said, turning and looking up.

Také's face appeared at the top of the stairs. "I made too much for one person. It's suppertime, so won't you join me?"

"Thank you. I'd be happy to."

Instant ramen in one hand and dried sardines in the other, he climbed the stairs, Tora at his heels.

Také's living room was the first room at the top of the stairs. The next room was her bedroom, and the one next to that she called the guest room. Not that she ever had any guests. The guest room served as storage space.

Both floors had a toilet, but the upstairs was a bit more compact, having no kitchen, bath, or laundry area. Instead, just outside the window there was a clothes-drying platform with a fine view. It might have been called a *veranda* or a *balcony*, but it was made of unfinished wood and looked like a slatted drainboard with a railing. There was no more fitting term for it than *clothes-drying platform.*

"May I come in?" Majime said politely.

He stepped into the room and stopped short. Out on the clothes-drying platform stood a display of silver pampas grass and round white dumplings, the traditional accompaniments for autumn moon viewing. Ah—so tonight was the harvest moon. All the while he'd been struggling to fit in at his new job, the seasons had continued their stately progression.

Tora nibbled some dried sardine from Majime's hand and meowed at the still-invisible moon. Majime opened the window a crack for him, and he slipped outside.

Také invited Majime to sit down, and he joined her at the little table covered with dishes: steamed spinach, boiled chicken and taro, cucumber salad, and more.

"I've got some of these, too," she said, setting out croquettes she must have picked up at the store. "Young people need to eat."

She served him miso soup with tofu, then piled a generous mound of rice in his bowl. All the dishes (except the salad, of course) were piping hot. She must have timed her preparations to his arrival and then casually invited him up.

"It looks delicious," he said gratefully, and for a time occupied himself solely with filling his stomach. She said nothing while he ate. He finished munching the cucumbers and then asked, "Did you feel that I needed cheering up?"

"You do seem pretty glum these days." She sipped her soup. "Is it your job?"

"I have too many things to decide. I feel like my head's going to explode."

"Oh, dear. And your brains are your one strong suit."

Ouch, he thought, but it was true. Apart from studying and thinking, he really wasn't good at much else.

"That's the trouble." He looked at the plump grains of rice, lit by the overhead light. "Back in the sales department, my job was clearly defined. All I had to do was go around to bookstores. The goal was clear, and I only needed to apply myself, so it was comfortable in a way. Making a dictionary's not like that. Everybody has to put their heads together to come up with ideas, and all the tasks have to be divided among us."

"Well, what's wrong with that?"

"Thinking is no problem, but conveying my thoughts to other people is hard for me. The simple truth is, I just don't fit in."

"Mitsu, be honest. When in your life did you ever fit in? You've always got your nose in a book, and you've never brought a single friend or girlfriend here."

"I don't have friends or a girlfriend."

"Then why let it bother you now all of a sudden, if you don't fit in?"

Why, indeed.

All his life, he'd been pegged as a weirdo. Both in school and at work, people had kept their distance. Occasionally, out of curiosity or goodwill, someone would speak to him, but his response would be so off the mark that they would disappear with a slight smile. He always thought he was responding honestly and openly, but people never seemed to warm to him.

The pain of such encounters had driven him to the pages of books. No matter how poor he was at communicating with people, with books he could engage in deep, quiet dialogue. There was an added benefit:

if he opened one during free time at school, his classmates would leave him alone and not try to strike up a conversation.

Reading did wonders for his grades. He grew interested in words as a means of communicating thoughts and feelings, and majored in linguistics at college. But however knowledgeable about language he became, he was no better at using it to communicate. Sadly, he couldn't seem to do anything about this, so he'd given up and more or less accepted his lot. Being transferred to the Dictionary Editorial Department had given him hope.

"Mitsu, you want to get along with your colleagues, don't you?" Také asked. "You want to get along with them and make a great dictionary together."

Majime looked up in surprise. He did long to communicate, to connect. The maelstrom of emotions he felt boiled down to that desire, he realized. "How did you know?"

"Mitsu, you and I are *tsu-ka*. We're in perfect sync." She pushed the lever on top of the electric kettle and filled the teapot. "But what are you doing fretting about something so childish at your age? You're a silly Billy who thinks too much."

Chastened, he fell quiet and concentrated on polishing off his croquette. While eating, he thought about that expression, *tsu-ka*. Why should the idea that two people were on the same wavelength be expressed that way? The full expression was "one says *tsu*, the other *ka*." He'd read about the etymology once in some book, but as he recalled there was no definitive answer. Dictionaries were better off staying away from etymologies unless they could be proven beyond all doubt. Words mostly just sprang up without any how or when, anyway.

Still, it bothered him. Why not "one says 'good,' the other 'morning'" or "one says 'horse,' the other 'carriage'"? What did *tsu* and *ka* mean anyway? The first one resembled *tsuru* (crane), and the second one sounded like the cawing of a crow. Maybe a woman changed into a crane and flew up into the sky, as in the folktale, and a crow said hello?

"You change lightbulbs for me when I ask you to, don't you, Mitsu?"

"Of course." Pulled back to reality, he took a quick look around. Which bulb was out? He tried to change them *before* she asked, but he must have missed one.

"And if I invite you to supper, you come up without any hesitation." She was watching the thin steam rise from her teacup. "That's all you need to do. Rely on people and let them rely on you. Do it with the people at work, not just me."

He realized there was no burned-out bulb, that she was being tactful and warmly sympathetic.

He thanked her for the meal and then, as a token of gratitude, offered her the packet of instant ramen.

Majime offered to clean up and took the dishes downstairs to the kitchen to wash. Také, having already taken her bath, retired to her bedroom for the night. He generally showered before leaving for work. Tonight he decided to turn in early, rather than staying awake to think about the dictionary or how to be more socially outgoing.

He poured fresh water in Tora's saucer, then piled more dried sardines in the cat's food dish and set it on the kitchen floor. Tora never did more than snack in the lodging house. Také often wondered aloud who else might be feeding him, but Majime had an idea that Tora was self-sufficient in that area. Despite his bulk, he was a crackerjack hunter. Time and again Majime had seen him triumphantly strolling along the canal with a sparrow or a dragonfly in his mouth.

He went back to his room and laid out his futon, then called softly for Tora. He waited a bit, but Tora didn't appear. Usually the big cat spent the night curled up at Majime's feet. Where could he be?

He lay down and pulled the lazycord to turn off the light. Thinking Tora might yet come, he stayed awake, staring at the ceiling. The window was slightly open.

There in the darkness, the lapping of the water in the canal became the murmur of a limpid brook. The wind blew away the clouds, and on the window were the shadows of leaves in the moonlight.

Suddenly he heard Tora. Somewhere he was emitting low sounds that might have been either threatening or placating. Majime sat up in the bluish-white moonlight and listened. Definitely Tora. Where was he? What was he doing?

Worried, Majime crawled out of bed and put on his glasses. The air had chilled. He picked a pair of socks off a nearby stack of books, gave them a quick sniff, and put them on. He went to the window and peered down at the canal, but to his surprise, Tora's meows were coming from overhead. Také must have shut her window before going to bed. Of course she had. Tonight was cold.

Majime tiptoed up the stairs to rescue Tora. The second-floor hallway was dimly lit. The sound of Také's deep breathing filtered from her bedroom. She was unaware of Tora's faint cries. Fortunately, every upstairs room had a window that opened to the clothes-drying platform, so there was no need to wake her up.

He slid open the door to the room where earlier they'd eaten supper and went in. Neither of them bothered to lock their doors anymore, since it was only the two of them. He entered the room, which was unexpectedly bright in the moonlight. He went to the window and looked out. The silver pampas grass and dumplings were gone. Had she cleared them away? Or had Tora eaten them? Wondering, he opened the window, and Tora's cries became more distinct.

"Okay, don't worry." He swung his legs through the window and out onto the platform. "I'm coming to get you." Intending to call the cat by name, he looked toward the far end of the platform, where for some reason the pampas grass and dumplings had been moved. A young woman was standing there with Tora in her arms.

Surprise made Majime's throat constrict, and he emitted a strange "urk." Slowly the young woman, who had been gazing up at the full moon, turned her head to face him. She'd been beautiful in profile, and she was no less beautiful seen straight on, he thought irrelevantly—and froze. As if by sorcery, his muscles and heart went rigid. He was incapable of speech.

The young woman smiled, her long black hair swaying in the breeze. "Oh, I'm so glad. You've come to get him."

The easy, faintly mischievous tone sounded familiar. Was this Také, rejuvenated by the moonlight? His mind reeling with age-old stories involving shape-shifting and apparitions connected to the moon, Majime staggered over to the bedroom window and looked inside. Také was fast asleep, mouth agape.

Then who was this? He fell back on his rear.

Tora twisted out of the young woman's arms, leaped down on the platform, then came over and rubbed against Majime's shins.

"So sweet!" she said. "Got a name?"

"Majime."

"Funny name for a cat."

"No, I'm Majime. The cat is Tora."

His mother, who saw him in the most favorable light possible, might conceivably call him sweet, but who else in their right mind would? He turned red at his mistake and then at his excessive self-consciousness. She tilted her head, clearly puzzled.

Seizing his chance, he asked, "Who are you?"

"Kaguya." (Shining Night.) "I just arrived today. Nice to meet you."

He gazed up at the young woman, her figure silhouetted against the great full moon.

"All right, Majime, what're you mooning about?"

Nishioka poked him, and Majime hastily brought his thoughts down to earth. If he wasn't careful, when he opened his mouth the name "Kaguya" might slip out, along with his soul.

Ignoring Majime's flustered appearance, Nishioka peered at his desktop. "What're you working on, anyway?"

Nishioka was the biggest reason Majime felt out of place in this department. The tempo of his conversation; the fluctuating distances—both physical and psychological—that he maintained with coworkers; the precision of his work—all were beyond the bounds of Majime's understanding. Every time he came into contact with Nishioka, he flinched.

"Um, nothing in particular . . ."

"*Ren'ai.*" (Love. Romantic attachment.)

Nishioka's sharp eyes had caught the entry Majime had been examining, and he proceeded to read the definition aloud: "'*Love* (noun): a feeling of special affection for a particular member of the opposite sex that causes exhilaration and the desire to be alone with that person and share a sense of emotional intimacy, including, if possible, physical intimacy, so that one fluctuates between a state of despair when unfulfilled and, on rare occasions of fulfillment, one of delight.'"

"Oh, I know this one!" said Nishioka. "It's from *The New Clear Dictionary of Japanese*, right?"

"Yes. Fifth edition."

"The one that's famous for its quirky definitions. So what's the story?"

"Beg your pardon?"

"You can't fool me!" Nishioka rolled his chair closer and laid an arm across Majime's shoulder. "You're in love! Fess up."

"No, I was just thinking." Majime straightened his glasses and pushed them back to the top of his nose, where they'd been before Nishioka jostled him. "It's certainly a unique definition, but I wonder if it's appropriate to limit the object of romantic love to 'a particular member of the opposite sex'?"

"Whoa." Nishioka removed his arm and slid his chair back to his own desk. "Are you by any chance one of those people?"

What people? What was he talking about? Letting Nishioka's comment pass, Majime began to thumb through the various dictionaries on his desk. They all had an entry for *ren'ai*, but in every case it was defined as an emotion between a man and a woman. In light of reality, such an explanation was hardly accurate.

On the example collection card, he drew a double circle to signify "a word of high importance that should definitely be included." In the column for comments he wrote, "Just between men and women? Check foreign dictionaries as well."

Only then did the significance of Nishioka's question penetrate his brain.

"No, I don't think so," he said. "Probably not."

"What are you talking about?"

"So far everyone I've ever felt a desire to 'share a sense of emotional and physical intimacy with' has been a member of the opposite sex. But I've yet to experience a state of delight on a 'rare occasion of fulfillment,' so in that sense I haven't yet had a complete experience of love, which is why I qualified my statement by saying 'probably not.'"

Nishioka digested this for a few seconds, then burst out, "Are you telling me you're a virgin?"

Mrs. Sasaki, who had just then entered the office, shot them a frosty look and raised her voice: "Professor Matsumoto and Mr. Araki are here."

Weekly staff meetings were held to hammer out the editorial policy for *The Great Passage*. The planned number of entries was around 230,000, making it a medium-sized dictionary similar in scale to *Wide Garden of Words* and *Great Forest of Words*. Some ingenuity would be needed to make *The Great Passage*, a latecomer to the field, attractive to users.

"We need to come up with definitions in line with contemporary sensibilities," Professor Matsumoto was fond of saying.

Araki, though now officially retired, came to the meetings as overseer. He advised, "Let's put in all the proverbs, technical terms, and proper nouns we can. Our dictionary should function as a mini-encyclopedia, too."

To meet these demands, Majime busied himself day and night, checking file cards. First, he searched for words included in existing dictionaries and marked those cards with a double circle. These words represented the basic building blocks of the Japanese language. Words found in small dictionaries got a single circle; those in medium-sized dictionaries, a triangle. The marks provided a rough guideline for whether or not to include a word in *The Great Passage*. Those with a double circle could not be omitted without a strong reason, whereas those with a triangle could conceivably be left out. Naturally, the data acquired from existing dictionaries was only for reference. Ultimately the team would make its own selection based on *The Great Passage* editorial policy. They would gather every kind of word—archaisms, neologisms, loanwords, technical terms—and sift through them one by one.

Majime divided up the cards with Mrs. Sasaki. Together they flipped through dictionaries of every description until their fingertips had been worn so smooth they had trouble picking up things. In the meantime, Nishioka mostly goofed off, taking breaks in nearby coffee shops and going to singles parties.

At one of their weekly meetings, Majime looked around at the assembled faces and made an announcement: "I think one potential problem is that we're conspicuously lacking in terms from the fashion world."

"I think so, too." Nishioka folded his arms and leaned back in his chair so it squeaked. "We should include the biggest designers or at least the top three collections."

"Then why are there no file cards for them?" demanded Araki.

"Forgive me." Professor Matsumoto fingered his bolo tie in evident embarrassment. "That's beyond my field of expertise."

"Oh, I didn't mean you, professor," said Araki hastily. "I meant this nitwit Nishioka."

With a sideways glance at Araki, Majime wondered aloud, "What would be the top three collections? Stamps, cameras, and . . . the envelopes that chopsticks come in? No, I guess netsuke carvings would be more common."

"You've got to be kidding me," said Nishioka. "Everybody knows the top three fashion shows are in Paris, Milan, and New York. Envelopes for *chopsticks*? What are you talking about, Majime? God only knows how your brain works. It's a mystery, for real."

Nishioka looked at him as if he were some unusual bug, but Majime paid no attention. Something else had caught his interest. Nishioka had used the phrase *riaru ni*—for real—an expression based on English that was new to him. Was it often used? Then and there he filled out a new file card, marking it with the day's date. First occurrence in writing, unknown. In the comments column, he wrote, "Spoken by Nishioka."

Seeing Majime engrossed in making a new file card even in the middle of the meeting, Mrs. Sasaki sighed. "I'll get right on it and draw up a list of fashion experts," she said. "I'll ask them to help with selecting entry words and writing definitions."

"Dictionaries do tend to be written from the male perspective," Professor Matsumoto said mildly. "They're mostly put together by men, so they often lack words having to do with fashion and housework, for example. But that approach won't work anymore. The ideal dictionary is one that everyone can join in using together, men and women of all ages, interested in all matters of life."

"Come to think of it," said Araki, nodding, "we've never had a young woman here in the editorial department." He was quick to add, "Though of course, Mrs. Sasaki here is still quite young."

"Trying to pry your foot out of your mouth?" she said drily. "Don't bother. Majime, did you notice anything else this week?"

Majime shook his head and started to say something, but Nishioka raised a hand and cut him off.

"Majime here is a virgin."

All eyes turned to Majime.

After a beat, Araki growled, a blue vein pulsing in his forehead, "What possible difference does that make? Is there some problem, some reason a man can't edit a dictionary if he's a virgin?" He began to gather his papers in exasperation, preparing to leave.

In the face of Araki's outburst, Majime felt somehow impelled to offer an apology. "I'm sorry."

Nishioka, however, was unabashed. "A problem? Yeah, there's a problem. Just now he was sitting in a daze at his desk, looking up the definition of 'love.'"

Even in a daze, I get a lot more done than you do, Majime thought. But pointing this out would only aggravate the situation. Once again, he meekly apologized.

"Has a young woman caught your eye, Mr. Majime?" Professor Matsumoto inquired, holding his heavy black briefcase.

The briefcase was full of used books. On his way to Gembu, the professor liked to browse through the secondhand bookshops in nearby Jimbocho, picking up first editions of novels old and new. His purpose was not to read for pleasure but to search for sentences that might serve as examples of usage. In dictionaries, noting the first recorded occurrence of a word was a matter of great importance. Collecting first editions of novels had become a habit, part of his never-ending research.

"There's no need to go along with Nishioka's idea of conversation," said Araki.

"No, Araki, you're missing the point," returned the professor. "Falling in love and keeping company with someone—these are matters of great importance, especially for an innocent like Mr. Majime."

Hearing himself described as an "innocent," Majime felt his earlobes burn. He was quite aware of his own innocence, but never before had his love life, or rather his lack of it, been the subject of public debate. He didn't know where to look.

Ignoring Majime's discomfiture, the professor went on. "All of us have to give our utmost to the making of *The Great Passage*. Our time, our money, and our energy. That leaves the bare minimum for living. Everything else goes into the dictionary. 'Family trip,' 'amusement park'—I know the words, but I have no experience of what they represent. For Mr. Majime's sake, and for the sake of our dictionary, it's crucial to find out whether the young woman will understand that way of life."

They had been expecting an encomium on the preciousness and beauty of love, so this conclusion came as an anticlimax. At the same time, they regarded the professor with renewed respect and a slight cringe: Who else would judge a romance by whether or not it interfered with lexicography?

"Wait, professor," said Nishioka. "Are you saying you've never been to Tokyo Disneyland?"

"I have heard of the place, but to me it is unreal, a mere phantasm."

"Don't your grandchildren beg to go?"

As Nishioka and the professor continued back and forth, Mrs. Sasaki turned to Majime. "What's she like, your girlfriend?"

"She's not my girlfriend. We're not going out." He shook his head vigorously but weakened under the intensity of Mrs. Sasaki's gaze. "Her name is Kaguya Hayashi. She just moved into the same lodging house as me. She's my landlady's granddaughter."

"What?" Nishioka broke in excitedly. "You're living under the same roof? Whoa, steamy! Watch it, Majime, don't lose control."

"Follow your own advice." Araki whacked Nishioka on the head. To Majime he said, "And? Go on."

Majime was no match for Araki's gaze, either. Defeated, he started spouting information like a merlion, the mythical sea lion that spewed water. Everything he knew about Kaguya came tumbling out.

"She's the same age as me, twenty-seven. Came here to live with my landlady, Také, I think because Také's getting old. Before that she lived in Kyoto, undergoing training."

"Training? What kind of training?" asked Nishioka.

"As a chef."

Nishioka gawked. Before he could say anything, Majime said, "Yes, a female chef. There are such things."

"Where does she work?" Mrs. Sasaki sat down at her computer and opened a search screen.

"I think in Yushima, a place called Umenomi." (Apricot.)

Mrs. Sasaki typed a few words, reached for the telephone, and made a call. In short order she announced, "I reserved a table for four in Araki's name. I have to cook dinner at home tonight, so I won't be joining you." She thrust a printout of a map at Majime, excused herself, and left.

Araki nodded approvingly. "Doesn't look too expensive."

Nishioka checked the contents of his wallet.

Professor Matsumoto genially suggested, "All right then, let's be off and meet the girl who has won Mr. Majime's heart."

A clean white shop curtain hung at the narrow entrance to Umenomi. Along the edge were three apricots drawn in indigo.

They slid open the door, and the voices of two chefs behind the counter rang out a welcome: *"Irasshai!"* One was evidently the master, the other an apprentice in his early thirties. To their right was a counter of plain unvarnished wood with seating for eight. On the left were three tables with seating for four apiece. In the back was a raised area with low tables on tatami mats. The interior was clean and spruce, the air full of energy, the seats nearly full.

Kaguya emerged from the tatami area carrying an empty tray. Having the least seniority, she apparently did double duty, serving as waitress as well as chef. To Majime she was blindingly beautiful in her white coat and apron. Her hair was twisted up neatly in a bun, and she had on a small white chef's cap.

She called out a cheery welcome and swiftly approached the group standing clustered in the doorway. Araki, who was in the lead, said, "We just phoned in a reservation. The name is Araki."

"Certainly." Then, seeing Majime standing behind Araki, her smile brightened. "Oh, Mitsu! How nice, you came! Are these your coworkers?"

"Yes. The members of the Dictionary Editorial Department."

"Follow me, right this way."

She led the four of them to a table in the rear. They wiped their hands on moist hot towelettes and studied the menu, handwritten with brush and ink on *washi* paper. Everything from elaborate dishes to simple home-style cooking was available. They placed their orders and then slaked their thirst with beer.

Araki opened the conversation. "Well, this is a pleasant surprise."

"She's a lovely girl." Professor Matsumoto nodded, helping himself to *shimeji* mushrooms in a rich sauce and custardy deep-fried tofu served in a warm savory broth and garnished with scallions and grated daikon.

"She calls you Mitsu?" It was hard to tell if Nishioka was grinning or grimacing.

"That's what my landlady calls me, so Kaguya is just imitating her," said Majime, feeling uneasy.

He kept sneaking glances at the counter as unobtrusively as possible—though to the others his interest was evident. Kaguya was focused on the master as he worked, her eyes intent on his hands. Once in a while the senior apprentice would say something to her, and she would crisply perform the task assigned. The senior apprentice was good-looking, with clean-cut, even features. Majime became acutely aware of his hair, unruly to begin with and smooshed more than usual. For the first time all day, he had an urge to smooth it down. He picked up the moist towelette, but it had already cooled off. He put it back down, giving up on the idea of fixing his hair. He felt as if air were stuck in his throat like a gob of sticky rice cake. He could hardly eat anything.

Fortunately, Kaguya seemed unaware that he was acting strangely. Maybe he acted this way all the time so it didn't bother her anymore. She brought dish after dish to their table: sashimi, stewed vegetables, Miyazaki beef simmered in miso-flavored broth. Each time she would check whether they needed extra plates or refills on their drinks, without being at all intrusive.

"Majime tells us your name is Kaguya," said Nishioka, looking up at her, his head tilted at what he probably thought was his best angle. "'Shining Night.' A lovely name."

"Thank you," she said. "Though I'm not that fond of it myself. I always think it sounds like graffiti some biker might scribble on a wall."

"Not at all. Kaguya is the perfect name for one so beautiful."

Majime let out a yelp. Someone had just kicked his shin. Across the table, Araki was glaring at Nishioka, apparently trying to tell him to knock it off. He must have aimed at Nishioka's shin and kicked Majime by mistake.

"I happened to be born on the night of a full moon, that's all." Kaguya handled Nishioka deftly, dismissive yet civil.

"Ah, so even the moon celebrated the occasion of your birth," Nishioka said, undaunted.

Another kick on the shin. Unable to speak up and say, "Hey, that's my leg," Majime gritted his teeth in silence.

When they had finished all the food and the alcohol had pleasurably taken effect, they left the restaurant. The cool air, suggesting the approach of winter, barely registered.

"The food was tasty, wasn't it?" said the professor. "Next time Mrs. Sasaki will have to join us."

"If you liked the place that much, from now on we could eat there after our weekly meetings," suggested Araki.

"What?" Nishioka protested. "I can't afford that. How about alternating between there and Seven Treasures Garden?"

Their four shadows stretched out long on the pavement as they ambled in the dusk. Thinking the moon must be out, Majime looked up at the sky, but tonight there was no sign of it. The lambent glow on low-hanging gray clouds was the reflection of city lights.

Shoved back by Araki, Nishioka fell into step alongside Majime. "Sometimes I scare myself," he said with a sigh.

"Why is that?"

"See how Kaguya kept looking at me? That always happens. I feel bad about it, my friend, but there's not much I can do. Women are drawn to my magnetic charms. Don't hate me."

"Nishioka, you're an idiot," Araki said over his shoulder.

Majime also was taken aback. He thought it might be a joke and stole a look at his coworker's profile, but Nishioka was wearing a self-satisfied smile.

Where did he get such ideas? What if she *had* been looking at him? Wasn't it just because he kept on talking to her? Majime had gotten the distinct impression that Kaguya was responding to Nishioka's comments about her name and so forth only because she couldn't ignore a customer. She'd swallowed her annoyance and been gracious.

And yet for all he knew, a woman might well find someone like Nishioka attractive, someone who dressed smartly and had a take-charge attitude and a degree of charm. Majime felt some consternation. Rather than go out with someone who wore ordinary, tacky suits and was lackadaisical and forgettable—someone like him—she'd probably prefer to stay home petting Tora. In the midst of these arbitrary speculations on the workings of Kaguya's heart, Majime fell into depression. Nishioka's awed appreciation of his own appeal to women had reached a rarefied level, and Majime knew that his inexperienced self was unlikely ever to match it.

"Mr. Nishioka, why don't you move into Mr. Majime's lodging house?" Professor Matsumoto cheerfully suggested.

"Live in some ramshackle old place? No thanks."

"What a shame. It would be a fine chance to re-create the setting of Natsume Soseki's novel *Kokoro* in modern times."

"*Kokoro*?" Nishioka walked on a few paces, frowning. "Oh, yeah, I remember. Read it in high school. The one with the farewell letter that went on forever. It was hilarious."

"*That's* your response to Soseki's masterpiece?" Once again Nishioka had succeeded in rousing Araki's ire. "Tell me again, why are you in publishing?"

"Can I help it if I thought it was hilarious?" Nishioka folded his arms. "Seriously, if you were about to do yourself in, would you sit down and write an epistle that many pages long? Who would? And anybody who got a final testament like that by parcel post would freak out."

"Actually," said Majime, "I'm pretty sure he didn't send it parcel post. It was too bulky for an envelope so he wrapped it in a sheet of strong *hanshi* writing paper, sealed it, and sent it by registered mail. But it was small enough to fit in the narrator's pocket." Funny, he thought, now that Nishioka pointed it out, the letter the character Sensei had written to the narrator before committing suicide really was inordinately long and probably wouldn't have fit inside a sheet of *hanshi*, the smallest size of writing paper, or inside a man's pocket, either.

"Who was in charge the day they hired you? That's what I'd like to know," said Araki, sounding fed up.

But as far as Majime could tell, Nishioka was by no means a bad employee. Patience wasn't his strong suit, but his mind was unfettered.

Just now, without trying he had pointed out something genuinely strange about Soseki's classic novel. Maybe rather than being a plodder like himself, someone like Nishioka was better suited to lexicography. Maybe he was someone capable of uninhibited leaps who could see things in an unusual light.

Majime's steps became so heavy that his feet seemed to sink into the ground.

Nishioka wouldn't let the topic drop. "Tell me, why would *Kokoro* come to life if I moved into Majime's dilapidated digs?"

"Because that way the love triangle of you, Kaguya, and Mr. Majime would play out in a lodging house, just like the one in the book."

"Majime isn't much of a rival," said Nishioka teasingly. "No challenge there."

"You may know the concept of a love triangle in theory," responded Professor Matsumoto with a serious expression, "but until you have experienced it in real life, you have no idea of the suffering and pain it entails. You cannot use a word properly if you don't know precisely what it means. A lexicographer must tirelessly follow up actual experience with intellectual analysis."

If these words could be believed, the professor had been willing to see Nishioka and Majime mired in a messy love triangle just so they would gain firsthand knowledge of the term. The man was a fiend for lexicography. Majime shuddered. The professor's bag, stuffed with used books, took on an air of menace, as if filled with unholy passion.

"That's a terrific idea." Nishioka wasn't, apparently, getting the same dark vibe. "You're saying that for the sake of the dictionary we should go out and grab life by the horns. That puts Majime at a disadvantage, though, doesn't it? Him being a virgin and all . . . Go for it, Majime! You can do it!" He nodded, quite pleased with himself, as he offered this nonsensical encouragement.

Majime was bothered less by Nishioka's teasing than by a seeming inconsistency in the professor's remarks. "But sir," he said hesitantly, "didn't you tell us a while ago that you've never been to an amusement park? What about the need to experience the reality of *that* word?"

"Oh, well," the professor said airily, "I can't bear the noise. But you people are young with energy to burn. You should be out there experiencing love and amusement parks and all the rest of it."

In his place? Was that what he meant?

The others were taking the subway, so Majime parted from them at the station and began walking the rest of the way home. To benefit the dictionary, he wanted to win Kaguya's heart and taste the wine of love if he possibly could; and if she was willing, he'd be happy to go to an amusement park, too. Korakuen was a stone's throw away, after all. Yet to Majime the park might as well have been an ancient ruin in a remote desert. How could he tell Kaguya of his feelings for her? How could he get her to respond to them? First and foremost, how could he ask her out on a date? He didn't have the slightest idea.

It became routine for the dictionary editorial staff to alternate eating at Umenomi and Seven Treasures Garden after their weekly meeting.

One morning, after seeing Kaguya working in the restaurant the previous night, Mrs. Sasaki came out of the reference room and told Majime, as he was heading toward his desk, "I think she's a tall order."

"She?"

"Kaguya. Majime, you've got your work cut out for you."

"You think Nishioka is more her type?"

"Nishioka?" She snorted. "If there's a woman alive who thinks he's her type, I'd like to meet her."

What kind of man did appeal to women, then? Majime was even more confused.

"He's too shallow." With that single, devastating word, she dispatched the absent Nishioka. "It's not him you should worry about, it's the men she works with."

"What?" Majime did a quick mental comparison of the craggy-faced master and the clean-cut senior apprentice. "You think she likes that other apprentice?"

Mrs. Sasaki sighed pityingly and shook her head. "Listen to me." She looked as if she wanted to add "you ninny." "I'm saying Kaguya is wrapped up in her work. Getting her attention without interfering will be the hard part. Your approach has to be timed just right. It won't be easy. Can you do it?"

No. It was beyond him. Majime looked down and began sweeping up eraser bits on his desktop.

Just as Mrs. Sasaki was leaving, Nishioka came back in, carefully folding a handkerchief. He had apparently just washed and dried his hands. "Hey, this is no time to sit and pick your nose," he said seriously as he watched Majime clean his desktop.

"Did something happen?" Majime asked, still keeping at his task.

"I just overheard some news in the men's room in the main building."

"You went all the way over there to use the bathroom?"

"I had to take a dump. I like to do it in peace, someplace where nobody I know is around."

Majime was surprised to find Nishioka had such a sensitive side.

"While I was in the stall, I heard someone say *The Great Passage* is being canceled."

"What?" Majime was on his feet.

"Someone from sales, I think. They were gone by the time I came out, so I don't know who it was. You haven't heard anything?"

"No."

Majime hadn't been close to any of his coworkers in the sales department. He'd been an encumbrance. Nobody there would think to give him a heads-up if *The Great Passage* was about to run aground.

"Making dictionaries eats up money, that's the whole trouble." Nishioka leaned back in his chair, making it squeak, and looked up at the ceiling. "What do we do?"

Majime thought swiftly. Their frequent staff meetings had paid off, and editorial policy was pretty much set. If the project were aborted now, Araki and Professor Matsumoto would lose face. "We need to find out how determined they are to shut down the project," he said. "See if there's any room for negotiation. Meanwhile, we can establish a fait accompli."

"How?"

"Reach out to specialists across the board and ask them to contribute."

"Aha." Nishioka saw Majime's point and laughed appreciatively.

Normally, a number of steps had to be followed before outsourcing could begin. First, using the example collection cards, the final entry selections had to be made. Then the editorial policy had to be tightened, and a style sheet had to be drawn up. Contributions from upward of fifty people were necessary. Without guidance, the writing styles would be so different that it would take forever to sort them out. That's where the style sheet came in, with model entries showing what kind of information to include, using how many characters, and in what form.

Following their own style sheet, the staff would compose sample entries in consultation with the editor-in-chief, Professor Matsumoto. Doing so would indicate what adjustments to the style sheet were needed. The selection, naturally a small fraction of prospective entries, would have to include some with proper nouns, some containing numbers, and some requiring illustrations. The process of drawing them up and checking them would help determine the dictionary's quality and orientation.

Having model entries on hand made it possible to decide font size, layout, and design. The number of pages, total number of entry words, and cost would all come into focus. Normally, only then would requests for contributions go out, accompanied by guidelines and models. They had just started to create writing guidelines for *The Great Passage*, so under normal circumstances it would be premature to begin outsourcing.

But Majime thought they should go on the offensive. The world of lexicography was surprisingly small; few publishing companies even had dictionary editorial departments. So far they had reached out only to fashion experts, but that was enough to start a rumor that a brand-new dictionary was in the works. In that case, all they needed to do was fan the flames of this rumor. Sending out requests to experts in a variety of fields would show everyone within the company and outside of it that *The Great Passage* editorial staff meant business.

Yes, making the dictionary would cost money. But a dictionary was a publishing company's pride, and a valuable asset as well. Publishing a dictionary that people trusted and loved would set Gembu on a solid foundation for the next twenty years. Killing the project at this point would give rise to unsavory rumors. People would suspect that Gembu was struggling or that management cared only about short-term profit—outcomes they would surely rather avoid.

"Got a head for strategy, don't you?" said Nishioka. "Way to go." He started out the door, on his way back to the main building to see what further information he could pick up, and then turned around. "By the way, go ahead and use that approach to try to one-up me, if you want. Fine with me."

"Huh?"

"I mean with Kaguya. You'll need to pull off some kind of trick to stand a chance against me." He went off laughing.

That might very well be, but it begged the question: What gave Nishioka such boundless self-confidence? Some people really did hold themselves in high regard. Majime could only marvel, watching him go. Then he picked up the phone to convey the urgent news to Araki and Professor Matsumoto.

The Great Passage wasn't yet scuttled. They decided to go all-out to keep it afloat. Nishioka and Mrs. Sasaki selected contributors and made phone calls, or paid personal visits to solicit contributions confidentially. Araki, in between visits to his wife in the hospital, stayed busy sounding out people at the highest levels, gathering support and feedback, while Majime and Professor Matsumoto struggled to hammer out a style sheet.

To define one word, you inevitably had to use others. Whenever Majime thought about words, something like a wooden image of Tokyo Tower rose in the back of his mind: a precarious structure of words in exquisite balance, words supplementing words. However he compared existing dictionaries, and no matter how much data he gathered, just when he thought he had captured a word, it would slip through his fingers, crumble to bits, and vanish.

Majime stayed home that weekend to think about words. In the back room on the first floor where he kept his stacks, he spread books on the floor and racked his brain. Wasn't there some straightforward way to pinpoint the difference between *agaru* and *noboru*? They were both verbs meaning "to rise, ascend," sometimes but not always interchangeable.

"Still working on the dictionary?" said Kaguya, entering the room followed by Tora. "On a Sunday?"

"Meow," mewed the cat.

Kaguya crouched on the floor across from Majime. Umenomi was closed Sundays, so instead of leaving early in the morning to buy fresh produce as she did other days of the week, she stayed home. Although stunning in her chef's garb, she looked great in jeans and a sweater, too.

Majime felt his pulse rise. It struck him that this rise was connected to another meaning of *agaru*, "to get nervous." Being with Kaguya made him happy, but it put a strain on his heart.

"Um, it's pretty dusty in here," he stuttered.

"Am I bothering you?"

Tora maneuvered around the piles of reference materials and gave Majime's thigh an encouraging flick with his tail.

"No, you're not," Majime quickly said.

"I wanted to borrow a book on cooking, if you have any."

Just as he thought of nothing but the dictionary, she couldn't stop thinking of work even on her day off. And yet she never cooked at home. She said she didn't want to have to cook on her day off. "Listen to the girl," Také would say with a shake of her head. "With an attitude like that, she won't find herself a husband anytime soon."

In no position to entertain ambitions of tasting Kaguya's home cooking, Majime took the initiative and, when he had the chance, would prepare three servings of Nupporo Number One. Kaguya seemed to like the junky taste of the instant ramen and ate hers with relish. The thought that food he had prepared was entering her body, would become her flesh and blood, always made him lean slightly forward to watch as she ate.

If only she would stay in his room now and not be put off by him. Praying for this, he stood in front of the shelves and searched. Unfortunately, he saw no books on cooking.

"I'm afraid I've only got one that's remotely connected to cooking."

With slight dissatisfaction, she regarded the book he held out: *The World of Fungi*. On the cover was a photograph of a bright-red mushroom growing in damp earth. It didn't look edible in the least.

"I'll collect more books on cooking from now on," he said apologetically.

"I'll take a look at it, anyway." She flipped through the pages, tucked *The World of Fungi* under her arm, and stood up. "It's a nice day. You want to go somewhere?"

"Where?"

"How about Korakuen?"

His heart started pounding hard enough to knock his soul right out of his body. This must be what was meant by the phrase *ten ni mo noboru kimochi*, "being on cloud nine," literally "rising to heaven" with joy.

In that moment, the difference between *agaru* and *noboru* became clear. Words that had been floating in chaos swiftly grouped themselves into interlocking sets. In his mind's eye he saw an *agaru* tower and a *noboru* tower, each one soaring high in perfect, beautiful balance. Forgetful of Kaguya's presence in the room, forgetful of her invitation, he pursued the thoughts unfolding in his mind at bewildering speed. Controlling his excitement, he murmured, "That's it. That's it."

Agaru emphasized the *place* reached by upward movement, whereas *noboru* emphasized the *process* of upward movement. When inviting someone to "come on up for a cup of tea," you used *agaru*, never *noboru*. That's because the focus was on reaching a place suitable for drinking tea—the interior of the house, a step up from the outside—rather than the process of moving indoors. For "to climb a mountain," the reverse was true; the correct verb was definitely *noboru*, as the emphasis was on the action of physically moving up the face of the mountain toward the summit, not just the moment of reaching the summit.

Then what about that expression *ten ni mo noboru kimochi* (a feeling of rising to heaven)? Majime ruminated on the feeling he had experienced a moment before. *Noboru* was correct, not *agaru*, because his joy still had room to grow; he hadn't yet attained heaven itself.

Then he thought of something else. Elation was described by the compound verb *mai-agaru*. Why not *mai-noboru*? He knelt on the floor and folded his arms, pondering. In that case, the emphasis was on the elation itself, wasn't it? And since elation was by definition a higher plane of feeling than normal, it was more appropriate to use the verb that implied attainment of, rather than transition to, that plane.

Having come to a satisfactory resolution of the issue that had been nagging at him, Majime unfolded his arms. Only then did he notice that Kaguya was nowhere to be seen. Alarmed, he went out into the hallway. The first floor was silent. Maybe she'd taken offense at his clamming up. Maybe the invitation to the amusement park no longer stood. He mounted the stairs, heading for the second floor.

The sound of her laughter sounded from Také's room. Také seemed to be chiding her. Maybe she was laughing her head off at him for being such a *bokunenjin* (dummy). For once Majime found himself concerned about losing his dignity. He cringed. The idea that the woman he loved might ridicule him made him unbearably sad. At the same time, he couldn't help wondering about that word *bokunenjin*. What was its origin? It sounded vaguely like a Japanese rendition of a Chinese name, like Motakuto for Mao Zedong, but that probably wasn't right.

Working up his courage, he opened the door. Kaguya and Také were munching rice crackers and watching television. The screen showed highlights of a popular daytime variety show.

"That emcee isn't really into it, is he?" Kaguya was still laughing. "It makes it all the funnier!"

"Keep eating all those rice crackers and you won't have room for lunch."

After this mismatched exchange, the two women simultaneously took a sip of tea. Majime stood transfixed in the doorway, sensing the mystery of the blood bond between this pair, who outwardly looked nothing alike. Realizing that Kaguya had been laughing at somebody's antics on television flooded him with relief.

Finally she became aware of his presence, turned to him, and smiled.

"All done thinking?"

"Yes. I'm sorry."

"Okay, shall we go, then?"

He was astonished. She'd been waiting until he came out of his reverie. This revelation was so astounding that Majime was less overjoyed than dumbstruck. Ignoring his apparent distracted state, she put a jacket over her shoulders and pocketed her wallet and phone.

"You coming, Grandma?"

"Where?"

"Korakuen Amusement Park."

Také looked from her granddaughter to Majime. She pressed the top of the electric kettle and filled her teapot with hot water. Majime looked at her pleadingly.

All of a sudden Také clutched her side and bent over in evident pain.

Kaguya patted her back in alarm. "What is it, Grandma?"

"My spasms. You know how I always get them."

"What are you talking about? What spasms?"

"You know. Spasms."

Majime bent over Také and helped her right herself. "Are you okay?" he said.

She turned to him and blinked. She probably meant to wink, but it didn't come off just right. "I'll be fine," she said. "I just need to go lie down for a while. You two run along without me."

"But Grandma . . ."

With a burst of strength so powerful that spasms seemed impossible, Také shoved the hesitating Kaguya out the door. "Never you mind me. Have a grand time spinning around, getting tossed in the air, and plunging back to earth."

That was her way of describing the rides. Her act was a bit phony, Majime thought, but he looked her thankfully in the eyes. She winked both eyes at him again.

And so Majime and Kaguya set out for Korakuen Amusement Park. Tora stuck his head out from under the heated quilt and meowed once, as if in blessing.

On that Sunday, the amusement park was crowded with young families and couples. Over the loudspeaker came the announcement of a live-action show. A roller coaster thundered by overhead.

It was still early afternoon. Majime hadn't been to an amusement park since grade school, and he looked around in agitation. "Roller coasters nowadays are something, aren't they?" he said. "Bigger and twistier than they used to be. Scary."

"Grandma was trying to be nice to us, don't you think?"

Another mismatched conversation. He looked at her. She was looking up at him, her dark eyes sparkling with determination and some kind of emotion. His chest hurt. He knew he needed to say something, but he also knew that no matter how big a dictionary he consulted, he would never come up with the right words.

"Which ride do you want to go on?" he asked, looking away.

She let out her breath, feeling perhaps that he had dodged the question. "That one."

She pointed to the merry-go-round. Getting on one of the gaudily painted horses would be embarrassing, but at least it was better than the roller coaster. The constant noise of shrieking over their heads made him nervous, so he quickly nodded.

They rode the merry-go-round three times and in between wandered through the park. They didn't talk much, but there was no awkwardness, either. It felt calm. When they sat on a bench, he stole a look at her profile. She seemed to feel peaceful, too. She was chewing her sandwich, watching as a pair of small brothers dragged their parents toward a big trampoline.

"Have you got brothers and sisters?" he asked.

"One older brother. He's married and lives in Fukuoka. Works for a company there."

"My parents have been living in Fukuoka for a long time now, ever since my dad got transferred."

"Brothers and sisters?"

"I'm an only child. I only see my folks once a year, if that."

"That's what happens after you grow up."

Then they talked about where in Fukuoka their respective family members lived, what to eat in Fukuoka, and which brand of seasoned cod roe was best as a souvenir. They exhausted the topic rather quickly and fell silent again.

There was the sound of a ride starting up. Screams, whether of joy or of fear, filled the air, along with cheerful music.

"Let's go on that."

She caught him lightly by the elbow and indicated a huge Ferris wheel. Her hand soon left his elbow, but the impression of her slim fingertips and their gentle pressure lingered in his mind.

The Ferris wheel was ultramodern, without central spokes, just an enormous wheel rising into the sky.

All the rides Kaguya had chosen were slow-moving. He wasn't sure if it was because she couldn't handle screamy ones herself, or if she was looking out for him as someone who was clearly not the screamy type. There was no line, so they climbed right into one of the little carriages and watched as the sky slowly opened up before them and the city spread out beneath their feet.

"I wonder who invented a ride like this," Kaguya said, looking out the window. "It's fun but a bit lonely, I always think."

Majime had just been feeling the same thing. Even though they were thrown together in this narrow space—or rather, because the space was so narrow—he was keenly aware of the impossibility of touching her or looking her in the eye. Even away from the confines of earth, the two of them were still separate. They saw the same scenery and breathed the same air, but they could not come together.

"Sometimes when I'm preparing food, I feel like it's a Ferris wheel ride." She put her elbow on the edge of the window and rested her cheek up next to the pane.

"What do you mean?"

"Because no matter how fine a dish I make someone is, it goes around once and then out."

Strange notion, comparing a Ferris wheel ride to the ingestion and excretion of food. Yet the kind of emptiness and loneliness she'd described applied no less to lexicography. However many words were gathered, however they were interpreted and defined, no dictionary was ever truly complete. The moment you thought you had captured words in a volume, they became a wriggling mass impossible to catch hold of, slipping by you, changing their shape as if to laugh off the compilers' exhaustion and passion, and issuing a challenge: "Try again! Catch us if you can!" All Majime could do with a word's endless motion and vast energy was capture it as it was, in one fleeting moment, and convey that state in written form.

However much food you ate, as long as you were alive, you would experience hunger again, and words, however you managed to capture them, would disperse again like phantoms into the void.

"But you would still choose to be a cook, wouldn't you?" he said.

Even if no one could ever stay full forever, he was sure she would go on giving her all to her abilities in the kitchen as long as there was even one person who wanted to eat good food. And even if no dictionary could ever be perfect, as long as there were people who used words to convey their thoughts, he would pursue his calling with all his might.

Kaguya nodded. "Yes, I would. I love it."

Majime looked at the sky, which was changing to evening colors. The little carriage they were riding in reached the top and slowly began its descent toward the ground. Soon they would be back where they'd started.

"Of all the rides in the amusement park," he said, "this is my favorite." Despite the loneliness, he liked its quiet, persistent energy.

"Mine, too."

Majime and Kaguya smiled at each other like conspirators.

"So you didn't tell her you like her, and you didn't even get to first base? What the hell did you go to the amusement park for, then?"

Berated by Nishioka at work, Majime sat moaning at his desk.

Nishioka wasn't the only one fed up with Majime's deliberateness. That morning, Také had lamented, too. "Then what was the use of my coming down with chronic spasms?" she had demanded.

Lacking any reply, all Majime had been able to do was chew his *takuan* pickle as quietly as possible. Kaguya had long since left for work.

Now Nishioka wouldn't let up. "This is no time to play games! She's probably getting it on with somebody at work, you know."

"No, she isn't."

"How do you know?"

"Because I asked her if she was seeing anybody, and she said, 'No, work keeps me busy, and I was never interested.'"

"And you believed her, you stupid ass!" Nishioka was merciless. "She meant she wasn't interested in *you*. Wake up! You don't fold, you tell her, 'Even so, I want you to be my girlfriend.' Why do you think they have love hotels next door to Korakuen?"

Kaguya hadn't said, "I'm not interested." She'd used the past tense: "I was never interested." Still, Majime wasn't so full of himself as to assume this meant she was now interested in him. He wanted to raise various points of objection to what Nishioka was saying, but he held his tongue. This was no time to be sparring.

Although it was still working hours, Majime was busy writing a love letter. He didn't need Nishioka or Také to tell him he'd dropped the ball. He was painfully aware of this, but in front of Kaguya words wouldn't come. He'd demonstrated that already. Since he couldn't tell her how he felt even while riding in the carriage of a Ferris wheel, it wasn't ever going to happen—not unless a desperado held him at knifepoint and yelled, "Say it! Who do you love? Out with it!"

If he couldn't say the words, he could write them. Once he'd decided on that, he'd wrapped up the day's work at top speed and was now bent over a sheet of stationery.

> *Greetings*
>
> *Cold winds are blowing, a reminder of the swift approach of winter's frosty skies. I trust that you are well.*

Nishioka had been watching from the side, chin in hand, as Majime penned his love letter. Now he leaned forward. "Too stilted, Majime. Not even corporate apologies are that stiff and wooden."

"It's no good?"

"Loosen up a little, make it fun. Who writes letters nowadays, anyway? She has a phone, doesn't she? Send her a text message."

"I don't have her contact information. Even if I did, I'd have to text her from work. That's pretty unromantic, isn't it?"

"Your not having a cell phone in the first place is what's unromantic. Go get one. Otherwise I'll change your nickname from Majime to Busui." (Unromantic.)

"Majime isn't my nickname, it's my real name."

As they bickered, a deep voice resounded. "Are you two getting any work done?"

They looked up. Araki stood with his hands on his hips in the office doorway, glowering. "You think we have all the time in the world to get this dictionary finished, is that it?"

"No, boss." Nishioka sprang up and offered Araki his chair. "We're hard at work, absolutely."

Majime swept the unfinished love letter into his desk drawer.

"You're here even though there's no meeting today?" said Nishioka.

"I just extracted a commitment from the board." Araki remained standing and removed his black scarf. "With certain conditions, *The Great Passage* has been given a green light."

Majime and Nishioka looked at each other, wary now. No matter what the company said, they were determined to see *The Great Passage* through to publication. They'd pushed ahead with their plans while the project was in limbo, seeking a fait accompli. What conditions were being imposed now? This could spell trouble.

"First, we have to revise the *Gembu Student's Dictionary of Japanese*. Second—"

"We can't do that," Majime interjected. "How can we revise another dictionary when we're in the middle of creating a brand-new one from scratch? We need to focus on *The Great Passage* and nothing else."

"Nobody on the board has ever worked on a dictionary," said Araki. "That's why they can make such a demand."

"Revising a dictionary is just as much work and takes just as much time as making a new one," Nishioka said. "You know that better than anyone, boss."

"Regardless, we have to do it." Araki grimaced. "Making *The Great Passage* will cost money. They want us to help pay for it. That's the long and short of it."

Revised dictionaries sold well. Given the choice between a revised edition and an unrevised edition, most people would choose the one with more up-to-date information.

Gembu Student's Dictionary of Japanese was a smallish volume that Araki and Professor Matsumoto had put together, with solid sales among elementary and junior high school students. That must be why the company had ordered yet another revision, following on the heels of a major overhaul done just the year before.

"What will Professor Matsumoto say?"

"He'll probably go along with it. The process of revision is bound to help in making *The Great Passage*." Araki sounded as if he were trying to persuade himself of this. "And Majime, since you're new to dictionary making, instead of plunging right into *The Great Passage*, you should get your feet wet with the *Student's Dictionary* first."

Araki had knocked himself out planning *The Great Passage*. Now that a damper had been put on the project, he should have been feeling more frustrated than anyone, yet he was making the best of it. The advice to gain experience made sense, too, so Majime was forced to swallow his words.

"There's something else, isn't there?" he asked. "What is it?"

Araki made a noncommittal noise and looked away, scratching his chin as if troubled. "Nothing. Nishioka, come with me," he said, and left the room.

Majime and Nishioka exchanged looks again.

"What's up?"

"Who knows?"

From the corridor, Araki barked, "Nishioka, are you coming?"

"Coming, boss!" To Majime he said, "I don't know what's going on, but I've gotta go. Lock up when you leave."

Now Majime was alone in the office. He spread out the unfinished love letter on his desk, but all he could think about was Araki and Nishioka. He took his teacup out into the corridor, planning to make himself a cup of hot tea.

The shadowy corridor was empty. He put his ear to the door of the reference room, but he couldn't hear anything. They must have left the building. He went into the old kitchenette, prepared his tea, and returned to his desk.

With dusk setting in, the room felt quieter than usual. He switched on the fluorescent light overhead. The shadows deepened until the bookshelves lining the walls looked like a black forest.

He patted the cushion on his chair and sat down. Sipping his tea, he thought about what to write next. Everything was up in the air. No telling where either the dictionary or his love life might be headed. He sat in a room overflowing with books and words, but which of them might provide a way out of this impasse? He didn't know.

But that didn't mean he should sit back and do nothing, petrified. If he did that, nothing would change. Feeling the weight of the bookcases bearing down on him from behind, he picked up his pen. Slowly and carefully he proceeded to fill in the space on the white sheet of paper in front of him, giving form to his feelings.

By a little after eight he was finished. Nishioka hadn't come back. Majime laid the missive on Nishioka's desk, but then hesitated—he certainly didn't want to create the impression that the love letter was intended for Nishioka. He attached a note: "Please give me your comments."

He turned out the light and locked the door, then made sure the reference room was locked and the gas was off in the kitchenette. No one knew quite how or when the practice got started, but it had become customary for the last person out to make sure the doors were locked and there was no danger of fire. Nothing in the office had any monetary value, but the materials they had gathered and the words they had accumulated were priceless.

Majime dropped off the key with the custodian on his way out of the building. His breath made a thin, white cloud. Time to get out a warmer coat. Burying his chin in his scarf, he headed home.

When Majime got back to the lodging house, he bumped into Také, just emerging from the bath.

"You're home. How was work?" Her cheeks were flushed pink.

It occurred to Majime that although he and Kaguya lived under the same roof, they kept such different hours that he had never seen her fresh from the bath. He found this regrettable. Then he felt embarrassed for thinking such a thing and said an inward apology—though whether he owed an apology to Také or to Kaguya, he wasn't sure.

"Fine, thanks."

"It's cold today, isn't it? Why don't you come up for tea?"

"Thanks, I will."

He washed up before going to Také's room. As he sat down at the *kotatsu* table heater, he let out a sigh. He felt something soft and heavy on his lap. Tora had been sleeping in the warmth under the *kotatsu.*

"I guess you two had a nice time at the amusement park," said Také, deftly setting out tea and a small dish of lightly pickled Chinese cabbage. "Kaguya told me about it. She sounded pleased."

"Did she? I hope she had a good time."

Majime reached for some Chinese cabbage with a toothpick. His heart was pounding so loud it was almost embarrassing. Také might not approve of his feelings for Kaguya. Why would she? He and his books had taken over the entire first floor, and now he was trying to get her granddaughter in his clutches, too. "Give him an inch and he'll take a mile," she must have been thinking. But he wasn't trying to get Kaguya in his clutches—he sincerely wanted a relationship with her, that's all. If she was willing.

"I couldn't keep up my end of the conversation too well, so I was afraid she might have been bored."

He spoke with humility, aiming to stay on Také's good side. Finding his emotions hard to control, he crunched the pickled cabbage rapidly. Little noises like those made by a hamster nibbling leaves filled the room.

"She's turned chicken," said Také with a sigh.

"Chicken?"

Majime swallowed and tilted his head, considering this. The Kaguya he knew was always in command of herself. The adjective *chicken* struck him as inappropriate.

"Yes, ever since she broke up with her old boyfriend. He wanted to marry her, but she turned him down. Wouldn't go with him on an overseas assignment. Said she wanted to devote herself to becoming a chef."

"Well, I've got no plans to go overseas." He half-rose from his seat. The statement ended in a yelp when Tora scratched him in protest.

"She's got such a one-track mind. I don't suppose many men would find her appealing." Také sighed again. "And she's not in the market for anyone, either. All she wants to do is focus on her career. She was seeing someone else in Kyoto, but that didn't last."

Kaguya had come to Tokyo to live with Také probably because she'd reached a certain stage in her training in Kyoto, but Také seemed to feel responsible for her happiness.

"Being a chef means lifelong training and discipline," said Majime, trying to cheer her up. "The person she almost got engaged to wasn't going to be posted overseas permanently, was he? If he'd really wanted to marry her, they could have lived apart for a while, or they could have put off the marriage until the time was right. There are any number of ways around that problem."

He was getting heated. He felt jealous and riled. Here he couldn't even get a relationship going with Kaguya, and some other guy had let slip a chance to marry her? And that made her turn chicken? His blood boiled.

"You know," mused Také, "someone like you might be just the ticket for her."

He looked up eagerly. "You really think so?"

"I do. Someone who's a bit fuzzy on top and has his own world, I mean. Someone who wouldn't be in a hurry to interfere with her world and what she wants to do. I think it's better if two people don't expect too much of each other. Live and let live."

This struck him as a rather lonely prospect, but maybe she was praising him? He hesitated a little, but remembering Také's previous advice about relying on people, he decided to go ahead and rely on her.

"Then put in a good word for me, would you, without making too much of it?"

"What? But I don't know how she feels, and it's not easy to be casual about a thing like that."

Majime jumped up, flew downstairs, and came racing back with an armful of Nupporo Number One. All he owned was books. Instant noodles were the only incentive he could come up with. He didn't care how ridiculous he might seem.

"Please reconsider. Please help me out."

Looking at the heap of instant noodle packets on the tabletop, Také sighed yet again. "Well, if it means that much to you, I'll see what I can do."

She seemed to be stifling laughter.

The next day, for once Nishioka was already at his desk when Majime arrived.

"Well, Majime, I read your love letter."

"And? What's the verdict?"

"It's fine! Go right ahead and give it to her." He also seemed to be stifling laughter.

How come people laugh when I'm dead earnest? Confused and wretched, Majime took back the fifteen sheets of stationery and filed them in his briefcase. "What did Araki say yesterday?" he asked.

"Oh, that." Nishioka started up his computer and began checking his e-mail. "Nothing."

"But . . . he must have wanted to tell you the other condition for continuing with *The Great Passage*."

"Nah. He just wanted to gripe about the board, let off some steam. I had to go out drinking with him till late. It was kind of a pain."

Majime studied Nishioka's profile dubiously. He was pretty sure he'd heard Araki say, "Second . . ." Had he misheard? If all Araki wanted to do was gripe about work in some bar, why had he asked only Nishioka to come along? *Maybe it's because I haven't been here very long yet. Maybe with me around he wouldn't feel free to say what was on his mind.*

Here he was worrying about feeling distanced from his friends, like a junior high school girl. Of course he'd never been a junior high school girl, so this was pure supposition. He was aware that his personality made people generally uncomfortable, which was a major reason why he never seemed to fit in. Yet he had thought the atmosphere at work was becoming more relaxed, that lately even he and Nishioka were getting along. He was quietly disappointed.

As he skimmed his e-mail, Nishioka was humming to himself and saying things like, "Oh, boy, Professor Saijo, the historian, responded right away." If only he, Majime, were more like Nishioka, cheerful and outgoing, and didn't put up fences to keep others out. Then everything would go more smoothly—his work and his love life, too. He was well aware that Nishioka, though he might sometimes come across as unfeeling, would never deliberately set out to hurt another person.

"All right." Nishioka stood up, jacket in hand. "I'm off. I'm going to go give a little nudge to the contributors we haven't heard from yet."

He must've only just arrived. This seemed hasty.

"There's still time," Majime said. "Why the rush?"

"You never know. They may not be exactly sure how to write what we asked them to. It's important to be on top of potential problems before they arise . . . Check this out!"

Proudly he spread out a piece of paper showing the teaching schedule of every university professor they had invited to be a contributor. Majime had to admit that this certainly would make it easier to visit them efficiently, during their office hours. How had Nishioka found time? The prospect of calling on contributors seemed to energize him.

"That's amazing," Majime said. It crossed his mind that there was plenty of work to be done right there in the office, but he didn't say so. He didn't want to undermine Nishioka's newfound enthusiasm.

"When I get back, let's go over the schedule for *Gembu Student's Dictionary.*"

"Sure."

Majime put on black sleeve protectors and pulled up the file cards he'd been assigned for the day.

"Majime."

Hearing his name called, he looked up. He'd thought Nishioka was gone, but he was standing in the doorway.

"Yes?"

"Have more confidence. Anyone who's as serious and diligent as you are is bound to succeed in whatever he does."

Majime set down his pencil in amazement.

"I'm behind you one hundred percent," Nishioka blurted and then disappeared out the door.

Something must have happened. Even Majime, who Také had said was "fuzzy on top," could tell. Either Nishioka had come down with a sudden fever or Araki had said or done something to him. It had to be one or the other.

When Kaguya came home late that night and found Majime crouching at the foot of the stairs, she seemed surprised, falling back against the front door she had just closed.

"What are you doing there?"

"Sorry, I didn't mean to scare you." As she stood in the tiled entryway with her shoes still on, Majime knelt down on the wooden floor in front of her and handed her the bulky love letter. "Please read this."

"What is it?"

"Just a token." Realizing he was beet red to the tips of his ears, Majime hurriedly stood up. "Anyway, good night."

He flew back to his room, closed the door, and burrowed under the covers. He heard her continue upstairs. Once she read the letter, she might come right away with her answer. His heart pounded; his temples felt like they'd turned to stone. He had poured his soul into those pages. Whatever her answer, he would accept it calmly. He lay in his futon and stared up at the ceiling, waiting. Outside on the clothes-drying platform, Tora meowed. He heard Kaguya's window open and shut. All was quiet. A fish jumped, or perhaps a twig fell, making a tiny splash in the canal.

He waited until his cold feet were warm, but she never came.

He watched as the window slowly filled with the bright light of morning.

A week went by with no response. Just as before, they scarcely saw each other. On Sunday she went to take in a demonstration by a famous chef at a hotel, or some such event, and was out the door early in the morning. Was she avoiding him? He never should have resorted to a form of communication as maddeningly slow as a letter.

He moped the time away. Yet even though he was moping, he didn't let up at work; being able to stay focused was one of his strengths. He talked with Professor Matsumoto about how to proceed with a revision of *Gembu Student's Dictionary of Japanese* in tandem with the work on *The Great Passage*.

"Any time you edit a big new dictionary, there are bound to be setbacks along the way." Professor Matsumoto took the company's decision calmly. "But regrettably, there are not enough hands on deck. This could mean years before *The Great Passage* is finished."

"Are they serious about our dictionary or not?" Mrs. Sasaki usually kept her feelings to herself, but for once she let her frustration show. "They don't give us the staff we need, and now on top of everything we have to revise another book, too? They're just waiting for us to abandon ship."

Araki and Nishioka exchanged looks, Majime couldn't help noticing. More than Kaguya's failure to reply had been weighing on Majime this past week. There was something strange about Nishioka.

He'd told him about handing the letter to Kaguya, and also that he had yet to receive any response. Since Nishioka had reviewed the letter for him, he felt he owed him a report. But whenever he brought it up, Nishioka either just grinned or offered cold comfort: "Give it time. She's not going to ignore a love letter, now, is she?" He was busy revising the work schedule for the dictionary, calling on contributors, and so on. Under normal circumstances he'd have been all over Majime with questions, clamoring to hear the latest developments. Something was definitely up. Majime found Nishioka's newfound diligence somehow ominous.

He tried to lift the general mood by saying something positive. "Think of our predecessors, pioneers who compiled great dictionaries single-handedly. At least we have each other. Let's not give up, let's carry on."

"Well said." Professor Matsumoto nodded, looking at Majime approvingly.

"Uh, this is hard to bring up, but . . . ," Nishioka began gingerly. "It looks like this spring I'm being transferred to advertising."

"What?"

"Why?"

Professor Matsumoto and Mrs. Sasaki raised their voices in astonishment. Nishioka gave a small laugh and looked down.

Gloomily, Araki explained. "Company policy. They don't want to spare people for our department."

"This is a calamity." Professor Matsumoto clutched the knot on a cloth-wrapped package on the desk. "Then *The Great Passage* may not be finished in my lifetime."

"And I was just saying how understaffed we are!" Mrs. Sasaki shook her head irately, and, perhaps from built-up stress, her neck made a loud cracking noise.

Nishioka was being transferred? Majime was speechless. Araki worked part-time, Professor Matsumoto was a consulting editor, and Mrs. Sasaki was a contract worker. So the only one in a position to negotiate with the company and head the project was now him, Majime!

This was no time to be going on about predecessors who'd made dictionaries single-handedly and how noble they were. Responsibility for the entire Dictionary Editorial Department at Gembu was about to land on Majime's shoulders.

Reeling from shock and loneliness, Majime finished work and returned home. He slurped down some Nupporo Number One and then retreated to his inner sanctum and his books. He couldn't sleep. He didn't own a television set. He had no hobbies. The only way he knew to calm himself was by reading.

He sat upright in the dusty night air and took a deep breath. His hand reached toward the shelf and took down the four-volume *Sea of Words*. A pioneering dictionary compiled single-handedly in the Meiji era by Fumihiko Otsuki. The man had poured all his assets and time—indeed, his whole life—into completing *Sea of Words*.

Have I got that much drive and determination?

He laid a volume, purchased in a secondhand bookstore, in his lap and carefully turned the musty pages. His eyes fell on the entry *ryorinin* (cook), written in old-fashioned orthography. The definition read: "One whose occupation is cooking. A *chujin*." *Chujin* was an old-fashioned word for "chef," one you hardly came across anymore. Any dictionary, no matter how well made, was destined to go out of date. Words were living things. If someone asked him whether *Sea of Words* was of practical use in the present age, in all honesty he would have to say it had grown outdated. And yet, the principles and passion that informed *Sea of Words* would never be old. They remained vibrantly alive, in other beloved dictionaries and in the hearts of lexicographers.

The entry *ryorinin* naturally made him think of Kaguya. The definition used the word *waza*, which could mean "occupation or job" but also went far deeper; it was closer to "a calling." A *ryorinin* was someone called to cook; someone who felt compelled to prepare food to satisfy the stomach and the heart; someone chosen to do so. The character for *waza* could also be read *go*, a Buddhist term meaning "a karmic bond." Kaguya, Fumihiko Otsuki, and probably Majime himself were each possessed by nothing less than a bond from past lives.

Majime indulged in a reverie. If Kaguya returned his feelings, how deliriously happy he would be. If she even so much as smiled at him, he would be thrilled to death. This was no mere figure of speech: having never gotten much exercise, Majime had little faith in his cardiovascular system and was not sure that his heart could withstand the impact of a Kaguya smile.

He never should have given her a love letter. She was immersed in her chef's training, possessed by it. He didn't want to stand in her way. He himself was bound to the editing of *The Great Passage*. He knew what it meant to be caught up in work, to be possessed. Her failure to answer his love letter was a sign of confusion. He shouldn't have done anything to cause her a moment's uneasiness. He should have kept his feelings—his love—tucked away in his heart.

He heard the quiet sound of the front door opening. She was home. Despite his best intentions, he jerked to his feet like a puppet on strings. His feet traveled of their own accord out of the room and into the hallway.

"Kaguya." His voice was hoarse.

Midway up the stairs, she turned and looked back. She was wearing a black coat and her hair was down. Perhaps she was tired; her eyes, always dancing, looked sleepy for once.

"Give me your answer."

"My answer?" She slowly blinked.

"Yes. If the answer is no, just tell me. I can take it."

"Wait. Are you by any chance talking about that letter you gave me the other day?"

"Yes, I'm talking about the l-l-l—" Majime choked, his nervousness at a peak, but managed to get the words out. "Love letter."

She froze, looking back at him, and made a sound somewhere between "mwa" and "nha." Her cheeks reddened, she said softly, "I'm sorry," then she turned and went up the stairs.

An apology. Was that a rejection? Then why blush? Why not break his heart with gut-wrenching words and actions?

She'd looked adorable.

Perversely, he couldn't stop thinking of the look on her face when she'd said she was sorry. Sad, anguished, adorable. Maddeningly adorable. Flooded with emotion, he stood stock-still in the hallway, oblivious to the cold.

Considerable time went by. Clad only in pajamas, he was chilled through, but when she came back down carrying a bath towel and a change of clothes, he was still there. Seeing him standing frozen at the bottom of the stairs, she looked surprised.

"I'm sorry, I have to take a bath," she said quickly and slipped past him.

That made two apologies. Majime finally began to recover his power of movement. Slowly he went back to the stacks, picked up *Sea of Words* from the floor, and returned it to the shelf. Then he retreated to his room, opened the window, and slid onto his futon, under the covers. He pulled the lazycord and turned off the light. The wind coming through the window rapidly lowered the room temperature.

"Tora," he called.

No answering meow.

He'd been staring up at the dark ceiling. Now, overcome, he closed his eyes. Even that wasn't enough, so he covered his eyes with an arm. No darkness, however black and dense, could blot out the way he felt now.

"Tora, Tora." He gave a sigh ending in a little sob. The name he really wanted to call out was different.

The bell at the end of the lazycord tinkled. He must have dozed off. So many things at work and at home had shaken him emotionally that, without his realizing it, fatigue had built up inside him, and he'd let go of consciousness as if to escape.

Through the comforter he felt a faint pressure and warmth. Tora. He reached out to stroke the cat's fur, groping with the arm that had lain across his eyes.

"So you came."

His fingertips sensed something quite different from cat fur.

"Yes, I came."

Majime made a strangled sound of surprise and hurriedly tried to get up, but could not. Kaguya was actually lying across his stomach. She crawled forward, brought her face near his. Letting his fingers stroke her hair, damp from the bath, she smiled in the dim light.

"After getting a letter so carefully written and so heartfelt, how could I not come?"

Shot through the heart, Majime was incapable of coherent speech. Was he dreaming? He swallowed several times and finally managed to work the muscles of his throat. "I gave it to you a pretty long time ago."

"I know. I'm so sorry. I wasn't sure if it really was a love letter or not."

Kaguya's fingers traced his cheek. Perhaps because she always did the washing up, her fingertips felt rough.

"My boss said, 'Who reads Chinese? Forget it,' and my coworker just laughed."

"You showed it to them?"

He hadn't written it in Chinese, but perhaps his style had been a bit stiff and ornate. It embarrassed him to think any eyes but hers had seen that letter containing everything in his heart, words that had gone in empty circles and been needlessly abstruse.

"Grandma kept saying, 'Go ask him in person.' But you seemed the same as ever, so I just couldn't be sure."

Of course he'd been the same as ever—nerve-racked. From the moment he'd first met Kaguya, he'd been nerve-racked. All because of his feelings for her. His next words were the most heartfelt of his life: "I love you."

"At the amusement park, there were any number of times when I thought maybe you cared." She laid her forehead against his chest and let out a breath of relief. "But you never said or did anything to show it."

"I'm sorry. I'm not used to this."

"Don't apologize. I thought I'd just wait and see what happened. It was mean. I came to make amends."

"Amends?

"Yes."

Kaguya looked up and their eyes met. Hers were smiling; Majime smiled, too. His heart was racing, but fortunately it didn't burst or stop. Her face came nearer, soft lips touched his. Cautiously, taking care not to make a sound, he breathed in the sweet scent of her hair. This was no dream.

"Why are you so tense?"

"Sorry," he said again. "I'm not used to this."

"Do you need to be?" she asked in a tone of wonder.

At that, Majime worked up his courage and took action. His whole body, including his brain, told him he wanted her, not only with his passion but also with his intellect.

He sat up, bringing her with him, and then had her move to one side while he pushed back the comforter. He reached for her hand, and without his needing to pull, she came of her own accord and covered him. He put his arms around her. She felt lithe and soft.

"By the way," she said, "next time you write me a love letter, make it a bit more modern, will you? That one took too long to decipher."

"I'll work on it."

He remembered he'd forgotten to close the window, but soon the cold no longer concerned him.

As if to erase the mood spilling from the room, Tora's meow sounded over the canal. His majestic roar that made all the neighborhood cats fall in line. It was a moonlit night.

Kaguya's eyes, shining with a moist blue light as she gazed at him, were incomparably beautiful.

CHAPTER 3

Aha. The minute he entered the office and saw Majime's face, Nishioka knew.

"Morning, Majime. Something good happen?"

"No, nothing special."

Majime didn't look up and kept correcting manuscripts for *The Great Passage* with a red pencil.

Written contributions to a dictionary are a rather special case, editorially speaking. Unlike in those for magazine articles or short stories, an author's unique voice or style of writing gets little respect. That's because in a dictionary, concision and precision are what count most. Dictionary editors freely alter submissions to unify the style and enhance the accuracy of explanations. They confer with contributors as much as possible, but contributors enter into the project understanding that what they write is subject to change. The burden and responsibility weighing on editors is all the greater as a result.

Majime looked impressive as he sat at his desk wielding his red pencil, seemingly deep in concentration—but more likely he was just embarrassed. This was the conclusion Nishioka reached after observing him from the neighboring desk. Majime was putting on a show of single-minded focus, but now and then his mouth twitched and he bit his cheek as though suppressing a smile. His eyes were bloodshot, suggesting he was short on sleep, and his skin had an unwonted glow.

No doubt about it.

In high school one of the guys would occasionally come into the classroom with skin looking like this. Never did Nishioka expect to see a colleague pushing thirty come into the office with the same telltale luster.

"Nothing special, huh?" *Yeah, right,* Nishioka thought. *Oh, you pulled a fast one, all right, Majime.* He removed his suit coat and slung it over the back of his chair to keep it from wrinkling.

He'd seen it coming a mile off. Women were mysterious creatures, apt to choose someone so unlikely you could bash your head in trying to figure it out. Good looks, a hefty bank account, a social personality—the seemingly obvious reasons rarely counted for much. No, experience had taught Nishioka that a woman attached supreme importance to whether or not a man put her first. Most men, if told by a woman, "You're really sincere," would suspect she was having a bit of fun at their expense. But apparently women actually did consider "sincerity" to be high praise—and by "sincerity" a woman meant someone who would never lie to her and who would save all his tenderness for her alone.

No way. Sure, he'd like to be that way, but really, no way.

No woman had ever praised Nishioka for his sincerity. He lied when the occasion called for it, and he was tender, or not, depending on his mood. Wasn't that being truly sincere, goddamn it? Take it or leave it. Inevitably, his relationships suffered. In the end, guys like Majime were the ones women went for. Ho-hum guys with only their seriousness to recommend them, but with a touch of charm for all that, and a passion, whether for their work or hobby.

With a sigh, Nishioka got to work and began churning out e-mails to potential contributors. This was no time to be sitting around in a daze. The branches of the cherry trees were still bare, even now preparing for the coming spring. He needed to get as much done as possible before his pending transfer. He owed it to Majime, who was by no means a skilled negotiator. When Majime had first come, Nishioka had taken one look at him and thought, *Here's a fellow who's never going to go far in the world.* He'd also thought he'd be a good fit for the department. Before that he'd been pretty worried, even though he himself had tipped off Araki to Majime's existence.

He'd first heard about Majime from Yoko Yokkaichi, a friend of his in sales. She and Nishioka were from the same batch of hires, and they got along pretty well. They'd once worked together organizing a company party, and every few months or so they went out for a drink. That day they'd been sitting in the basement cafeteria at lunchtime.

"Our new guy is creepy." She'd paused as she was eating curry and frowned. "We heard such good things about him, too. A graduate degree in linguistics, supposed to be brilliant."

"Creepy? Like what?"

"Like his hair's always a total mess, for one thing."

"Might be another Einstein."

"He's always straightening up his desk, and the office shelves, too."

"Sounds like a handy fellow."

"Yeah, but he's more like a squirrel hiding nuts or something. I mean, he scurries around like some furtive little animal. And making the rounds of bookstores to push new titles is tiring, right? But he always comes back loaded down with books he picked up at secondhand shops. I mean, you start to wonder, does he go to all the places he's supposed to or not? Before payday, he eats instant ramen out of the package, doesn't even bother to cook it. I'll bet all those used books are the reason he runs out of money. Don't you think?"

"How would I know?"

"Doesn't he sound creepy?"

"Different, I'll grant you that."

"First you, now this new guy . . . Makes you wonder about our company's hiring policies!"

After this lament, Yoko finished her curry, then rinsed off her spoon by stirring it in her glass of water. She was a cheerful, bright young woman, attractive except for this annoying quirk.

"Oh, my god." She set her spoon on the tray, looked behind Nishioka, and lowered her eyes. "He's right behind you. What if he heard me?"

Nishioka turned casually and looked behind him. At a table a slight distance away, a lanky fellow had just gotten to his feet. Sure enough, his hair was jumping every which way. One hand held an empty plate, the other a yellowed paperback. Eyes glued to the page, he started off toward the tray return counter. And proceeded to bump into a potted plant. Dust from the leaves swirled in the air as all eyes turned to him. Without adjusting the glasses that had slipped down his nose, he bowed apologetically to the plant.

"I bet he wasn't listening," Nishioka said, turning back to face Yoko.

The guy was lost in his own world. Exactly the type Nishioka had the most trouble dealing with.

"So what am I doing, getting involved like this?" Nishioka murmured, looking at Majime, who was sitting across from him slurping soba noodles. After finishing the morning's work, he had invited the perennially broke Majime out to lunch at a noodle joint near the office. "My treat," he'd said. Majime modestly ordered a platter of *morisoba*, plain cold noodles with a dipping sauce. He seemed to be enjoying them.

"Involved in what?" Majime asked.

He couldn't very well say, "You." Instead he brushed the question aside. "Nothing."

Having devoured his noodles, Majime was now pouring *sobayu*, the hot water the noodles were cooked in, from a little teapot into the rest of his dipping sauce to make a tasty drink. Nishioka had had a bowl of *oyako domburi*, rice topped with a chicken-and-egg mixture simmered with onions. He looked on restlessly as Majime finished his meal.

"Hey, Shiny."

"Who, me?" Majime put a hand to his head. "I've still got plenty of hair, I think."

"How's it going with Kaguya?"

"Fine, thanks." Majime was noncommittal at first, but under Nishioka's steady, piercing gaze he realized the futility of evasion. He set the teapot back on the table and answered formally. "It's hard to believe, but apparently she's had feelings for me, too. She didn't want to interfere in my dictionary work or let anything get in the way of her training as a chef, so she felt torn, she says, and let things slide."

"Oh, yeah? How about that. Well, congratulations on losing your cherry."

The noodle shop was a favorite lunch spot of Gembu employees, so he had the grace to say this last bit in a lowered voice, but Majime nodded without embarrassment.

"We talked it over and decided one reason we get on so well is we both have something we don't want anyone interfering with."

"How about that," Nishioka said again, thinking, *Good god. No doubt about it, Majime is the right man for both the department and Kaguya.*

Nishioka had never been that absorbed in anything. And probably never would be.

Whatever he made of the smile on Nishioka's face, Majime returned it with a sunny yet rather abashed smile of his own.

Ever since Majime's arrival in their office, Nishioka had had an uneasy feeling. A sense that he was going to get sacked. Over the years he'd done his best. Not that he had the least interest in or feelings about dictionaries, one way or the other. But as long as he'd been assigned to work on them, he'd applied himself to the task at hand. Work was work. He'd learned to put up with Mrs. Sasaki's snippiness. He'd done his homework on Professor Matsumoto, taking note of his habits and food preferences. And he'd acquired the knack of taking in stride Araki's singular fastidiousness about words. Yet Araki was always on his case.

"Nishioka, the word *kodawari*, 'fastidiousness,' can't be used in a positive sense. People use it to refer to a craftsman's pride and joy in his work, for example, but that's an error. The original meaning is 'finding fault, being a stickler.'"

A perfect description of you when it comes to dictionaries, so hey, my use of the word was right on target! Mentally he lodged this protest, but all he said was, "Yes, boss."

Dictionary makers tended to spend their time holed up in the dimly lit office. He had tried to do what he could to lighten the mood so everyone could do their work and enjoy it. In the five years he'd been in the Dictionary Editorial Department, he'd found his place, his raison d'être. He'd felt a glow of affection for the department and for people who loved dictionaries beyond all reason.

Majime had changed everything. Araki had made no secret of his high hopes for the newcomer. Professor Matsumoto never said anything, but he seemed to take a positive view of Majime's work. Even Mrs. Sasaki, who was curt with everyone else, treated him with a certain easy familiarity, like a mother or an older sister—completely unlike the way she treated Nishioka.

Not much he could do about it. Majime's passion for dictionary work was nothing short of phenomenal. Less than a month after Majime arrived, Nishioka had been forced to admit it: the guy was made of different stuff.

Majime was no smooth talker, yet he had a keen sensitivity to words. Like the time Nishioka, in talking about his nephew, whom he'd just seen for the first time in a while, commented, "Kids today are sure precocious." All of a sudden Majime had said, "Wait!" and reached for the nearest dictionary. Nishioka had used a word for "precocious," *omase*, that could apply to either boys or girls, but a similar word, *oshama*, was for girls only. How to explain this difference in nuance, Majime wanted to know. He was always coming up with things like that, so conversations with him tended to get derailed. That day, too, Nishioka had ended up helping him make file cards for both *omase* and *oshama*, looking through dictionary after dictionary.

The file cards Majime wrote seemed to give off a light of their own on the shelves. He faithfully filled in gaps in the vast collection of cards written previously by Professor Matsumoto, Mrs. Sasaki, and the rest. His powers of concentration and endurance were prodigious. If Nishioka called out to Majime when he was writing guidelines or file cards, Majime didn't hear. He would sit at his desk for hours, often skipping lunch. He worked with such energy the black sleeve protectors he wore might have given off sparks as they rubbed against the paper. His unruly hair seemed only to grow wilder, in defiance of the laws of gravity.

"Lately it's gotten harder to pick up things," Majime said one day with a wry laugh. He'd finally worn his fingerprints smooth, like the others. Only Nishioka's fingerprints, despite his five years on the job, remained intact.

Majime seemed to live on a higher plane, unconcerned with his appearance and reputation, yet when it came to words and dictionaries, he was implacable. He would turn over a problem in his mind endlessly until satisfied, and at editorial meetings he gave his opinion forthrightly.

All of which spelled trouble, Nishioka felt. A dictionary was a commodity. Sure, you had to devote yourself to the making of one, but at some point you had to draw a line. Various factors shaped a dictionary: the company's intentions, the timing of the release, the number of pages, the price, the team of contributors. And however perfectionist you tried to be, in the end words were alive, in constant flux. No dictionary could ever achieve true completion. If you got too attached to the work, you could never bring yourself to let it go and finally make it public.

Despite the envy and jealousy Majime aroused in him, Nishioka found him impossible to dislike. Majime's zeal meant he needed someone to keep a watchful eye on him. Who but Nishioka could look out for him and see to it that all their work finally came to something, that the department delivered the goods?

After he left, what would become of the Dictionary Editorial Department, and of Majime? Anxiety lit a fire under Nishioka. He stayed in constant touch with contributors, collected manuscripts when he could, and urged those who had not yet made their submissions to do so by the deadline. Such tasks weren't up Majime's alley. Or maybe Nishioka was getting worked up over nothing. Maybe after he was gone the department would manage just fine. Just maybe Majime, with his burning passion for dictionaries and his finely honed sensitivity to words, would help *The Great Passage* see the light of day.

Thus ruminating, Nishioka fretted in solitude.

At Umenomi, the lovers' behavior grated on Nishioka's nerves, made him want to lurch for the door. Majime avoided Kaguya's eyes more than ever, but should their fingertips happen to touch when one of them passed a dish to the other, he turned beet red. Kaguya called him "Mitsu" more often, but perhaps to avoid giving any impression of favoritism, the hors d'oeuvres she set before him were clearly smaller in quantity than those she served anyone else.

For crying out loud, what is this, junior high? Nishioka wondered. *What the hell are they trying to prove?*

Araki, Professor Matsumoto, and Mrs. Sasaki had also picked up on the new closeness between the lovers. "Tackle dictionary making with the same determination," counseled Araki. "Too bad there won't be a reenactment of *Kokoro* after all," said Professor Matsumoto with a sigh. "When did all this happen, for heaven's sake?" said Mrs. Sasaki. One by one they offered teasing congratulations, while Majime hunched over and made shy, noncommittal noises.

"So you weren't making any headway with her after all, eh, Mr. Nishioka?" Mrs. Sasaki gave him a look.

He forced a smile. "Majime had the jump on me. Living under the same roof with her and everything."

"You're a big talker and that's all."

"That's what's good about Mr. Nishioka!"

Nishioka refilled Professor Matsumoto's glass in gratitude. "Someone who understands me!"

"Being a big talker is what's good about him?" Mrs. Sasaki rolled her eyes. Then, turning to the counter, she called for two more bottles of sake.

Kaguya was watching intently as the master grilled striped mullet with salt, so the other apprentice, whose name was Saka, brought over the order. He didn't go out of his way to be friendly, but his good looks were striking.

"Hey, Saka," Nishioka said. "You work with Kaguya. Doesn't it bother you at all?"

"Doesn't what bother me?"

"There she is, cute as a button and dedicated to her work, and now look." He gestured with his chin at Majime. "Hooked up with a guy who'll never amount to a hill of beans. Doesn't it seem like a waste?"

"Nishioka, you're drunk." Upset, Majime waved his hands over the table as if to dispel the words Nishioka had spoken.

"I'm a married man," said Saka, one eyebrow raised in faint amusement.

Nishioka clucked his tongue faintly, as if to say, "What if you are? Go get her."

"But I'll say this," Saka went on, looking at Majime. "If you do anything to stand in Miss Hayashi's way, you'll get a drubbing from me." With a smile at the corner of his mouth, he added, "She is my protégée, after all," and returned to the kitchen.

"What a sweetheart!" Mrs. Sasaki said, her cheeks flushed.

Even Araki was impressed. "*That's* what is meant by 'a man's man.'"

Majime, meanwhile, was holding forth with Professor Matsumoto. Did the professor think the word *drubbing* was related to *drumming*?

"He's a chef, after all," said the professor lightly. "I'm surprised he didn't threaten to dredge you in flour and boil you in oil!"

Nishioka was not amused. "Last orders!" he announced, ready to bring the evening to an end. "Who wants Inaniwa udon noodles, and who wants rice with tea? A show of hands, please."

Majime raised his hand for the noodles.

Nishioka plodded home to his apartment in Asagaya.

"Hi, Masa." Remi Miyoshi greeted him from the living-room sofa, where she was lying down watching television.

Nishioka stood looking down at her, coat in hand. "Butt-ugly as ever, aren't you?"

"Hey! You think you can say anything and people won't get hurt. You're an idiot, you know that?"

Remi sat up and checked the manicure and pedicure she had given herself, to see if her nails were dry. The color was pearl beige, studded with tiny glittering stones.

Nishioka apologized, while thinking about how useless her skills were.

Their relationship had changed the night of the company party. He liked her, and after getting drunk he had ended up taking her to bed. The next morning, seeing her face without makeup, he'd been stunned. Her big, lustrous eyes were now narrow slits, she'd lost 70 percent of her eyelashes, and her eyebrows had vanished like mist. To be frank, she was a dog. The sight surprised him, but he still liked her. Also he was impressed by her mastery of the art of makeup and moved by the effort she was willing to put into making herself attractive.

Ever since, they'd been in and out of each other's apartments. Remi removed her makeup in front of him, and he spoke his mind freely around her. But if anyone had asked, "So are you and her an item?" he'd have been stuck for an answer.

He still went to singles parties and sometimes, if things worked out, slept with other women. Sometimes he'd go on seeing the other woman for a while, though never for very long. Remi never said a word. When she sensed he had another woman, she stayed away. When the other woman disappeared, she came back. Apparently she saw other men now and then, too. He wasn't sure if he should ask, so he kept quiet. Back when they had been in college, they could talk about anything. It was funny to think that sleeping with someone could put distance between you.

Whoever he is, I'll bet he doesn't know what she looks like without her makeup on, he would tell himself to lift his gloom. But why be gloomy in the first place? Was it jealousy based on feelings of love, or just a childish desire to have her to himself? He wasn't sure. Anyway, their nowhere relationship kept right on going nowhere.

Now, having apologized, he explained, "It's just that after seeing Kaguya up close tonight, the difference kind of hit me over the head."

"Kaguya? Who's she?"

"Works in a restaurant we go to sometimes."

"A stunner, huh?"

"Way beyond ordinary. A perfect ten."

"Not the world's most tactful guy, are you? Good grief!"

She puffed out her cheeks and came at him as he sat on the sofa, delivering a body blow. With her cheeks like that, she was more moon-faced than ever. At the same time, he had to admit that her warmth beside him somehow helped him relax.

Her hair smelled nice. Must've used his shower without asking, like always. It was his shampoo, but on her he always thought it smelled sweeter. Even though she'd just rammed him, her eyes were laughing, so he felt comfortable saying, "I was comparing you to someone way beyond the ordinary, so we're cool, aren't we?"

"Comparing me to *anyone* is rude!"

For a while they tussled on the sofa.

How did Majime act with Kaguya? Nishioka lacked much imagination, so he couldn't come up with a very precise mental picture. Somehow he imagined Kaguya smiling happily as she looked up at Majime—that was all. "A beautiful woman palls in three days." That's what people said, but maybe Majime would go on to marry Kaguya, while he ended up with Remi here. Now, was that fair?

Remi gently bit his lower lip, bringing his attention back to matters at hand. He was staring straight into her narrow eyes from close up. He was darned if he knew how she transformed them every morning. She huddled over the bathroom sink with her makeup kit, and when she came out, they were big and beautiful. Magic.

"She's not really just a waitress, is she?" asked Remi, sounding wan.

Indeed, she was a cook, not a waitress, but that didn't seem to be where Remi was going.

"What do you mean?"

"You've been kind of down lately. She's not just a pretty waitress. There's something more." Sitting on the sofa with her arms around her knees, Remi let her gaze drop to his chest. "You sure you're not smitten?"

She had keen instincts. That might be one reason why their funny relationship had lasted so long. He opened his arms and pulled her close.

"You know me better than that," he said lightly. "You know I'm never serious."

Remi stirred slightly in his embrace and stole a look at his expression. She looked like she was thinking, "I know you scare easy."

He started to enjoy himself. *Enough with the upward glances,* he thought. With a face like hers, it just looked as if she was giving him the evil eye.

"I'm going to go take a bath," he said, and stood up. "You working tomorrow?"

"You know I am."

"Get to bed."

He was still a bit tipsy, so he decided to take a shower instead of a bath. As the hot spray struck him, he wondered, had she read his mind? Just as she'd said, Kaguya meant more to him than just a "pretty waitress." Of course he wasn't in love, nor did he seriously want to take her to bed. He'd just wanted to beat Majime. If Kaguya had chosen him over Majime, his sense of inferiority might have eased. A crazy dream, that's all it was. He hadn't really believed it might come true, hadn't done anything to make it happen, either.

Nishioka had his pride. Unable to get deeply involved in much of anything, and incapable of getting a satisfactory evaluation at work, he was constantly comparing himself with others and feeling he fell short. He didn't want anyone to know that side of him. Not even Remi, who knew all there was to know about how disgracefully lackadaisical he was. His useless pride had become so swollen that the expression "caring nothing for appearances" could never, ever apply to him.

He rubbed hair restorer into his scalp as a precaution and carefully towel-dried it before heading to the bedroom. Remi lay stretched out on the far side of the smallish double bed, her eyes already closed.

Nishioka crawled into the empty space and let out a sigh. Sleeping in the same bed with Remi was a little cramped, but he didn't really mind. He switched off the light on the nightstand. After a moment his eyes grew used to the darkness, and with just the light from the streetlight seeping through the space between the curtains, he could see into the corners of the ceiling. Blue night shadows, in contrasting shades of light and dark.

"If something's bothering you, you can tell me, you know."

He'd thought she was long asleep. He turned to face her. Her eyes were still closed.

"If I know you, you're just pretending nothing's wrong out of silly pride."

Sheesh. Who do you think you are, my girlfriend? Or what, you're trying to be my mother or my big sister or something? You know what you are? You're somebody I have sex with. Period.

He was frustrated beyond measure. The words rose in his throat, and he was on the verge of spitting them out when for some reason he looked at her sleepy, fleshy expression as she lay beside him halfway dreaming. He found himself stroking her hair.

"Do I seem that down?"

"Uh-huh."

"Want me to show you I'm not?"

"Turkey."

She thrust out an arm to distance herself from him, smiling as if tickled. Before he knew it, he was smiling, too. He pulled her head close, a bit roughly, and cradled it in his arms. He buried his nose in her soft hair and sighed again. This time it was more like a long, deep breath.

Even as they fell into their separate slumbers, they could hear each other's hearts beating.

Revision of *Gembu Student's Dictionary of Japanese* was in full swing.

Even after steering a dictionary safely through to publication, Professor Matsumoto never let down his guard. "That's the real starting point," he liked to say. Day by day he busied himself making new file cards filled with bothersome turns of phrase or young people's slang.

Revision started with a review of those cards. Which ones were suitable for inclusion in the revised edition of the *Student's Dictionary*? And which words included in the current edition had to be taken out? Removing a word from a dictionary was more unnerving than adding a new one. Even if a word was seldom used and all but obsolete, there still might be people who wanted to look up its meaning.

They held cautious deliberations. Professor Matsumoto and Majime made most of the judgment calls on which words to keep or drop. Readers' comments and requests were also taken into consideration. Dictionary users' opinions were a particularly valuable tool for improvement. After all, dictionaries aren't made only by editors-in-chief, contributors, and editorial staff. They are perfected over a long period of time using the collected wisdom of readers.

Adding or deleting entry words often necessitated adjusting the word count in surrounding entries. Definitions had to fit neatly on the page, with a minimum of empty space. Sometimes fine adjustments had to be made over several pages to fit everything in as attractively and readably as possible.

Some words referred the user to another entry, but if that second entry had been deleted in the revised edition, the user would be left high and dry. Such a calamity would seriously damage the dictionary's trustworthiness, so careful checks were made to ensure that revisions didn't give rise to contradictions or discrepancies. Everyone pitched in on this task, not just the professor and Majime, and they were joined by proofreaders from inside and outside the company. Day after day was spent reviewing the vast number of galleys, red pencils at the ready.

The appropriateness of usage examples for new entry words also had to be verified. Twenty graduate students in humanities courses, students of Japanese language and literature, were hired as part-time assistants. The students' job was to make sure all the quotations were accurate and all the examples of usage appropriate. Their schedules weren't set. They could come and go as they pleased, whenever they could spare time from their studies, punching time cards to document their hours worked. They sat at a large desk that had been brought into the office and checked examples with materials on the shelves behind them. Mrs. Sasaki was in charge of overseeing reference materials and assigning work to the part-timers, and Araki oversaw what they did.

The office was suddenly full of life and activity, but for Nishioka time hung heavy. He was leaving in the spring to join the advertising department. Even if he became involved in the revision process, he would have to leave before it was finished, so he felt awkward and hesitant about jumping in.

Instead, he decided to rearrange the office. He was the one who brought in the large desk for the students, lugging it from the storage room on the first floor. Actually, since it was too heavy for him alone, he had enlisted the custodian's help. He also reorganized the reference room and brought newly empty shelves into the office, where they were useful for storing the voluminous galleys.

In the course of moving all that furniture, the door to the office got in the way. It was an antique door with brass knobs, but Nishioka decided it had to go. He borrowed a screwdriver from the custodian's room and removed the hinges. The wood beneath was fresh and lustrous, unaffected by the passage of time.

"How old is the annex?" Nishioka asked Araki.

"It was built right after the war, so it's over sixty years old now."

A door that had been there that long ended up being removed by him, who'd only been around five or six years. How ironic. He apologized silently to the door, wrapped it carefully in packing material, and laid it in the storage room. Without the door, you could see right into the office from the corridor, but nobody seemed to mind. Everybody but him was absorbed in the work of revision, and only dictionary staff used the annex corridor anyway.

For days afterward, Nishioka's back ached. Sneezing took courage. To stand up and sit down, he had to place both hands flat on the desk, regulate his breathing, and talk himself through it: *Here we go, you can do it, easy does it.*

Majime seemed concerned. One morning when Nishioka came in early, he found the cushion Majime always used fastened to his chair seat. A small tube of ointment lay on his desk with a get-well note attached: "Feel better."

"It's not hemorrhoids!" He picked up the tube and threw it on Majime's desk, then thought better of it. Majime had made the gesture as an expression of sympathy, after all, and besides, you never knew—he might need hemorrhoid ointment someday. He retrieved the tube and stuck it in a drawer.

When Majime came to work a bit later, he was carrying a new cushion with a floral pattern. "My landlady sewed it for me."

Jeez, you might have given me the new one! Nishioka thought, but Majime looked so pleased at the sight of him sitting on the hand-me-down cushion that he just thanked him and let it go.

Progress on *The Great Passage* was held up by the work they had to do on *Gembu Student's Dictionary of Japanese.* Even so, sample pages came back from the printer, and Professor Matsumoto, Majime, and Araki spent a good deal of time brooding over them.

Sample pages were printed using finished layouts, of which there were still precious few. Even though the number of samples was necessarily limited, seeing entries arranged on pages as they would be printed and bound gave the dictionary makers a useful preview. Were the size, font, and spacing of characters adequate? Was the placement of figures and illustrations pleasing to the eye? Were numbers and symbols easy to make out? The sample pages were invaluable aids to making the dictionary more readable and enhancing its functionality and appearance.

The three men hovered around the samples, frowning with concentration, yet somehow buoyant. No doubt it gave them a thrill to see *The Great Passage* taking concrete shape at last, even to this minuscule extent.

"Doesn't using white numbers in a circle against a black background make the numbers harder to read?" the professor wondered aloud.

"What's this lame sketch of a toadstool doing by the mushroom entry?" asked Araki.

"Oh, I drew that," said Majime. "The actual illustration wasn't ready, and I thought we should have something to fill the space."

"You didn't have to go and make them print it up like this."

"That's supposed to be a mushroom?" said Professor Matsumoto. "I thought it was a strawberry."

"Come on. It's right there next to the word 'mushroom'! Don't gang up on me."

Nishioka again felt out of the loop. It would be years before *The Great Passage* was complete. Worse, there was no telling when the company might put up another roadblock. The project might end up falling by the wayside after all. Either way, whether it got finished or went up in smoke, he wouldn't be around when it happened. He wouldn't share in either the joy or the pain. Even though he'd been here from the start, before Majime ever came along.

The source of the bitter emotions that rose in him unceasingly like water pouring out of a hot spring was all too clear: jealousy. Compared to Majime, he didn't give a damn about the dictionary, but he couldn't shake off his resentment. He couldn't get over the feeling that he'd gotten off track at work. He felt a swell of panic.

All he had to do was pull his weight in the advertising department—a place where Majime would never succeed, not even if he did handstands and turned somersaults. But Nishioka would do fine. He had faith in his ability to work equally well wherever he was put. Let them send him to advertising. He'd find a way to put a feather in his cap.

But actually, advertising interested him about as much as dictionaries. How could he find something to get excited about? Something he could commit to, no holds barred. He had no idea. People like Professor Matsumoto, Araki, and Majime were alien to him. His friends in school had all shied away from getting deeply involved in anything, and Nishioka thought it was bad form to show too much enthusiasm. His father had been a company worker, but whether he'd liked his job or hated it, Nishioka never knew. He'd just done it because it was his job. He did it for the sake of his family, for the sake of the company, for the sake of earning a salary and making a living. All perfectly natural.

These people so entranced by dictionaries were outside the bounds of Nishioka's understanding. He couldn't even be sure they thought of their work as work. They spent huge sums of their own money on materials, ignoring the limitations of their salaries. Sometimes they stayed in the office looking up things and never even realized they had missed the last train home. They seemed filled with a mad fever. And yet you couldn't really say they loved dictionaries, either—not given the way they studied and analyzed them with such stunning concentration. There was something almost vindictive in their obsession, as if they were going after an enemy, getting the goods on him. How could they be so wrapped up in making dictionaries? He found their obsession mysterious, with even a whiff of bad taste. And yet—if only Nishioka had something that meant as much to him as dictionaries did to Majime and the rest. Then surely he would see everything differently. He would see a world of such dazzling brightness it would hurt.

Next to him, Majime had various types of dictionaries spread open on his desk. He'd brought in a magnifying glass from somewhere and was using it to make minute comparisons of numbers and symbols, his hair flying every which way as usual. Nishioka almost reached out and gave him a whack on the back of his head.

"Well, I'm off to the university." He sprang up and felt a bolt of pain shoot up his back.

Seemingly oblivious to Nishioka's muffled groan, Majime kept looking through his magnifying glass. "Goody," he said absentmindedly. "See you tomorrow."

Goody? What the heck was that supposed to be? *Goody?*

Nishioka left the office in high dudgeon, but as he had to avoid sudden, painful movements, he crept with the stealth of a burglar.

Pale winter afternoon sunshine lit up the mosaic-tiled stair landing. Nishioka climbed to the fourth floor of the old, imposing staircase, holding on to the wooden railing, and went to the door of the professor's office. Before knocking, he took off his coat and laid it neatly over his arm, following proper etiquette. With one hand he massaged the small of his back, and with the other he knocked.

In answer to the response from within he opened the door and found the professor, a specialist in medieval Japanese literature, just finishing lunch at his desk.

"Oh, Mr. Nishioka!" The professor swiftly wrapped up the lunch box in a large handkerchief.

"I'm sorry to interrupt you at lunchtime."

"It's fine. I just finished. Have a seat."

Nishioka pulled up a chair covered in books and perched on the edge. "Does your wife make your lunch for you?" he asked sociably.

"Ah, well." The professor uneasily stroked his fine head of silver-gray hair. "If it's the dictionary entries you're here for, I'm afraid they're not done."

"Please do finish them by the deadline, if you would." Nishioka then sat up straighter. "I came here today to let you know that next year I will be transferring to the company's advertising department.

Someone else from the Dictionary Editorial Department will work with you from now on."

The professor frowned slightly and leaned forward. He looked either concerned or eagerly curious, Nishioka couldn't tell which.

"So the rumor is true?" he asked.

"What rumor would that be?"

"I heard that Gembu isn't on board with the new dictionary. That must be why they're reducing staff."

"Not at all." Nishioka smiled. "If that were true, we would hardly be asking you to write contributions for us."

"Good to know." The professor seemed to take this at face value, but shrewdly added, "I hate to say it, but considering the work involved, writing dictionary entries certainly doesn't pay. Of course, dictionaries are invaluable and I intend to do my best, but you need to understand that my time is taken up by meetings and academic conferences and such. I have very little time to myself. Which is why I would be disturbed to find the Dictionary Editorial Department had bitten off more than it can chew."

"Sir, only you can help us with entries relating to medieval Japan. When the time comes I'll be back to introduce the new member of the editorial staff. Thank you for your understanding." Nishioka bowed politely.

College professors. If they weren't babes in the woods who knew nothing outside the covers of their books, they were political savants with one ear always to the ground. But when it came to reconnaissance, Nishioka himself was no slouch. He knew full well that those boxed lunches were prepared not by the professor's wife but by his mistress. And if he had to, he was prepared to use that information to get the entries on time.

Worn out by his encounter with the professor, who looked so distinguished on the outside and was such a sleazeball on the inside,

Nishioka went home and got into a hot tub. Almost immediately, he fell asleep. The next thing he knew, he was sputtering in water that had cooled to lukewarm.

Later he poked his head into the living room. "Hey! You didn't notice I was in the bath too long? I nearly drowned!"

"Oh, no!" Remi never took her eyes off the television. "I did think you were taking your time, but I was busy so I didn't go check. Sorry."

On the screen, a comedian was yammering about his favorite electrical appliance. A weird show, Nishioka had always thought, but when it was on he couldn't help getting caught up in it. Listening to the guy go on about people and things he cared about was annoying and ridiculous, but there was something about it that amused Nishioka at the same time. Before he knew it he found himself drawn in, interested despite himself. Kind of like the way he felt around Majime and the others.

The program ended, and they sat on the sofa sipping hot tea.

"So what do you think about dictionaries?" Nishioka asked casually. He offered the conversation topic the way you might fill an empty space with a potted plant.

His surprisingly serious expression gave her pause.

"What do you mean?"

"Oh, you know. What kind do you like, what kind did you use in school, that kind of stuff."

"Huh?" Her eyes grew so wide, you'd have thought she'd been startled by a voice from the dead. "You mean some people have likes and dislikes about dictionaries?"

Right. Of course. That's how normal people react. Nishioka thought perhaps he'd caught the dictionary bug at work, after all. The thought scared him a little, but it was reassuring to know that Majime and the rest, all of whom could spend hours debating which dictionaries they liked and why, were really cranks.

"Some do."

"Yeah? I couldn't even tell you the name of the one I used to use."

She set her cup on the coffee table and drew her legs up onto the sofa, arms around her knees. "But now that you mention it, back in junior high the expression 'fish and chips' came up in our English textbook, and I didn't know what it meant."

"Oh, right, you grew up somewhere out in the sticks where there were no pubs."

"Give me a break. I was in junior high. What would I know about pubs?" She gave his knee a little kick and went on. "Anyway, I looked it up in the dictionary, and what do you think it said? *Fisshu & chippusu.*"

Nishioka hooted. "Some help. They call that a definition?"

"I know! Isn't it awful?" She laughed, too, and rocked back and forth on her bottom. "Masa, make a good dictionary, okay?"

With painful swiftness, a hot lump rose in his throat. The reason he'd stayed with Remi all this time, stuck it out, hit him with force: he loved her. She drove him crazy sometimes, but he could never—would never—let her go. *I love you, Remi. You may be no beauty, but you're adorable to me.*

He opened his mouth to say the words, but he heard his hoarse voice say something completely different. "I can't." It wasn't just his throat now—even his eyes felt hot. He looked down. "I'm being transferred to advertising. I'm off the team."

It was demoralizing to sound like a whiner. Pitiful. But finally he'd been able to get it off his chest. Finally he had been able to give voice to how demoralized he felt, the sense of emptiness that had been like a small sharp stone cutting into his flesh.

Remi sat silent and motionless for a moment. Then without a word she drew his head to her breast, as if scooping up a flower fallen onto the water.

The professor sent in his entries at the end of February. Nishioka opened the attached file, read it over, and groaned. The professor had been asked to write definitions for terms relating to medieval Japanese literature as well as encyclopedic entries for major authors and works. Nishioka had given him guidelines and models, yet every entry was over the word limit and full of personal opinions.

His offering for Saigyo was typical:

> **Saigyo** (1118–1190) A priest and a poet who was active from the late Heian period through the beginning of the Kamakura period. Born with the name Sato Norikiyo. Served as a guard to retired emperor Toba, but at the age of twenty-three, for reasons of his own and over the protests of his weeping child, he became a priest. From then on he traveled all over the archipelago, writing numerous poems. "Let me die in spring/under the cherries in bloom/and let it be/in Kisaragi month/at the time of the full moon!" This poem is familiar to one and all. Any Japanese person would be deeply moved by the scene Saigyo paints and share his wish. In his works Saigyo created a unique poetic style that skillfully evokes nature and human emotion, shot through with a sense of life's ephemerality. He died in Hirokawa Temple in Kawachi.

Well, Nishioka thought, *I'm Japanese, but this poem doesn't particularly move me.* Perplexed, he printed out the document. A dictionary was supposed to be precise. Was it all right to write "any Japanese person"? What if other people who failed to be moved sent in complaints?

Probably the professor's thoughts had gone along these lines: "February is almost over. In classical poetry, the second lunar month is Kisaragi—the month that comes up in that poem by Saigyo. That reminds me, I'm supposed to write something for the new Gembu dictionary. Might as well do the entry for Saigyo right now." He then sat down and dashed off this text. Nishioka was annoyed that the writing was so perfunctory.

"Hey, Majime. Take a look at this." He handed the printout to Majime, who was sharpening a red pencil with a penknife. Majime took the paper respectfully in hand and held it before his face like a new pupil the teacher had called on to read aloud.

The half-sharpened pencil rolled across the desk. The tip was still round, despite Majime's intense efforts to whittle it to a point. The wood bore gouges—the blade hadn't been put to effective use. *Jeez,* Nishioka thought, *the guy's all thumbs,* and he started to sharpen the pencil for him.

As Majime pored over the paper, Nishioka silently whittled. It was still morning, so the part-time student workers hadn't shown up yet. Only he and Majime were in the office. The room was still.

He pared the dry wood and gradually exposed the red core, sharpening it to a point. He liked sharpening pencils with a penknife or a box cutter. The pencil core made him think of bone marrow. Something secret . . . a hidden life force . . . never-ending. In elementary school, he used to use freshly sharpened pencils that smelled fragrantly of wood to draw pictures of robots and monsters in his notebook. He felt he could draw better when he sharpened them by hand, so he had never used a pencil sharpener.

It made him nostalgic, remembering those old drawings. He hadn't thought about that notebook in twenty years. He held up the pencil to inspect his handiwork. The tip was so narrow it seemed to melt into the air. Satisfied that he hadn't lost his touch, he thought, *Majime ought to buy himself a pencil sharpener. After I leave, he's likely to cut off a finger with this knife.*

Majime grunted and laid the paper on his desk. He twisted his hair with his left hand while his right hand groped blindly on the desktop. Nishioka put the pencil between his fingers, and Majime looked up.

"Thank you. You know, this needs drastic revision."

"Thought so."

"Did you get the guy's permission to revise what he wrote?"

"Well, of course. When I first went to see him I told him we might have to make some changes. But he can be difficult." Nishioka peered at the entry. "To be on the safe side, I guess I'd better let him know about any changes we make."

Majime nodded, picked up the red pencil, and set to work.

"First off, there are too many unnecessary words. And subjective opinions have no place in a dictionary. It should just be the facts. Also, he's written the poem using modern orthography, which is not how Saigyo wrote it."

"Do we even need the poem?"

"We can think about it again later, but for now I think it's okay to leave it out."

> **Saigyo** (1118–1190) A poet and priest of the late Heian and early Kamakura periods. His religious name was En'i, his lay name Sato Norikiyo.

"Wasn't Saigyo the name he took as a priest?"

"No, that's his pen name. His name as a priest was En'i."

"Okay. This is already a lot better. What else should we fix? The line 'for reasons of his own' is full of holes."

"Yes, it is. Some say he decided to become a priest because the death of a friend made him feel the frailty of life, others say it was because of an unhappy love affair. There are various theories but no one knows for certain."

"How could they? I bet he himself couldn't have put it into words all that easily."

"That's right," said Majime with a faint smile. "What lies deep inside the heart can be a mystery even to oneself."

"And what about 'over the protests of his weeping child'? Who was watching, I'd like to know?"

"That part is vague, so let's cut it. Okay, this still needs work, but how about something like this?"

> A palace guard of the retired emperor Toba, he entered the priesthood at twenty-three. After that he traveled the land writing poems on nature and human emotions, creating his own poetic style. The eighth imperial anthology, *Shinkokinshu*, (ca. 1205) contains ninety-four poems by Saigyo, more than by any other poet. His poetry collections include *Sankashu*. He died in Hirokawa Temple in Kawachi.

Now it was sounding like a dictionary. Nishioka looked admiringly at the corrected text, but Majime seemed still unsatisfied.

"Defining 'Saigyo' only by explaining the man is hardly enough, though."

"You mean the word has another meaning?"

"It also means *fujimi*, as in 'invulnerable, immortal.'"

"How come?"

"There was a time when people liked to paint pictures of Saigyo looking at Mount Fuji. The characters for 'looking at Mount Fuji' are also read *fujimi*, so both meanings became associated with him."

"A lame joke."

"A play on words."

Nishioka felt discouraged. Why would people want to paint pictures of Saigyo looking at Mount Fuji in the first place? He had no idea. What would be fun about painting some itinerant priest?

"Besides that—"

"There's more?"

"Oh, yes. Since Saigyo traveled his name also took on the meaning of 'wanderer' or 'pilgrim.'"

Nishioka took down a volume of the *Great Dictionary of Japanese* from the shelf and looked up Saigyo. Majime was right. After the man himself, various associated meanings were listed. Evidence of the affection people had for Saigyo, how close they felt to him.

"What else?" he said, sneaking a look at the page. He felt like testing Majime.

"I think the mud snail *tanishi* used to be called *saigyo*. And there's a Noh play called *Saigyozakura.*" (*Saigyo and the Cherry Tree.*) "Wearing a traditional bamboo hat pushed back on your head is called *Saigyo-kazuki*, and carrying a bundle wrapped in a *furoshiki* cloth and tied on the diagonal on your back is *Saigyo-jiyoi.* We also might need to include *Saigyo-ki.*" (Saigyo Memorial Day.) "That refers to February 15, the day he died—a word used in haiku to indicate that time of year."

Nishioka thumbed through not just the *Great Dictionary of Japanese* but also *Wide Garden of Words* and *Great Forest of Words* to verify what Majime had said. Beyond impressed, he was in awe. "Man, don't tell me you sat down and memorized a bunch of dictionaries?"

"As if anybody even could." Majime hunched his shoulders apologetically. "Anyway, we won't have space in *The Great Passage* for all these meanings. Which ones do you think we should include?"

"I vote for 'wanderer, pilgrim' and 'invulnerable, immortal.'"

"Why?"

Faced with Majime's quiet question, Nishioka folded his arms and looked up at the ceiling. He had voted by gut instinct, so being asked to defend his choices left him at a momentary loss.

"I guess it's because not many people use traditional cloth wrappers or bamboo hats anymore. But suppose I'm carrying something wrapped in a *furoshiki* on my back, tied on the diagonal, and I run into a buddy of mine and he says, 'Hey, that's *Saigyo-jiyoi*!'"

"Hmm, that's not happening anytime soon."

"That's just a hypothetical example. When he says that, I think, *Aha, so this way of carrying something is* Saigyo-jiyoi*!* Or what about this. Say the company sends out a memo: 'Employees are requested to forgo briefcases and use *Saigyo-jiyoi*.'"

"That's never happening."

"Like I said, these are hypotheticals. When I get the memo, I say, 'What's *Saigyo-jiyoi*?' Somebody explains, and I get the picture. What I'm saying is, the meanings of both *Saigyo-jiyoi* and *Saigyo-kazuki* are easy to guess from context, and if somebody describes them in words, they're easy to visualize."

"Ah. So you're saying there's little practical need for them in a dictionary."

"Right. Same goes for *Saigyozakura*. Chances are, anybody who sees or hears the word will already know it's a Noh drama. Nobody starts a conversation or a letter right off the bat with 'Now, take *Saigyozakura* . . .' As long as someone could guess it was a Noh drama, all they'd have to do is look it up in a dictionary of Noh."

"And Saigyo Memorial Day is self-explanatory. But what about calling mud snails *saigyo*? There I think you'd have a hard time figuring out the meaning."

"Who calls mud snails that anymore? Nobody. If they did, all you'd have to do is ask them what they were talking about."

"Pretty cavalier, aren't you?" Majime seemed to be enjoying this.

Nishioka plowed on. "But the idea that 'Saigyo' also means 'invulnerable' I think has to be included, along with its origin in the image of Saigyo looking at Mount Fuji. Suppose you were reading and came upon a character who goes, 'I am Saigyo! Bwa ha ha.' Unless you knew 'Saigyo' was a synonym for 'invulnerable,' you'd be totally confused."

"And for the same reason you think we should include the meaning of a wanderer or pilgrim, right?"

"Well, it's partly that." Nishioka hesitated slightly. "Suppose an actual drifter is leafing through a dictionary at a library and comes across an entry for the word *saigyo* that says 'a wanderer or pilgrim (after Saigyo, the itinerant priest-poet).' Think how he'd feel. He'd tell himself, 'So Saigyo was just like me! Even in the old days, there were people who never stayed put.'"

Nishioka became aware of Majime's eyes on him and turned to look. Majime had swiveled his chair around to face him.

"I never thought of it that way before." Majime's voice was full of admiration.

Embarrassed, Nishioka quickly added, "It's probably no basis for including words in a dictionary, I realize."

"You're wrong." Majime shook his head, his expression intent. "Nishioka, I'm so sorry you're leaving. We need you to make *The Great Passage* a really human dictionary."

"Yeah, right," Nishioka said dismissively, and swiped the paper back. With Majime's red-pencil corrections as reference, he typed the professor an e-mail informing him of the changes. He stared at the computer screen and tried not to blink, afraid he might cry tears of happiness.

If anybody but Majime had told him such a thing, he'd have thought they were just saying it to make him feel better. But he knew Majime's words were heartfelt. He'd always thought of Majime as a lexicographical genius but also as an awkward weirdo he had nothing in common with. He still thought so. If they'd gone to school together, they never would have been friends. Which was exactly why what he said meant so much. Majime was incapable of flattery. Since Majime had said it, Nishioka could believe it: he was needed. He wasn't deadweight after all. He felt a burst of joy and pride.

Majime had turned back to his desk with an unconcerned look on his face, little suspecting that he had been Nishioka's salvation. He was twisting his hair with his left hand while making corrections on another entry. Majime always came straight out with what he thought; he seemed unaffected by what he had just said. Whereas Nishioka, though happy, was all but squirming with embarrassment.

Majime was one of a kind. Nishioka knew that now as never before.

When he showed up at the professor's office in answer to the summons he had received, he again found the professor just eating lunch at his desk.

"Nishioka, what's the meaning of this?" barked the professor.

"I beg your pardon?" Standing in the doorway, Nishioka spoke politely and respectfully.

"That e-mail from you yesterday. What did you mean by rewriting my text?"

"I believe that when I asked you to write for us, I mentioned that there might be some revisions."

"Did you?"

Nishioka smiled courteously and said nothing.

"Nothing you said ever led me to expect radical changes of this order."

If you don't want us to rewrite it, get it right the first time. How did you expect us to use that crap you sent? What's the matter, old man, you've never opened a dictionary?

Still smiling, Nishioka replied, "I am very sorry. However, it's necessary for us to ensure that all the entries are uniform in style. I hope you will be so kind as to give us your consent."

"Are you the one who made those corrections?"

A pause. "No." He decided to be up-front. "I consulted with my colleague, Majime."

"Fine. Then let your Majime write all the entries. I'm washing my hands of the whole thing. It's not my work anymore."

"Sir!" Nishioka rushed over to the desk. "Please don't say that. Majime is someone you can trust. After I leave the editorial department, he'll work with you in absolute good faith. All we had to do was make stylistic changes once we had your text in hand. He and I are both grateful." Of course, rather than simply stylistic changes, it had been more of a complete overhaul. Unlike Majime, Nishioka could lie like a trooper. He lowered his voice and said confidentially, "To tell you the truth, contributions from other people have had to be much more drastically revised."

"Is that so?" The professor's attitude softened a little. With a sidelong glance at Nishioka, who maintained a humble stance, he wrapped a handkerchief around his lunch box—packed not by a loving wife but by his mistress. "Anyway, it's most unpleasant having one's writing tampered with."

What kind of literary genius does this guy think he is? Despite the thought, Nishioka remained a smiling statue, determined to ride out the professor's displeasure. If the professor backed out now, they would be up a tree.

Dictionaries, like any product, needed name recognition as a guarantee of quality. Having Professor Matsumoto's name on the cover as chief editor was one example. Of course, Professor Matsumoto was genuinely involved in the compilation of *The Great Passage*, but often people like him just lent their names without actually doing any work. Contributors had to be trusted scholars in their respective fields. Since their names were listed at the end of the dictionary, people in the know could tell at a glance whether the selection was appropriate or not. One measure of a dictionary's precision and rigor was the roster of contributors.

This particular professor might not have been such a great choice, Nishioka now realized, and yet he was a recognized authority on Japanese medieval literature. His name would add cachet. If he would just leave the editing of his manuscripts to Majime, all would be well.

"Well, as long as you properly apologize I'm prepared to accept the suggested revisions," the professor said, sipping his tea. "I'm not saying you *have* to prostrate yourself."

"Prostrate myself?"

Dogeza, the most abject form of apology in the book—getting down on all fours and striking the ground with your forehead. Damn.

A smile hovered on the professor's lips. He knew Nishioka was in no position to resist what he said and was enjoying badgering him. Nasty. Nishioka looked down at the dusty floor. He'd just gotten this suit back from the cleaners, too. But if *dogeza* was what it took to make the professor happy, he'd do it all day long.

Just as he had resigned himself to kneeling down and his muscles began to respond, a bolt of reason went through him. He froze. Was *The Great Passage* such a shabby dictionary? What was the point of his prostrating himself in abject apology if he didn't even mean it? With Majime, Araki, and Professor Matsumoto knocking themselves out to make a first-rate dictionary, how could humiliating himself in front of this jackass make any difference? The dictionary was above such shenanigans.

Nishioka reconsidered. Hell no. He wasn't going to let the professor get his kicks. Instead of kowtowing he laid a hand on the professor's desk. Right next to the lunch box. He bent down, put his face close to the professor's ear, and said, "Oh, that was a good one, sir."

"Wh-what do you mean?" The professor faltered, flustered at having his personal space invaded, and tried to push his chair back. To keep him from escaping, Nishioka laid his free hand on the back of the chair, fixing it in place.

"I get it," he said. "You're not the type of man to go around putting people's sincerity to the test. You only mentioned me prostrating myself as a joke, isn't that right?"

"I never—" Sensing that something ugly had come over Nishioka, the professor mumbled a disclaimer.

"But I don't much care for such jokes. I don't think people should put each other to the test." Okay, he had tested Majime's knowledge about Saigyo, but never mind. He continued in as deep and threatening a voice as he could muster. "Now, let's suppose you had a lover."

"What?" The professor almost jumped out of his chair.

"Just for fun." This *was* kind of fun. Nishioka let a sly smile play about the corners of his mouth. "Why so jumpy?" Casually he slid his hand over and laid it on the lunch box. "Actually, I happen to know that you do have a lover. I know who and where she is, and all you're doing for her, too."

"But how?"

"Making a dictionary requires help from all sorts of people. Knowing how to gather information is part of my job."

Nishioka hadn't just randomly made the rounds from one professor's office to the next. He'd made a point of visiting the lounges where the research assistants hung out and being generous with little gifts. Now his thoroughness was paying off.

"But I'm not going to use that information to make you accept the revisions. I would never do such a thing. Like you, I understand the meaning of dignity." Nishioka lifted his hand off the lunch box and straightened up. "I hope I've made my meaning sufficiently clear."

The professor nodded silently.

"Thank you. Then we will proceed with the revised version as planned."

His business here finished, Nishioka did an about-face and headed for the door, maneuvering around piles of books. As he grabbed the doorknob, a sudden thought came to him and he turned around.

"Sir."

The professor looked at him, quailing like a small animal.

"Majime is going to make a dictionary that people will love and trust for years to come. Your name will be on it—but he'll be the one who really writes your entries."

The professor couldn't let this pass. Hearing the truth spelled out, he turned pale. "How dare you!" he blustered, his voice shaking with anger. "What are you saying?"

"I'm saying that you just made a very wise choice, going for appearance over substance. Good day."

Nishioka closed the door behind him without a backward glance and started down the corridor. That parting shot might have been too much, he thought, but he couldn't keep from laughing as he walked along.

Damn, he felt good. He didn't give a flying frittata now whether the professor stormed into the office or even quit the project. Either way, *The Great Passage* would sail along, steady on its course. The determination of Majime and the other editors was firmer than the earth's core, hotter than magma. Even if they and the professor argued, they would take it in stride and charge ahead toward completion of the dictionary.

Come spring Nishioka would gone. If there was trouble, Majime would have to handle it. *Sorry,* he thought. *Hang in there, buddy.*

While mentally dodging responsibility for future consequences of his clash with the professor, Nishioka pledged to himself that he would choose substance over appearance. Araki often said, "A dictionary is the product of teamwork." The meaning of that statement was now clear to him. He wouldn't be like the professor—dash off any old thing and have his name on the dictionary as a matter of form. He'd do all he could to aid completion of *The Great Passage*, wherever in the company he was assigned. Getting his name on it wasn't the point. Even if all trace of his time in the Dictionary Editorial Department vanished and Majime said, "Nishioka? I kind of remember somebody by that name," it didn't matter. All that mattered was putting together a fine dictionary. He would still be in the same company, and he would do his utmost to support the team going all out to make *The Great Passage* the best it could be.

Nishioka went down the stairs and out the door. The pale white light of a winter afternoon lit up the campus. Leafless branches of a gingko tree made cracks in the sky.

He would respond to the passion of others with passion of his own. Until now he had avoided doing so out of sheer embarrassment, but something had changed. Having made up his mind, he felt a thrill of excitement.

Back in the office, Nishioka gave Majime a full report on his run-in with the professor. Majime stopped what he'd been doing to listen and, when Nishioka was finished, looked at him with respect.

"Wow! You're like an extortionist!"

The gap between his awed expression and his choice of words left Nishioka bewildered.

"That's your response?"

"Absolutely. If it had been me, I'd have gotten down on all fours or eaten out of the palm of his hand." The use of irony was not in Majime's skill set. He apparently meant this as sincere praise.

"Listen, Majime."

"What?"

Nishioka swiveled his chair to face Majime, sitting knee to knee with him. The chair cushion had slipped out of place, and he took time to set it to rights before going on. Majime waited. Finally Nishioka sat down again and said seriously, "What I'm saying is, because I bungled it he might come back and cause trouble."

"I doubt it." Majime said. "As you said, he'll choose appearance over substance."

"What if he quits?"

"Let him. I really couldn't care less."

The cold tone took Nishioka by surprise.

"Sorry," said Majime, smiling wryly. "I can't help it—I expect others to be at least as committed as I am."

Nishioka nodded. The more you took a project to heart, the more your expectations of others on the team were bound to rise. The same way that if you loved someone, you wanted them to love you back.

At the same time, he found the depth and intensity of Majime's commitment to the dictionary remarkable. Meeting his expectations and demands would be no easy task. Majime looked easygoing, but his soul was on fire. Nishioka let out a small sigh. Kaguya might find she had bitten off more than she could chew, getting involved with this guy. And if a new hire came to the Dictionary Editorial Department, that person would have their work cut out for them, too.

Ease up, Majime, he thought. *Otherwise everyone around you is going to end up choking. Expectations and demands that weigh too heavy are poison. You'll be worn down in the end, when you don't get what you're looking for. You'll wind up exhausted, resigned, and alone, unable to trust anyone.*

As Nishioka pondered, the late afternoon passed into evening, and soon it was quitting time. Majime, unusually for him, prepared to leave on the dot.

"Going home already?"

"Tonight Kaguya has sole charge of one item on the menu. I thought I'd go to Umenomi and try it out." He cheerfully stuffed reference materials and a sheaf of manuscripts into his briefcase. "Want to come?"

"That's okay," Nishioka said, shooing him off.

Majime went around to each student worker and apologized for leaving first. Finally he was gone. Nishioka turned back to his desk and set to work. The details of his replacement were uncertain. Majime might be the only full-time employee in the department for some time. With the faint sound of the part-timers working in the background, Nishioka bestirred himself. If put upon by someone like the professor today, Majime would be hard pressed to deal with it. Somebody had to help him handle such scenarios. Nishioka wanted to leave a record of all he knew to help his successor.

He began typing up all the information he had gathered about the various contributors—their quirks, their likes and dislikes, their foibles, their academic stature, their private lives, trouble that was likely to occur and how to deal with it. He made it as detailed as possible. When he'd finished, he printed the document and put it in a file with a blue cover. Since the information was sensitive, he deleted the computer file and marked the blue file with a magic marker: **Top Secret: View Only in Dictionary Editorial Department Office**. It ended up being a pretty voluminous file, but something was missing.

Nishioka thought it over and then had an idea. He opened his drawer and took out the love letter Majime had written. When asked to critique it, he hadn't missed the opportunity to make a copy. Fifteen sheets of paper. Made him laugh every time he read it.

One of the college students gave him a funny look as he sat laughing silently to himself. Nishioka hastily composed his expression and began hunting for a hiding place. A bookshelf would be ideal, but if he stuck it between two books, somebody was sure to find it right away. He pretended to examine the rows of books while carefully selecting a place to hide the love letter. In the end he stuck it under a bookend on the shelf holding miscellaneous titles like *How to Write a Letter* and *All You Need to Know about Weddings and Funerals*.

After concealing the love letter, Nishioka returned to his desk and added a new sheet of paper to a clear pocket in the blue file. On it were the words: "Worn out by dictionary editing? Ready to be cheered up? Drop Masashi Nishioka a line: masanishi@Gembushobo.co.jp."

That would do it. He put the top-secret file in a conspicuous place on the bookshelf. Then he stretched and reached for his briefcase. It was after nine, and most of the student workers had gone home. He called out to the two remaining part-timers.

"Let's call it a day and go get something to eat. My treat."

"All right!" said one enthusiastically. "I vote for Chinese."

"Korean barbecue sounds good to me," said the other.

They punched their time cards, chattering with excitement.

"Whoa. You want me to go broke? Make it ramen or a beef bowl."

"What?"

"No way!"

Despite their disappointment, they were laughing.

Nishioka checked to make sure the gas was not on and switched off the lights. Since the office door was gone he locked only the reference room. The vast number of words waiting to be set in order made their presence felt even out in the dark corridor.

"You two enjoy working on the dictionary?" Nishioka asked as they walked toward the exit.

"Sure," said one. "Don't we?"

"Yeah," agreed his friend. "It was tedious at first, but once I get into it I lose track of time."

Same here, Nishioka silently concurred.

People with a finite amount of time at their disposal, setting out together across the broad, deep sea of words. The voyage was scary but enjoyable. He didn't want it to ever end. To get closer to the truth, he wanted to stay on board that ship forever.

Out on the street, the students started a game of rock, paper, scissors to decide between ramen and a beef bowl. Nishioka looked on, smiling.

An idea popped into his head: maybe he would propose to Remi. How would she feel? What would she say? He had no idea, but he was done averting his eyes from his real feelings. No more masquerading. For a pretty long time now he'd had no desire to sleep with anyone else, and that wasn't going to change. He wanted her to know it.

Dinner was ramen. That meant he'd have to propose with garlic on his breath, but with Remi he was past worrying about such things. He sent her a quick text message: Hey. Where RU? If @ my place, W8 for me. If @ home, can I come over? I'll eat first. CU

At the Jimbocho intersection, the cell phone buzzed in his pocket to let him know he had a new message.

Hey. I'm home. Come anytime. No hurry. I'll W8.

He smiled and reread it. No emoji. Her messages were always the same, surprisingly terse. All the same, he felt as if he could hear her voice. He felt warmed. There it was again, the mysterious power of writing, of words.

"All right," he announced, "just to liven things up, you can each have a hard-boiled egg with your toppings."

"What's this, all of a sudden?" said one of the students.

"How about an extra-large bowl with roast pork topping?" said the other.

"Go for it."

Nishioka put away his cell phone and went into the ramen shop with the students, his spirits high.

CHAPTER 4

For the first time in her three years at Gembu Books, Midori Kishibe set foot in the annex, located in a corner of the company grounds, and promptly sneezed three times.

She was allergic to dust and sudden temperature changes. Entering rooms that hadn't been adequately cleaned or that were a different temperature gave her sneezing spells and a runny nose. The annex was the kind of place that might give her a hard time. As soon as she opened the heavy wooden door, she felt the chill in the dim corridor. The air smelled musty, like a library.

This was nothing like the modern main building. Could she really be in the right place? She'd always known about the annex, but assumed it was some sort of storage facility. The Western-style wooden structure was so old-fashioned. Yet once inside, she could tell that despite its age, the building was currently being used. The floorboards and the staircase railing were worn to a deep amber. The walls were white plaster, the ceiling high and elegantly arched. Her nose itched, but no dust bunnies lay in the corners. The building was clearly in daily use and kept up well.

"Excuse me," she called down the corridor. "Hello?"

"What is it?" said a voice beside her, making her jump.

She timidly looked and realized that nervousness and poor lighting had caused her to overlook a small window just inside the door, where now a custodian or security guard was peering out at her. A faded piece of paper taped to the window was hand-lettered RECEPTION. Just beyond the window was a small room where the man had been sitting, watching television in the breeze from an electric fan.

The entrance to the main building had a metallic reception counter with a smiling woman to greet visitors. *What a difference,* Kishibe thought, and started to announce herself. Before she could get a word out, the man waved his right hand carelessly.

"Second floor," he said, twice, before closing the window and turning back to his show.

She decided to follow his instructions and go on up to the second floor. Her footsteps rang out in the corridor. In the main building, her high heels clattered pleasantly on the tile floor, but on this wooden floor the sound was muffled. She thought it sounded like a bird pecking for food.

Every time she stepped on a riser, the stairs creaked. *Have I gained weight? My waist size hasn't changed, but lately I've been pigging out on snacks from all the stress.* She tiptoed the rest of the way up.

The second floor was a little brighter, thanks to light coming through the windows. Only one of the doors leading off the corridor was open. She headed for that one.

As she drew closer, she saw the door wasn't open but had in fact been removed. Inside, bookshelves lined the walls and every desk was buried in piles of paper. She sneezed three times. She hesitated to go into the room. It had to be full of dust. Also, there was a strange moaning coming from inside. A low and continuous sound. *Like a tiger in labor,* she thought.

As she gingerly peered inside, a voice behind her said, "Oh, we've been expecting you!"

Kishibe turned with a squeal of surprise to find a woman standing in the corridor that moments before had been empty. She was slender and bespectacled, and seemed high-strung.

"Um, I—"

"Yes, yes, I know."

Once again, Kishibe was cut off and prevented from introducing herself. The woman slid past her into the room, maneuvering around stacks of paper.

"Director! Director Majime!"

As if in response, the moaning stopped. After a bit, the pile of papers farthest back in the room gave way to reveal the figure of a man.

"Over here. What is it, Mrs. Sasaki?"

Apparently he had fallen asleep at his desk. When he stood up, there was a red line on his cheek from the paper he had dropped his head on. He too was thin, but unlike the woman named Mrs. Sasaki, he had a disheveled air. His shirt was wrinkled and his hair, which looked naturally curly, was thick and unruly.

About forty, she thought, taking note of the wisps of gray mixed in with that explosive hair. *And he's this careless with his appearance? Hmm. And he's the one in charge. Maybe that explains what they say about this place—that it's a paper-eating money pit.*

The man scrabbled around on his desktop without a scrap of dignity. Finally he found what he was looking for—his glasses. With these in place, he seemed to finally notice Kishibe, and began groping on his desktop again.

Now what's he doing? Unsure whether she should speak or remain silent, Kishibe stole a look at Mrs. Sasaki, who was standing perfectly still, as if in a trance, not rushing the man. Kishibe had no choice but to wait for him to do something.

"Found it!" he announced happily, and approached Kishibe with a silver card case in hand. To reach her he had to skirt around piles of paper on the floor, so this took a bit of time. "I'm Mitsuya Majime. How do you do?"

The business card he held out was printed with these words:

Mitsuya Majime
Director, Dictionary Editorial Department
Gembu Books, Inc.

He was pretty tall, so he was bending down to look at her. The eyes behind his glasses looked sleepy, but they were dark and shining.

Quickly she brought out her card case from her suit pocket—the same case she'd bought when she'd first come to work at Gembu, full of excitement. Hermes Box Calf leather. Inside were her brand-new business cards.

"I'll be working with you now," she said. "My name is Midori Kishibe. I look forward to learning a great deal from you." She had never heard of two people in the same company exchanging business cards.

Mrs. Sasaki introduced herself, without offering a card. "My name is Sasaki. I work mostly in the reference room next door."

Relieved, Kishibe put her card case away while she greeted Mrs. Sasaki. This proved that the director had indeed acted bizarrely. There was no need to exchange business cards with your new boss.

No one else was in the office. She thought the others must have stepped out, but no, it seemed it would just be the three of them: Majime, Sasaki, and Kishibe.

"Besides us," Majime said cheerfully, "Professor Matsumoto serves as editor-in-chief, and Kohei Araki is a consultant."

With a staff of two, his title of director didn't amount to much, Kishibe thought, and yet here he was smiling away. She felt inclined to mock the apparently unambitious man, and simultaneously her eagerness to work here, scant as it had been, shriveled up. They were working on some big project, she'd been told, but now she felt as if she'd been exiled to a remote outpost.

Did I screw up somehow? Is this my punishment? Familiar thoughts returned, and her spirits flagged.

Since being hired at Gembu, Kishibe had spent three years on the editorial staff of the glamorous fashion magazine *Belle*. Many publishing companies put out fashion magazines targeting women in their twenties, and *Belle* ranked among those with the most robust sales. The staff lived up to its reputation as one of the leading departments in the company.

An avid reader of *Belle* since college, Kishibe had been excited to be assigned there and had done her best to fit in. She followed the example of her snazzy colleagues and kept up with the latest fashions, taking care to dress as well as she could within her limits; you couldn't really judge how good an item of clothing was until you wore it and lived with it. Even after the page proofs were done and she went home exhausted, she never skipped her skin care regimen. Before interviews, she read boring celebrity autobiographies cover to cover. She'd worked hard at her job without losing her drive—even after her college boyfriend dumped her, saying, "You're the type who can make her way alone."

So why had she been transferred to this godforsaken corner of the universe—the furthest conceivable place from interviews with Hollywood stars and behind-the-scenes wrangling among top models? What was she supposed to do in a department as far removed from her old one as the Crab Nebula was from Earth? What *could* she do? She felt lost.

Unaware of her state of mind, Majime and Mrs. Sasaki were chatting breezily.

"Just now I was having a bad dream," said Mrs. Sasaki.

"That reminds me," Majime said. "I dreamed that when the second proofs came back I found some characters that weren't *seiji*."

"Oh, no! That's awful, even in a dream."

"A nightmare."

Seiji? She wasn't sure what the word meant. She sensed their brisk chatter was from another world. Hesitantly, she spoke up. "Um, what should I do?"

"Find your own work to do," her old boss used to say, but fashion magazines and dictionaries were worlds apart. Until they showed her the ropes, she'd be of no use here.

"Just take it easy," said Majime.

She felt let down, as if they didn't want her, but apparently he hadn't said this to be mean.

"We're planning a welcome party for you," he added earnestly. "Your mission for today is to have your stomach and liver in good working order by six this evening, that's all."

"Your things are over there," said Mrs. Sasaki, pointing to a corner where several cardboard boxes were neatly stacked. "Take whatever desk suits your fancy. If we need help, we'll let you know." With that, she left the room.

She must have gone back to the reference room, or whatever they called it. Maybe, seeing that the director wouldn't be good at welcoming a new employee on his own, Mrs. Sasaki had kept an eye out for her arrival so she could step in and help. Her manner was a little brusque, but she seemed nice enough.

Whatever desk suited her fancy? She looked around the room, at a loss. Every desk was piled high with books and papers.

Majime had already returned to his seat. His desktop was covered with a particularly huge amount of paper—galley proofs? Even his computer huddled uneasily beneath a pile of papers, sticking out like a visor. The floor all around his desk was piled high with stacks of books so tall that when he sat down he was nearly hidden. His desk looked like a fortress or the cave of some hibernating animal.

Kishibe peered at Majime between the books in his stronghold. Tied to the seat of his chair, she noticed, was a worn floral-patterned cushion. She hesitated over how to address him. Since it would be only the two of them in this room, "Director" seemed a bit awkward.

"Mr. Majime?"

"Yes." He looked up from the book in front of him, which was filled with hieroglyphics like those carved in ancient Egyptian temples. Surely he was just looking at them, not reading them? She faltered a bit, unable now to bring herself to ask which desk to use.

Majime, his head still raised, waited patiently for her next words.

"What does *seiji* mean?"

On the spur of the moment she changed her question, and instantly regretted it. This was probably some jargon connected with dictionaries. Majime seemed a bit eccentric; he might be the type to blow up. *You don't know a simple thing like that? What kind of ignoramus did they send me?*

Even though she was feeling scared, he answered in the same mild tone. "Basically, it means a proper character, one based on the *Kangxi Dictionary*."

She still didn't understand, and what on earth was the *Kangxi Dictionary*? She'd never heard of it. Apparently sensing her distress, Majime laid the book in his lap, pulled a piece of paper from the nearest pile, and started scribbling on the back.

"For example, if you type *sorou* on the keyboard and press the language conversion key, the computer will generally come up with this character. But if you look at actual printed materials, the word is almost always written this way. It gets changed to the proper form in the proofreading stage. The second one is the proper form, and the first one is an informal variant."

Kishibe looked closely at the two characters, comparing them. At a glance they seemed identical, but then she saw it. "So the two tiny horizontal lines in the middle are supposed to slant down."

Now she remembered that sometimes in an article for *Belle*, the proofreader would correct the form of a character. Two things counted in a fashion magazine: whether product colors were printed correctly and whether shopping information was up to date. She had never really thought about the meaning behind those proofreading corrections, never realized they had to do with writing the character in its proper form.

"But when you write the character by hand, the variant is fine." Majime looked down at the hieroglyphics in his lap. "Japanese has so many homonyms that it's easy to write the completely wrong character, and those mistakes creep in, too. *Seiji* means not merely the correct character, but the correct form of that character for print. Dictionaries have to put priority on using *seiji*, although characters in the *joyo* or *jinmeiyo kanji* tables are listed in their new forms."

Joyo *or* jinmeiyo kanji *tables?* She didn't know what those might be, but she got the point: dictionaries were made by following detailed rules and lavishing extreme care on each character's form.

I wonder if I can make a go of it here. Her head was spinning. Perhaps because Majime had yanked out a piece of paper before, the pile of papers on his desk chose to collapse, burying his hands.

Kishibe sneezed five times. She wanted to blow her nose, but she had a feeling it was going to take a while before she located a box of tissues in this office.

Before unpacking, Kishibe decided to do some cleaning and tidying.

Since it was early July, she feared they wouldn't be selling flu masks at the convenience store, but they were—probably because new strains of pandemic influenza popped up regardless of season. She found just the ones she wanted, of nonwoven fabric. She bought work gloves, too, and as soon as she got back she set to work, wearing two masks as protection from the dust. Majime offered to help, but she politely declined. They had only just met, so it was a bit presumptuous of her, but somehow one look told her he wouldn't be much use.

Majime backed off, returned to his desk, and resumed work. What he might be doing, she had no idea. He had his nose in that book about hieroglyphics and was taking notes. She took a casual look and saw scribbles such as "The king's bird flies toward night." Could he really be reading hieroglyphics?

The cleaning was more satisfying than she had expected. She arranged books with books, papers with papers, galleys with galleys, and piled them on the big work desk. Once they were organized, she asked Majime to decide what could be discarded. Books went over on the bookshelves, papers she filed in the filing cabinets, and everything that had been judged waste she tied in string and set out in the corridor.

The galleys, which had to be stored, were more trouble. Apparently to make a dictionary, galleys had to go back and forth between the editorial department and the printer five times. After the first proofs had been corrected, they were returned to the printer, and when the next batch reflecting those corrections came back, they had to be checked again, the process repeating five times in all.

When she had worked on the magazine, if there was no particular problem, they only checked the proofs a single time. At most they would check a second proof. So when she saw "fifth proof" stamped on the galleys, she was floored. Printing up galleys wasn't free. *So that's why a dictionary requires an inordinate amount of time and money,* she realized.

Paper was piled up all over the place because they were checking galley proofs for a revised edition of the character dictionary *Wordmaster*. Organizing them was tricky because third, fourth, and fifth proofs were mixed together. She separated them by proof, put the pages in order, and bundled them together. The proofs formed such thick piles that she divided them at arbitrary points and fastened them with clips.

She spent almost her entire first day working like this and succeeded in clearing only the immediate area around her desk. Piles of unorganized *Wordmaster* proofs still covered the work desk.

She was pleased with her handiwork, however, and having looked at so many proofs she now had a fair idea of the kinds of editorial changes being made. Satisfied, she turned to the cardboard boxes containing her things and opened them. She put her writing things, files, and computer on a desk as far away from Majime's as possible. Unpacking took far less time than cleaning up. She was the type who couldn't relax unless everything was in its place; that was partly why she had brought so little with her.

At a little past five thirty, Majime stood and stretched. "Shall we be off?" He looked around, nodding. "It looks a lot better. You even put the reference books in their proper places."

She took off her mask and said proudly, "I worked in the library all the way from kindergarten through high school. You develop a feel for it. But be sure to let me know if I got anything wrong."

"Miss Kishibe, I can tell you're suited for dictionary work."

Majime sounded so impressed that she quickly waved her hands in protest. "Oh, no. I don't know anything about *seiji*, and I've always left proofs to proofreaders."

"All that sort of thing you can learn." He smiled. "It may sound obvious, but working on a dictionary differs considerably from working on a magazine. If someone asked me to check the colors on a color proof for a magazine, for example, I wouldn't have the foggiest idea what to do."

"What makes you think I'm suited for dictionary work?" she ventured to ask, eager for any boost to her self-confidence.

"Because you're so efficient at putting things away."

"Oh." She was disappointed. She wished he had found something to praise that sounded a bit more professional. And if this department was full of people suited for dictionary work, then why hadn't things been put in their proper places to begin with? It made no sense.

Majime picked up on her misgivings. He gave an embarrassed laugh. "Usually things are more organized here. The problem is that just as we were finishing up *Wordmaster* proofs, we had to start editing the *Sokéboo Encyclopedia*, so everything's been at sixes and sevens."

At sixes and sevens? He actually uses that expression? The oddness of it struck her. As she was pondering it she stood with a stupid expression on her face and failed to reply. Then she realized he had just said something even stranger than "sixes and sevens."

"Sokéboo?" she parroted, thinking she might have misheard him.

"That's right." He looked at her quizzically. "Don't you know Sokéboo?"

Of course she did. Socket Booster, aka Sokéboo, was a video game and anime series popular with children and adults alike. Ten-year-old Socket Booster traveled the universe, befriending all manner of creatures on the planets he visited. The creatures of the universe were of every imaginable shape, ranging from adorable to grotesque, and vivid in coloration. Some of them were more popular than Socket Booster. Even Kishibe, who had never played the game or seen the anime, was familiar with several of the characters.

What possible connection could there be between Sokéboo and this department? She wanted to ask, but Majime went around checking that everything was turned off and then, after he had called to Mrs. Sasaki in the reference room, the three of them left the building.

The rainy season hadn't ended yet. The sky over Jimbocho was lit by a tapestry of gray clouds reflecting illuminated buildings and car headlights. Majime went swiftly down the subway stairs.

Nobody had told Kishibe the location of her welcome party. Majime made no sign of telling her now as he charged ahead obliviously. This wasn't the time to ask about Sokéboo. If Mrs. Sasaki hadn't been there, she might have gotten lost.

She studied Majime's appearance from behind. He was still wearing black sleeve covers over his shirtsleeves. She couldn't believe anyone would go out dressed like that. What did he think about fashion, about maintaining one's appearance? Nothing, probably. She sighed. Where was his suit coat? Had he left it in the office?

"He always looks like that." Mrs. Sasaki, walking alongside her, seemed to have picked up on Kishibe's internal monologue.

They changed trains once and arrived in Kagurazaka in about ten minutes. The *Belle* editors would have gone by taxi, since the company would pay and changing trains was a pain. Didn't these people ever use taxis? Majime and Mrs. Sasaki swayed back and forth with the lurching subway, and went up and down stairs without the least sign of discontent. Majime was carrying a heavy-looking briefcase. Now she remembered: before leaving he had crammed it with books. After spending all day chasing hieroglyphics, now he was going to go home and read some more.

Unbelievable. Kishibe sighed again.

They made their way through the maze of back streets in Kagurazaka and came to a little old house at the end of a narrow cobblestone lane. Square lanterns hung from the eaves. On the lanterns, which emitted a soft orange light, she read the words BACK OF THE MOON.

When they slid open the latticed door, a young man in chef's garb greeted them courteously. They removed their shoes in the vestibule.

Just inside was a room with a wooden floor, some fifteen mats big. On the left was a counter of unvarnished wood with five wooden chairs in front of it. There were also four tables seating four apiece. The seats were about 80 percent filled. The customers included businessmen entertaining clients as well as young couples, perhaps self-employed professionals.

"Irasshaimase." A woman chef behind the counter called out a welcome. She looked forty at most. Her hair was tied in a bun. She was very pretty.

The young man led their party up a staircase on the right. Upstairs was an eight-mat tatami room with an arrangement of snow flowers in the simple alcove. Across the corridor were two doors, one to the washroom and another to an employee lounge.

Two men were already seated at the table. Majime introduced them as Professor Matsumoto and Kohei Araki, the other members of the *Great Passage* team. When he introduced her in turn, she offered her business card to each man and said hello. Professor Matsumoto was bald and older, thin as a rail. Araki seemed a bit younger; he looked stubborn to her.

The young man took their orders for drinks and went back downstairs, soon returning with bottles of beer, sake, and hors d'oeuvres. Tiny dishes that could fit in the palm of the hand held sliced raw flounder with marinated kelp. The kelp flavor delicately permeated the fish, and with her first bite Kishibe realized she was hungry.

The welcome party proceeded amiably, with everyone pouring beer for one another. Professor Matsumoto sipped sake. Araki explained the Sokéboo mystery.

"At Gembu, it's the practice for all types of dictionaries and reference works to be made by the Dictionary Editorial Department. That's why Majime took on the *Sokéboo Encyclopedia*."

"The director is a real stickler, so we had our hands full," Mrs. Sasaki said. "We tried to tell him that the purpose of the encyclopedia was to explain the creatures of the universe in terms children could understand, but he wouldn't listen. 'If creatures on the planet Pekébo came to Earth, what would their average weight be in kilograms?' he'd ask, or 'It says in the guidelines that the aristocrats on planet Aum communicate by telepathy, but tell me in detail about the class system on Aum. And what does it actually mean to communicate by telepathy? Do they transmit language from brain to brain, or is it pictures or music or something else? And what about ordinary people? Do we assume that they communicate in words, the same as earthlings?' He'd fire off these detailed questions to the makers of the anime series and games. Finally they threw up their hands and said, 'Whatever you think will be fine. We'll go along with what you come up with.'"

"Mrs. Sasaki, I've never heard you talk so much." Professor Matsumoto shook his head with a look of admiration and surprise.

"Trying to curb Majime must have been hard." Araki looked at Mrs. Sasaki with sympathetic eyes.

Kishibe was astounded at this level of dedication to a child's dictionary of fictional characters. Why had someone like her, with no knowledge of dictionaries to speak of, been transferred to this department? The question had been nagging at her. Now she tried to think. Perhaps she was here to curb Majime, rein him in? It made sense. Without someone in the same room constantly keeping an eye on him, it sounded like he was liable to go way over budget.

"Well, one way or another the *Sokéboo Encyclopedia* has been a great success." Majime looked happy. "It's a credit to the Dictionary Editorial Department. We saved face."

"We were low man on the totem pole for a long time, but now we can really get to work on *The Great Passage*." Araki made a fist on the tabletop. "And we have Miss Kishibe on board now."

"What's *The Great Passage*?" asked Kishibe.

Professor Matsumoto explained. "It's a dictionary of the Japanese language that we've been planning for a long time. It's been thirteen years now since we started work on it."

"Thirteen years!" Kishibe was gobsmacked. "Thirteen years, and it's still not ready? What have you been doing all that time?"

"As I said, revising other dictionaries, making the *Sokéboo Encyclopedia*," Majime said.

"Not only that," said Professor Matsumoto. "You got married!"

"So he did," chimed in Araki. "I always thought it was a miracle."

Majime laughed shyly.

Kishibe was so surprised she didn't know where to begin. This geek was married? Her boyfriend had dumped her, and this guy had a wife? Life was unfair. But no, that wasn't the important thing. How in God's name could they have spent thirteen years making a dictionary and still not be finished? Wasn't that way too long by any stretch of the imagination?

"We couldn't help it," Mrs. Sasaki said, helping herself to some sea bream sashimi. "Time and again, the company forced us to interrupt work on *The Great Passage*."

"If a dictionary turns out well and attracts users," said Araki, "it can be highly profitable, but unfortunately the work is just too slow and painstaking. Companies are interested in quick profits, so it's hard for them to back making a new dictionary. Such a project requires a huge investment of time and money."

He drank the rest of his beer and ordered a refill from the young man who had brought them a side dish: fine strips of leek mixed with Szechuan pickles and chicken breast, seasoned with pepper. The mouthfeel was refreshing, and the spiciness encouraged everyone to drink more beer. This was more like a snack to go with drinks than true cuisine. Maybe they'd been eating and drinking with such gusto that the chef was having trouble keeping pace.

"The *Sokéboo Encyclopedia* is selling well, so now we can finish *The Great Passage*. We *must* finish it." Majime topped off everyone's glasses.

"Yes," Professor Matsumoto murmured, raising up his sake cup. "Otherwise my life will finish first."

This was no laughing matter. Unable either to agree or offer reassurances, everyone wore vague smiles and fell silent. Majime cleared his throat and said, as if pulling himself together, "Well, now Midori Kishibe has joined our team. Let's all join forces and do our best. *Kampai!*"

They'd been eating and drinking all this time, and he was finally getting around to proposing a toast? Strange. Usually such occasions started off with a toast. Everyone else seemed accustomed to drinking toasts whenever the mood struck. Four beer steins and one sake cup clinked together in midair.

"Excuse me for interrupting."

The woman chef who'd been behind the counter now appeared at their table. After distributing bowls of savory boiled vegetables she'd brought up on a tray, she seated herself formally on the tatami floor, turned to Kishibe, and introduced herself.

"I am Kaguya Hayashi, the owner of Back of the Moon. Thank you for coming tonight. I hope you'll come back often."

Before Kishibe could say anything, Araki laughed. "That could be a bit impossible. Tonight is our welcome party, so we splurged, but normally Seven Treasures Garden is more our speed. Right, Majime?"

"I'm afraid we're chronically short of cash. Sorry about that." Indicating Kishibe, he added, "Kaguya, this is Midori Kishibe."

"Well, you could come not just for work-related meetings, but on a date." Without a trace of a smile, Kaguya appealed to Kishibe.

I'm not dating anyone, Kishibe thought, but kept this to herself and smiled in acknowledgment of the invitation.

"How unusual!" Araki looked from Kishibe to Kaguya and back again. "Kaguya takes great pride in her work, but this is the first time I've ever heard her promote her restaurant to anyone so intensely."

Kaguya looked down in evident embarrassment. She looked as if she might start apologizing. She was pretty, Kishibe thought, but kind of . . . different. Still, she found her appealing.

"And this is Kaguya Hayashi."

Majime proceeded with his introductions—unnecessarily, Kishibe thought, since Kaguya had already said her name. Preoccupied with finding reasons to fault Majime's lack of sophistication, she missed his next words. Or perhaps her brain simply couldn't process them.

"My spouse."

A full five seconds went by before she said blankly, "What?"

Majime repeated the words. "My spouse."

Kishibe looked at him, then at Kaguya. He was beaming; Kaguya, solemn as ever, was slightly red faced.

Life was definitely unfair and absurd. Kishibe lodged an inward protest: *Dear God, who may exist somewhere. Why did you give this woman such outstanding cooking ability and then deprive her of judgment in men? That's awful. How could a beautiful creature like her end up with a guy whose hair is a mess and who wears covers on his sleeves?*

The next day, hungover, Kishibe dragged herself to work. Majime was already seated at his desk, carefully sharpening a red pencil by turning the handle on a pencil sharpener.

She greeted him and slowly took her seat, trying to avoid setting off vibrations that would make her head pound.

"You don't look very good." Majime raised his head and looked at her across the mounds of books and papers. "Come to think of it, you seemed pretty *meren* last night."

"*Meren*? What does that mean?"

"If you don't know a word, it's a good idea to look it up." He indicated a bookshelf, but she lacked the energy.

"What shall I do today?"

"Someone from the paper company will be coming by soon. I'd like you to sit in on the discussion."

Today of all days someone has to be coming in for a meeting. Here it comes, my first sneeze of the day. Oh, my aching head! I don't think I'm up to meeting anyone, not without an energy drink at least.

She excused herself, went to the nearby convenience store, and bought an energy drink said to be effective against hangovers. She drank it down as she left the store. A middle-aged man gave her a disapproving glance, but she didn't let it bother her.

Feeling a bit better, she went back to work. Majime was standing by the big desk next to a young man in a business suit. Setting aside the pile of galleys, the young man was spreading out sheet after sheet of paper.

"Sorry I'm late." Hurriedly she exchanged cards with the visitor. His read:

SHIN'ICHIRO MIYAMOTO
SALES DEPARTMENT
AKEBONO PAPER COMPANY

He looked to be about her age. He seemed the quiet type, but clearly he was patient and devoted to his work. His eyes, filled with the light of determination, impressed her.

A visitor this good-looking, and I have to be hungover. Worried that he might smell alcohol on her breath, she tried to talk without exhaling. This was not easy, but she didn't want to make a bad first impression.

Miyamoto had brought a variety of paper samples for *The Great Passage*. Majime was touching them, sliding his fingers over them, and turning them over. He ignored Miyamoto, so Kishibe tactfully came up with a topic of conversation.

"They're all extremely thin, aren't they?"

"Yes. Our company designed this paper for *The Great Passage*, and we're very proud of it. It's fifty microns thick and weighs only forty-five grams per square meter."

She didn't quite get the picture, but evidently the paper was very thin and lightweight.

Miyamoto went on. "And yet it has almost no show-through!"

"Show-through?"

"That's when words printed on one side of the paper are visible on the other side, which makes reading difficult."

According to Miyamoto, paper for dictionaries had to be as thin and light as possible without allowing show-through. That was because the number of pages in a dictionary was so much greater than in any other type of book. The wrong thickness of paper would make the finished book unwieldy and impractical, too heavy to lift.

"You said you designed this paper for *The Great Passage*," said Kishibe. "You mean this new product was specially made for our dictionary?"

"That's right. We received the order from Mr. Majime a year ago, and our technical staff and development team put all their energy into creating these samples. It's my great privilege to finally be able to present them today. Everyone at Akebono, including me, is filled with emotion at having finally reached this milestone."

Miyamoto spoke with intensity. Majime must have presented the company with a challenge of daunting difficulty.

"Is it common for new dictionaries to use specially ordered paper?"

"That depends. The *Gembu Student's Dictionary of Japanese*, for example, uses previously developed paper, but for *Wordmaster* our company came up with new paper. And as I say, we received the order for *The Great Passage* quite some time ago. We put enormous effort into creating something very special."

He flipped through a sheaf of paper and looked at her with pride. "What do you think?"

"Tell me what I'm looking for."

"The paper has a slightly yellowish tint with just a hint of red. We went through a lot of trial and error to come up with a color this warm."

Ah, another weirdo. Too bad. She stopped trying to speak without exhaling. "But a paper this thin has no other uses besides dictionaries, does it?"

"Oh, yes it does." He straightened the edges of the paper. "Of course, we wouldn't use specially ordered paper like this anywhere but in *The Great Passage*. But the challenge of developing thinner and thinner paper is very important for our company as it helps us advance technically. There's demand in all sorts of fields besides dictionaries: Bibles, for example, or insurance papers, or drug information leaflets, or industrial products."

"I see."

Kishibe was impressed. Now that she thought about it, the explanations that came tucked inside boxes of medicine were written on thin, neatly folded paper. She'd never really considered it, but evidently there was ongoing research and development to make all kinds of paper for all kinds of purposes.

Majime, who had been scrutinizing the paper samples, suddenly exclaimed, "There's no waxiness!"

Kishibe and Miyamoto turned to look at him in surprise, unconsciously drawing close together.

Waxiness?

Majime wore a deep frown, looking like writer Ryunosuke Akutagawa with a toothache.

"Miss Kishibe, would you bring over one of the medium-sized dictionaries? *Wide Garden of Words* would do."

As instructed, she brought over the dictionary from the bookshelf and laid it on the table. It was the latest edition.

"See here, Mr. Miyamoto?" Majime turned page after page, using only the ball of his thumb. "This is what I'm talking about."

Kishibe and Miyamoto peered at Majime's hands and exchanged puzzled glances.

"I beg your pardon?" Miyamoto said hesitantly.

Majime looked so severe now it was as if Akutagawa, his toothache raging, had turned his back on the world. "Don't you see how the page clings to my finger as I turn it? And yet the pages don't stick together, so I never turn more than a single page at one time. See for yourself." He passed *Wide Garden of Words* over to them, and they tried turning its pages.

"It's true!" said Kishibe.

"I see what you mean," said Miyamoto. "There is definitely a touch of moisture in the paper that allows each page to be turned easily, using only the ball of the thumb."

Majime nodded benevolently, pleased that Miyamoto had finally seen the light. "That's what I call waxiness. It's essential for dictionary pages," he said. "Dictionaries are bulky and unwieldy to begin with. We want the user to turn pages with as little stress as possible."

"I apologize."

Miyamoto looked down, then resolutely took down a copy of *Wordmaster* from the shelf. He turned page after page, apparently checking something. His expression was so intense, he looked fierce.

Deep down Kishibe was taken aback by all this fuss over mere paper. At the same time, Miyamoto's determination to help out with *The Great Passage* was a pleasure to behold.

He left off turning the pages, stepped out into the hall, and began talking to someone on his cell phone. When he came back into the room, he announced, "We'll redo the samples immediately. These sample pages definitely lack the waxiness of the paper we used in *Wordmaster*. One of our technicians just explained why."

Apparently a new paper machine had caused the problem.

"As you may know, making paper for specific uses requires careful adjustments to the pulp ingredients and sizing agents."

After this explanation, Majime nodded and said, "Yes, I see."

He hadn't heard anything he didn't already know, Kishibe realized, but he wanted to build up the younger man's confidence. She took note of this demonstration of considerateness. She doubted whether most people knew anything at all about such "careful adjustments," but she, too, nodded wisely.

Majime's stern expression softened a bit. "So although you made the appropriate adjustments based on your experience with *Wordmaster*, because your paper machine was new you weren't able to obtain the desired quality, is that it?"

"That's exactly right." Miyamoto hung his head. "Every paper machine has its quirks. Depending on the machine, the same formulation can produce slight irregularities. Not only that, the technician who supervised the paper for *Wordmaster* has since retired. I'm afraid we didn't pay sufficient attention to waxiness."

The only person on the planet who goes around paying sufficient attention to waxiness is Majime, Kishibe thought wryly.

Majime seemed won over by Miyamoto's heartfelt apology. "I'm glad you understand the problem," he said. "I look forward to your next samples."

"Thank you, sir!" A smile finally returned to Miyamoto's face. "I promise you we will produce paper that matches your highest expectations." He swept up the samples and was gone.

"A fine young man." Majime returned to his seat with a cheerful expression, and as soon as he sat down began writing something. Kishibe peered over his shoulder and saw that he was making a file card for *paper machine.*

Everyone connected in any way with dictionaries is daffy, Kishibe thought, vaguely appalled by the level of her new colleagues' commitment and unsure whether she could keep up with them. For now, she set about clearing off the big desk. Picking up *Wide Garden of Words*, she remembered the word *meren* that Majime had used before and looked it up. The definition read: "to drink a great quantity of alcohol; extreme drunkenness."

Now she understood. Majime had been telling her, "Yesterday you were rip-roaring drunk." Well, if that's what he meant, why not come out and say so? She started to get angry.

The definition was followed by an illustrative quotation from *Kanadehon Chushingura, The Revenge of the Forty-Seven Samurai*—the story of the 1703 vendetta carried out by samurai to avenge their master's death. But puh-leez! The example was incomprehensible, written in classical Japanese. A period drama, set centuries ago! Who in their right mind used a word like *meren* in this day and age?

He deliberately used a hard word to test my knowledge. Even though he knows perfectly well that I don't know much about words and I'm a complete amateur when it comes to dictionaries. That's just mean!

She felt frustrated and humiliated, on the edge of tears. But to break down and weep at such treatment would only add to her misery, so she fought back her tears and went on cleaning the office.

Majime still did not give her any assignments. He sat hunched at his desk, engrossed in writing something. Maybe he had forgotten she was even there. Maybe she could bawl or sneeze all she wanted, and it wouldn't make any difference.

She ate lunch, deep-fried horse mackerel, alone in the cafeteria.

She'd felt like talking to someone, so she'd peeked in the reference room on her way out, but Mrs. Sasaki had evidently gone out to eat. And today of all days she saw no one she knew in the cafeteria. Come to think of it, all her colleagues now belonged to an older generation.

She was fond of deep-fried horse mackerel, but today it tasted like sawdust.

When she was on the staff of *Belle* she'd been surrounded by plenty of editors and writers her own age. And the editorial team, except for the editor-in-chief, had all been women. There'd been some rivalry, but basically they'd looked out for each other, talked to each other, and worked extremely hard. During downtime they would share a laugh over frivolous topics like food and romance.

Only now, on her second day at her new post, did she realize what a needed diversion that had been.

In truth, Majime was really the only person in the Dictionary Editorial Department. It was bad enough that they had nothing in common to talk about, but on top of that he used unintelligible, archaic words when he did manage to talk. What was she supposed to do?

She thought back to what it used to feel like on the first day of classes. Wondering if she would fit in, filled with nervous anxiety, she would pick out as safe a seat as possible—an interim place to be until the homeroom teacher gave out assigned seats.

The biggest difference between the first day of school and now was the absence of any sense that something new was about to begin. Working at the company wasn't an obligation, but it had none of the freshness and excitement of a new school term. Maybe psychologically people just weren't built to work only for money. She sighed. The company's plans, her slipping into sheer habit and inertia—amid the need to reconcile these and other things, losing the pleasure of associating with colleagues was a blow. What could sustain her at work now? She felt herself losing her grip.

Yet she had neither the sense of adventure nor the personality to up and quit her job. She polished off her lunch and returned her tray and dishes, reflecting that all she could do was keep on working in the Dictionary Editorial Department with an eye on her winter bonus. She'd gotten her summer bonus just last month, but it was already gone, spent on shoes and clothes. She sighed again.

The moment she returned to the annex, her sighs changed to sneezes. Everything really just had become too much.

The task of straightening up the office finally ended on her third day of her new position. The amount of dust in the air began to decrease.

Kishibe removed her mask and relaxed at her own desk. Sipping on a cup of coffee, she opened a file with a blue cover.

On her way to the kitchenette, she had asked Majime if he wanted a cup of coffee, too, but all she got out of him was an indecipherable mutter. He never looked up from the old-fashioned book he was studying. She decided to let it go.

Next came her big discovery. She found a file on one of the bookshelves right at eye level and so easily accessible to anyone—and yet it was marked in big letters: TOP SECRET: NOT TO BE REMOVED FROM THE

DICTIONARY EDITORIAL OFFICE. *Certainly a bold way of marking something top secret,* she thought, and laughed aloud. Then, full of curiosity, she took the file in hand.

The contents turned out to be about contributors to *The Great Passage*. Data on university professors and researchers, mostly. For each person, the file listed not only their field of expertise and major published works but also their family structure, favorite foods, and how to deal with any trouble that might arise. A former employee had evidently compiled all this information for the benefit of his or her successor. Some of it was outdated, however. On the list of contributors she spotted the name of a famous psychologist who had been dead for several years. She folded her arms. Who on earth had put this together, and when? The paper was yellowing.

She flipped through the pages and at the very end found this note: "Majime is somewhat out of his element when it comes to interacting with outsiders. You, the newcomer to the Dictionary Editorial Department! Use this file to back him up and bring *The Great Passage* to completion. Wishing you the best of luck."

The department had been dreaming of the publication of this dictionary for more than a dozen years, moving forward slowly. In all that time, no additional personnel had been assigned here, she'd heard. That meant this file had been made for her eyes only. It must be the handiwork of whoever used to work here with Majime. When that person was transferred elsewhere, knowing Majime would be left high and dry, he had made this file so whoever replaced him could help deal with contributors. Not knowing when or even if he would be replaced, he had chosen this means of passing on his knowledge to an unknown successor—and that turned out to be Kishibe, who now felt even more daunted than before.

This was heavy stuff. Did being assigned here mean she had to become a fan of dictionaries? Apply herself to dictionary making with love and enthusiasm? Of course, nothing would be better than that, if she could manage it, but she sensed such a commitment might be beyond her. She wasn't at all sure she could communicate effectively with Majime, either. Could she live up to the expectations of whoever had cared enough about the department and its fate to make this file? Maybe not.

What to do? She looked at the last page, and there it was—the name of the file maker. A final note read: "Worn out by dictionary editing? Ready to be cheered up? Drop Masashi Nishioka a line: masanishi@Gembushobo.co.jp"

Nishioka? There was somebody by that name in publicity or sales, a guy about Majime's age. She searched her memory. She'd never spoken to him, but she knew him by sight. She'd seen him sauntering down the corridor in the main building. Belying his goofball air, he had four children and was a devoted father, she'd heard, although she had no way of verifying it.

She could hardly call herself "worn out." This was only her third day on the job. But she was more than ready to be cheered up, and she would love to have someone to talk to about her bewilderment and anxiety. Nishioka would probably lend a willing ear. Propelled by hope and expectation, she sent off an e-mail.

> Dear Masashi Nishioka: Allow me to introduce myself. I am Midori Kishibe, newly assigned to the Dictionary Editorial Department. I don't know the first thing about dictionaries, but I am willing to learn. I saw the top-secret file you made. Thank you for making what looks like a very useful resource. If it wouldn't be too much trouble, would you mind getting together sometime for a talk? I would love to pick your brain. Yours, Midori Kishibe

Nishioka happened to be at his desk. By the time she had made herself a fresh cup of coffee, he had already written back: "Howdy! Thanks muchly for the email." Even his writing style was goofy.

> But sorry—get together and talk? No can do. You'd only fall head over heels in love☆. Haha jk. Seriously, I haven't got anything to teach you about making dictionaries. Just go ahead and ask Majime. Ciao!

What an idiotic message for a man in his forties. Good grief. Now not only her nose but her whole body itched.

> P.S. I suggest you take a look at the bookends on the shelves. You're bound to find something to cheer you up. It'll show you a way out of your present funk. Now, for real, adios!

His style was the height of frivolity, but she decided to follow his advice.

The office was crowded with bookshelves, and there were bookends galore. What could he be hinting at? She went around shoving books aside and examining bookends one by one. While she did this Majime, quiet as a hibernating squirrel, remained wrapped up in his reading, oblivious to her actions.

On a shelf dedicated to miscellaneous information, she found something promising. Taped to the bottom of a metallic gray bookend—an ordinary one for office use—was a white envelope. The Scotch tape was discolored with age and had all but lost its adhesive strength.

Apparently the envelope had lain there for years, unnoticed and untouched. Nishioka must have hidden it. What could be inside? Driven by curiosity Kishibe opened the envelope on the spot. It contained a thick bundle of stationery. Xeroxed stationery, to be precise.

> *Greetings*
> *Cold winds are blowing, a reminder of the swift approach of winter's frosty skies. I trust that you are well.*

Who wrote this letter? To whom was it written? Was it something she should be reading? Worried, she checked the signature at the end—and in so doing realized there were fifteen sheets of stationery. A magnum opus, for a letter. At the end of the fifteenth sheet, she read, "to Kaguya Hayashi from Mitsuya Majime. November 20xx"

Holy cow. Stifling her excitement she returned to her seat. Kaguya Hayashi was the chef at Back of the Moon—and Majime's wife. Then this was what, a love letter? It sure didn't start out like one.

Casually she sneaked a glance at Majime, who was still in hibernating-squirrel mode. Only his unkempt head of hair showed between the stacks of books on his desk. Kishibe settled back in her chair and began to peruse the pages.

It was a love letter all right, at once earnest and ridiculous, and chock full of Chinese characters, making it hard to read. The sentences were awkward; Majime must have been extremely nervous when he wrote it. His very desperation to find some way of conveying his feelings led him around and around in circles so that he never got to the point.

> *There is the example in the ancient tale of a radiant princess named Kaguya (Shining Night) who descended to Earth from the moon, and indeed from the night I first encountered you I have felt such pain in my chest and found breathing so difficult that it is as if I myself were living on the moon.*

She read this sentence over several times and decided it meant, "I have loved you from the day I met you. You give me butterflies." Probably. But all he'd really needed to write was "I love you." What a lot of beating around the bush!

Reflecting Majime's fluctuating emotional state, the letter kept on rising and falling until it entered the climax.

> *If I were to write my present feelings in plain terms, I would sum them up this way: "Kaguya Kaguya, what shall I do with you?"*

What on earth was this? Wasn't this a reference to that poem by Xiang Yu, the ancient Chinese rebel? From the famous one he had written in desperate straits, surrounded by the enemy? Kishibe remembered reading it in high school in her classical Chinese class. The last line was addressed to his lover and started out: "*Gu ya Gu ya*"—which meant "Oh, Yu, oh, Yu." And, as she recalled, the whole line went: "*Gu ya Gu ya*, what shall I do with you?" Should he keep the one he loved with him in this time of imminent peril, or release her and allow her to live, knowing that a fate crueler than death might await her? The line conveyed the agony of a man at the limit of endurance, torn by his love for a woman. A powerful, unforgettable poem.

But what of Majime's love letter? He had probably congratulated himself on his cleverness in substituting Kaguya Kaguya for *Gu ya Gu ya*—but no! It wasn't clever. It was god-awful! She felt a rising tide of emotion, a confused mix of anger and hysterical laughter.

There was just too much of a gap between Xiang Yu, on the boundary of life and death, and Majime in the Dictionary Editorial Department, his hair sticking out every which way. The words "what shall I do with you?" couldn't help but differ in meaning and weight. She wanted to go back in time and wring Majime's neck for writing such a thing. It sounded as if he were taking on the persona of Xiang Yu only to insinuate "Kaguya, baby, I want to do something to you!"

After all that, he ended the long missive with these words:

> *This is all I have to say. Or no, this is not all I want to say, but if I tried to say it all, even if I lived 150 years it wouldn't be enough, and I would use up so much paper they would need to cut down every tree in the rain forest, so I will rest my pen here.*
>
> *I would be very grateful if after reading this you would let me know what you think. Whatever your response, I am prepared. I will take it solemnly to heart.*
>
> *Do take care of yourself.*

After undulating waves of hyperbole, beseeching, and declamation, the letter ended abruptly with a plea for her to take care of herself. Asked what she thought, Kaguya must have been at a total loss.

Out of the corner of her eye, Kishibe saw Majime get up. Hastily she shoved the pages into the space between her knees and the desk.

"Miss Kishibe, there's something I forgot to tell you."

"Yes?"

He came around her desk and stood beside her chair. She looked up at him, scarcely able to keep from going into convulsions at the thought of that love letter.

He seemed at a distance from the world, as if he'd lived for centuries in the Dictionary Editorial Department, as far removed from love and lust as a withered tree or a dried-up sheet of paper. And yet even he had once fallen in love, had yearned and written a love letter that didn't hold anything back, like some kind of midnight diary. And now look at him, a language expert immersed in the task of compiling a dictionary. To hide the spasm of laughter that came over her, she awkwardly pretended to go into a fit of sneezing. Judging from that letter, he was the last person who should give people language advice. He was certainly no master of language. His turns of phrase were clumsy; his ardor spun in circles.

Having got that far in her thinking, Kishibe experienced a revelation. Majime seemed unapproachable, but maybe when he was young he'd been much like her. Maybe he still was, for that matter, in his worries about his relationships with other people, his worries about whether he could properly edit a dictionary, and his general floundering about. She could imagine him upset at his inability to express himself or communicate with others, yet he was forced in the end to put his heart clumsily into words and trust that the other person would understand what he meant. Maybe his linguistic anxieties and hopes were the very thing driving Majime to make a dictionary chock full of words.

In that case, I can make a go of it here, too. I also want to know how to dispel my fears. If I can, I'd like to communicate with Majime in words, pass the time pleasantly with him at work.

Gathering a huge number of words together with as much accuracy as possible was like finding a mirror without distortion. The less distortion in the word-mirror, the greater chance that when you opened up to someone and revealed your inner self, your feelings and thoughts would be reflected there with clarity and depth. You could look together in the mirror and laugh, weep, get angry.

Dictionary making might actually be fun and important work.

Thanks to the love letter, Kishibe felt somewhat closer to Majime. For the first time since coming to the Dictionary Editorial Department, she felt optimistic.

Majime, unaware of Kishibe's inner transformation, was completely taken in by her theatrical sneeze.

"Caught a cold?"

"Maybe. What is it that you forgot to tell me?"

"Starting tomorrow, we'll be entering the final stage of editing *The Great Passage.* We'll use both floors of the annex. Mobilize everyone we can to check all the usage examples, and send material to press as we go."

"Really?" *Surely you didn't wait till the day before to tell me something so important . . .*

"Let's move the desks around and get ready," said Majime.

Ignoring her stupefaction, he rolled up his sleeves, black covers and all.

It took them all day to move desks and transfer materials. The custodian helped. Mrs. Sasaki copied instructions and laid out writing materials for the staff, which was expected to grow considerably.

By the time everything was ready, Kishibe's entire body ached.

"Nice to be young," said Majime enviously. "Right now all I can feel is back pain."

He shuffled off like an actor on the Noh stage, holding his back erect and sliding his feet along the floor. Actually, it looked to her as if that posture might put extra strain on the back.

After seeing Majime off, Kishibe composed a quick e-mail to Nishioka: "I found the document, and thanks to you I do feel better now. Starting tomorrow, the editing of *The Great Passage* moves into the final stage . . . but right now my muscles are so stiff I don't know if I'll be able to come to work."

Thanks largely to Majime's determination, work on *The Great Passage* had continued bit by bit over the past thirteen years. He, Araki, and Professor Matsumoto were 90 percent finished with definitions of general words. The remaining 10 percent consisted of neologisms that had been coined in the intervening thirteen years and words whose inclusion was still under debate. Majime and Professor Matsumoto would go over these together, and Majime would write definitions for those to be included.

Certain other words that had originally been marked for inclusion were now out of date. Kishibe and Mrs. Sasaki would go over these and decide which should stay and which should go.

"Once a word makes it into a dictionary," explained Araki for Kishibe's benefit, "it tends not to get cut. That's because it's better to have as many words as possible, including archaic terms. But if you're not careful, by the time of publication you can end up with a dictionary full of obsolete words."

"But including some obsolete words is okay." She nodded, looking at the bundle of draft definitions written according to the guidelines. Encyclopedic entries and technical terms were the province of college professors, who wrote drafts as requested. "I wondered why we were including the word *getabako*." Literally "*geta* box," the word referred to shelves in an entranceway for storing footwear; *geta* were wooden clogs formerly worn with kimonos or other traditional wear.

"Are you saying no one uses *getabako* anymore?"

"At the school I went to it was called *kutsubako*." (Shoe box.) "Ah, but come to think of it, our definition of *getabako* doesn't say, 'Same as *kutsubako*.' And *kutsubako* should be an entry word in its own right, meaning 'shelves or a box for storing shoes.'"

"Times do change," mused Araki. Then he shouted, "Majime! We've got trouble! An extra entry word!"

Gradually Kishibe became more used to reading dictionary entries. These were all now on hand. Majime had gone around to the various universities and research institutes to collect them in person.

"Mr. Majime, did you ever by any chance take a look at the top-secret file?" Kishibe asked.

Majime nodded, beaming. "Thanks to Nishioka, all my struggles and tactics worked out perfectly."

Then did he also know all about the concealed love letter? Cautiously she asked, "Did you look at the note on the last page?"

"It's embarrassing to admit." He scratched his cheek awkwardly. "Sometimes I would get discouraged and wonder if *The Great Passage* was ever really going to launch. At times like that, I'd take Nishioka up on his offer and e-mail him. He always was kind enough to take me out for a drink."

"Oh, I see . . ." The twisted closeness between the two middle-aged men boggled her mind. Wearing a strained smile, Kishibe turned tail and fled. So for Majime, Nishioka's e-mail address on the "top-secret" file led to an invitation to go drinking, and for anyone else it would lead to a revelation of the love letter's existence.

Having all the manuscripts finished didn't mean the dictionary was finished. All the entries had to be polished and trimmed as much as possible. With over two hundred thousand entry words, space was at a premium.

All usage examples had to be checked and double-checked. A usage example included a quotation showing a specific instance of the word in use along with the source. For modern words, rather than offer a quotation, they often invented illustrative sentences of their own. Every usage example had to be checked to make sure the sentence conveyed the appropriate meaning and any quotation was accurate. Over twenty college students were hired as part-time workers to do the job. Seated at the desks Kishibe and Majime had worked so hard to rearrange, they thumbed through reference works. As summer vacation came along, the number of student workers doubled.

When the checking was finished, the entire editorial staff worked on inserting instructions for font sizes, phonetic renderings, and the like. Everything had to be in accordance with the guidelines and conform to a single standard. If the font changed for no apparent reason, or if different symbols were used depending on the entry, users would be confused.

Then, finally, the dictionary pages would be ready to send to the printer. They began with words starting with the first kana in the syllabary and proceeded in order.

The submitted pages came back in the form of galley proofs. The editorial staff and proofreaders went over these with a fine-tooth comb, looking for typographical errors as well as interpretation issues, places lacking in clarity, and a host of other possible mishaps. The company brought in a huge number of freelance proofreaders in addition to in-house ones.

When everyone was satisfied that all was well, the galleys were returned to the printer's marked in red, and a second set of proofs was made. For a dictionary the size of *The Great Passage*, a minimum of five proofs was standard. Larger dictionaries often required as many as ten.

For the first two sets of proofs, they confined themselves to checking content and format; that was really all they could do, since some texts weren't finished and the entries were not in perfect order. With the third proofs, finally all the entries were put in order following the kana syllabary. Now, for the first time, they were able to survey the entire dictionary, and could look for redundancies and omissions, and decide where to insert illustrations.

On the fourth proofs, page layouts were determined and the placement of illustrations was tweaked. At this point, changes affecting the total number of pages were to be avoided. Major edits to the sentences or entry words would change the number of pages, and that in turn would push up the price of the dictionary. But sometimes a new entry word needed to be added at the last minute. Such things happened if a new American president took office, for example, or if a municipal merger took place. On the chance that such a thing would happen, a bit of white space had to be left until the very end.

Naturally, work on the galley proofs also began at the front of the syllabary. "That's why most dictionaries skimp on words toward the end of the syllabary," said Majime with a grin. "By the time they get to words starting with *ra* and *wa*, the publication date is near, and it's a battle for time. Words get left out just because there isn't enough help to do the checking or space to squeeze in one more on the page."

"Is that going to happen with *The Great Passage*, too?" asked Kishibe. What a shame that would be, she thought, after the years of labor the staff had put in.

"Well, after all," said Professor Matsumoto from the side, "we've been working on it for thirteen years now. We'll make sure we get every last word in, right down to the bitter end."

"There's an easy way to tell if you're slighting words at the end of the dictionary," said Majime. He lugged over a number of medium-sized dictionaries and lined them up in front of Kishibe, unopened. "Dictionaries have black markers called thumb indexes, like these, cut into the pages to locate entries starting at a particular section. As you can see, a preponderance of Japanese words start with sounds from the first three columns of the kana syllabary: those headed by *a*, *ka*, and *sa*."

Kishibe compared the various dictionaries. In each one, words from those first three columns took up more than half the pages.

"Whereas words from the last three columns, those headed by *ya*, *ra*, and *wa*, take up very little space. That's because few *wago* begin with those sounds."

"Wago?"

"Native Japanese words, as opposed to *kango*"—Chinese loanwords—"and *gairaigo*," (words borrowed from foreign countries other than China). "Anyway, when you line up words in order, you see most of them are concentrated at the beginning: words starting with *a-i-u-e-o*, *ka-ki-ku-ke-ko*, *sa-shi-su-se-so*. So if the lead word on the middle page of a dictionary starts with *su* or *se*, you know that the words chosen are evenly distributed throughout the syllabary."

"It's interesting that the center of the dictionary comes so far at the front of the syllabary." Kishibe folded her arms and looked at the black thumb indexes.

"Well," said Professor Matsumoto, "it's helpful to know that words aren't scattered evenly through the syllabary." He traced a thumb index fondly with a finger. "That's why, if you want to win at the word game *shiritori*, you need to pick words that end with *ra* or *wa* or some other kana from the end of the syllabary." He smiled. "The trouble is, it's hard to come up with such words on the spur of the moment."

"Even for you?" she asked in surprise.

"The ocean of words is wide and deep." He laughed. "I still have a long way to go before I can be like an *ama*, someone who dives down and fetches pearls."

The editing of *The Great Passage* went on seemingly without end.

Summer vacation came and went, and the student workers continued to haunt the office. Kishibe and the rest of the staff almost always took the last train home. Day after day they kept on checking entry words, making final calls regarding usage samples, adding phonetic readings of characters, and otherwise marking the proofs with red-pencil corrections. There was so much to do that Kishibe often felt like shouting out. Sometimes she would actually go into the annex restroom, shut the door, and let out a little scream.

Seeing her frustration, Mrs. Sasaki would point to the schedule and the work checklist and say comfortingly, "It's all right. We're doing fine. I know what has to be done, and if anything gets left out, I'll speak up right away. Just relax and do the work in front of you."

There was way too much work in front of her; that was the whole problem. She had to carry out various tasks simultaneously and wound up confused.

As she was tearing her hair out, Araki came around to give her warm encouragement. "For someone working on her first dictionary, you're doing fine, Miss Kishibe. Look at our Majime. All the time we worked on the *Sokéboo Encyclopedia*, he was in his element—he knew more about that world than we ever would. Now look at him."

Majime was sitting facing the galley proofs, head in hands. Once in a while he would raise his head and mime moving a box or something in midair. Had overwork finally driven him to playing with invisible blocks?

As Kishibe was flinching at this thought, Araki explained, "He's mentally figuring how much space the entries will take. How he can fit them all into a fixed number of pages by cutting a word here and a line there. It's like a complicated puzzle. Even he appears to be struggling."

There was more work not only in the office, but outside it as well. As head of the Dictionary Editorial Department, Majime was often called to meetings with the sales and advertising departments. He also had to consult with a designer and production editor to decide on the binding for *The Great Passage*. Kishibe fully expected him to cave under pressure from others and come back looking dejected, but he proved a surprisingly tenacious negotiator. When it came to his precious dictionary, he could apparently hold his own. He delayed the release date and worked up to the last minute to perfect the contents, and he didn't agree readily to everything suggested by outsiders, either, refusing to be pushed around and admirably sticking to his guns.

Kishibe also would have liked to attend the meetings with advertising, but the editorial department was shorthanded to begin with and couldn't spare two people at once. A major publication like *The Great Passage* called for a major ad campaign. Rumor had it they were going to plaster train stations with posters featuring a popular celebrity. The idea made Kishibe a bit nervous. Did Majime have any idea who was who in today's entertainment world?

Despite her anxiety, he would return from such meetings in high spirits.

"Did they come up with the name of a celebrity you particularly like?" she asked.

"No," he said, laughing shamefacedly, "I never heard of any of them. But that's all right. Nishioka's gung-ho and full of ideas."

That name again. Remembering his goofy e-mail, she sighed. Still, it was nice to think there was somebody in advertising who used to work here.

The Dictionary Editorial Department and *The Great Passage* both had long been the butt of jokes at Gembu, derided as "money pits," but now thanks to Nishioka's exertions the dictionary was set to make a smashing debut.

It was spring—Kishibe's second spring in the Dictionary Editorial Department. Since leaving the staff of *Belle* two years ago in July, she had toiled with the others for the past year and eight months, checking proofs for *The Great Passage*. Now the first part of the dictionary was on its fourth set of proofs, the last part on its third set. The end was not yet in sight. And yet the release date was set for early March of the following year. Spring vacation was when dictionary sales heated up, in advance of the new school year in April. People bought them to prepare for their own studies or as gifts. Would *The Great Passage* be ready in time? Its slow progress made Kishibe antsy.

Majime was sitting at his desk gazing at something, seemingly as insouciant as ever. Kishibe, checking the words beginning with *a*, was bothered by something and went to ask his opinion.

"Could I ask you something?" Standing next to him, she glanced down at his desktop. He was staring at a picture of a *kappa*, a traditional Japanese river imp. They had commissioned the illustration to accompany the entry word. It was drawn in narrow lines using a realistic style (not that she had ever seen an actual *kappa*), depicting a creature with a turtle shell and a fringe of hair, carrying a sake flask. True to folklore, the top of its head was bald.

"First let me ask you a question," he said, motioning for her to sit down in a nearby chair. "What do you think of this illustration?"

Difficult question. She was no judge of *kappa.* She studied the picture and said, "It's good, isn't it?"

Majime scratched his head. "Does a *kappa* carry a bottle of sake? I have a feeling it's Shigaraki-ware raccoon dogs who do that."

"Now that you mention it . . . The TV commercials for sake that show *kappa* with a sake bottle and cup may have imprinted that image on people's minds." Lately, Kishibe had come to appreciate the department's dictum to try to get to the bottom of anything that wasn't crystal clear in its meaning, rather than leave things vague or depend on mistaken assumptions. Leaving aside her own question, she went to the bookshelves and looked up *kappa* in another company's dictionary.

"The illustration in the *Great Dictionary of Japanese* doesn't show it carrying anything," she reported.

"That's what I thought." He folded his arms and nodded. "The one carrying a sake flask is the Shigaraki-ware raccoon dog, all right."

"It's okay, though, isn't it?" she said. "I mean, why shouldn't a *kappa* carry a sake flask?" She seated herself again in the chair by his desk. "After all, real raccoon dogs don't carry sake around, and we have no way of knowing what a *kappa* might or might not carry."

"All the more reason to be as accurate as we can." He said this almost to himself. "You could put an illustration of a raccoon dog figurine carrying a sake bottle next to *Shigaraki ware* in the dictionary, but not next to *raccoon dog*. That would be highly problematic. For the same reason, we can't put up a picture of a *kappa* holding a bottle of sake without any justification. Some people believe in *kappa*, and take them very seriously. We can't just . . . have any old thing."

Left to his own devices, Majime would probably go all the way to the folklore-rich city of Tono in Iwate Prefecture, supposedly the hometown of the mythical *kappa*, to capture one. She could just see him inquiring of his quarry, "Do you ever carry a sake flask?" Quickly she said, "There are various theories about the appearance of *kappa*, so I think it would be all right to leave it this way, but if it really bothers you, why not just ask the illustrator to erase the sake bottle?"

"Right. If I'd known it was going to be this much trouble, maybe I should have just gone with an illustration by Toriyama Sekien, the eighteenth-century folklore artist."

He turned to his computer and started to type an e-mail. He was going to politely ask the illustrator to correct the picture. Without a pause, he said, "What were you going to ask me?"

"It's about the entry for *ai*, 'love.'" She brought over the proof to show him. "I understand the first definition: 'A feeling of tender affection for someone or something irreplaceable.' But look at the sample compounds using the character *ai*: *aisai*." (Beloved wife.) "*Aijin*." (Lover.) "*Aibyo*." (Pet cat.)

"Is there something wrong?"

"There certainly is!" Her tone was bristling. "Listing *lover* right alongside *beloved wife* implies that you can have both at the same time, but the definition says this is impossible—because the object of one's affection is 'irreplaceable.' It's as if we're asking someone to choose between his lover and his wife! And while I'm on the subject, I object to equating love for another human being with love for a cat."

"Love is love, without any distinction or ranking. I love my cat as much as I do my wife."

"That may be," she said heatedly, "but I'll bet you and your cat don't have intercourse!" Then, feeling the eyes of the part-timers on her, she tried to make herself small.

It took a few seconds for her meaning to register with Majime; the word she had used, *seiko*, had various other meanings, including "succeed." He seemed to sift through the possible compounds, mentally trying out different combinations of characters. Suddenly he turned red and mumbled, "Well, no . . ."

"See?" Kishibe threw out her chest in triumph. "What's even stranger is the second definition: 'Being enamored of a member of the opposite sex, sometimes accompanied by sexual desire. Romantic love.'"

"What's strange about that?" Majime looked at her, trying to read her face. He seemed to have lost all confidence.

"Why limit it to a member of the opposite sex? If a homosexual person is enamored of someone and feels intermittent sexual desire for them, are we saying it's not love?"

"No, I didn't have any such intention. But does it really—"

"Matter?" She cut him off. "Yes, it matters. *The Great Passage* is supposed to be a dictionary for a new age. If we yield to the majority and stay bound to stale ways of thinking and feeling, how can we ever offer true definitions of kaleidoscopic words—words that are in constant flux but have underlying bedrock meanings?"

"You're right." Majime's shoulders sagged. "When I was young, I remember having the same doubts about the meaning of *ren'ai*, 'romantic attachment.' And yet somehow in the course of working on so many other things I forgot about it. I'm ashamed of myself."

Lately Kishibe had begun to feel more confident about her work on the dictionary. Majime often accepted her opinions, and he made her feel that he regarded her as a powerful ally. With a sense of relief and pride, she took back the proofs.

"Now that I think of it," he mused, "Nishioka said once that I should put myself in the shoes of the dictionary user and imagine whether the definition they encountered would boost their spirits. If a young person thinking he or she might be homosexual looked up the word *ai* in our dictionary and read, 'Being enamored of a member of the opposite sex,' how would they feel? I didn't have enough imagination."

"No," Kishibe agreed, "you didn't." Then, seeing his remorse, she added forgivingly, "But it's understandable. You're a member of the elite, someone who's always been on the winning side."

"The elite? Me?"

"Yes. You have a graduate degree and a beautiful, talented wife, and you're a leading expert on the editing of dictionaries. You don't seem to have any problems related to being a minority."

"Is that how I seem to you?" He gave a troubled laugh. "Anyway, I think your point about *ai* is well taken. Now, how to fix it?"

"Since you are so devoted to your cat, we'll leave in *aibyo*, 'pet cat,' and take out *aijin*, 'lover.' How's that? And we could change 'a member of the opposite sex' to 'another person.'"

"Sounds good to me. Professor Matsumoto will be here soon, so I'll ask him to go over the changes."

At that point Miyamoto called to say that the latest paper sample for *The Great Passage* was finished. "We have finally produced the ultimate paper!" he told Kishibe in triumph.

"Excellent," said Majime. Then he glanced around the office, where proofreaders and student workers milled around and a slew of galley proofs covered all the desks. "But there's no space here to spread out paper samples. Miss Kishibe, I'm sorry to trouble you, but would you go to the Akebono office and check the sample yourself? If you think it's good you can tell them to go ahead and start production."

Paper used in dictionaries was distinctive and needed in large quantity, so unless they started to make it at least six months before publication, it wouldn't be ready in time. Kishibe understood this, but she wasn't comfortable making such an important decision on her own.

"Can't you go instead of me?"

"No, because I have to discuss some things with Professor Matsumoto." He looked at her and nodded encouragingly. "You'll be fine. You're a dictionary editor of the first water. You make shrewd judgments and you know as much about paper as anyone, if not more, since you've been in on all the trials so far. I have full confidence in your judgment."

Charged with such an important mission, Kishibe left Gembu Books feeling slightly nervous.

The cherry blossoms were almost ready to bloom, but a cold rain was falling. She could just see her breath. Opening her plastic umbrella, she walked past the cherry buds, their color deepening in the rain, and headed for the subway.

She had spoken confidently to Majime just now, but in fact she was still far from sure of her abilities as a dictionary editor. Her insight about limiting the meaning of *love* to members of the opposite sex was based on a fluke. A boy in her college seminar had confessed at a drinking party shortly before graduation, "Know what? I'm gay." She and all his friends had suspected as much. Everyone who happened to be present when he said this had felt like saying, "Yeah, we know." They bit back the words, however, realizing that considerable anguish and courage had led up to the admission. So instead of "We know" they'd said things like, "Oh, yeah? Here, drink up," and continued their friendship as before. That experience was what had led her to question the definition. She was appalled to think that she had accused Majime of being a member of the elite, with no struggles or complexes of any kind. She turned red at the thought.

Just because I've finally started getting a little used to dictionary editing doesn't give me the right to sound off like that! She knew perfectly well that Majime suffered and agonized over his work at the helm of *The Great Passage*. She frequently saw him in the throes of anxiety. She wasn't a member of the elite in any sense, but she, not he, was the one who had lived oblivious to her own emotions, without cares or complexes to speak of. She had pursued her life and her career without thinking, drifting along like someone who comes to a fork in the road and unhesitatingly takes the easier way.

Working on the dictionary, delving into words the way we do, has changed me, she thought. Awakening to the power of words—the power not to hurt others but to protect them, to tell them things, to form connections with them—had taught her to probe her own mind and inclined her to make allowances for other people's thoughts and feelings.

Through her work on *The Great Passage*, she was seeking and gaining access to the power of words as never before.

The Akebono Paper Company building faced a main street in Ginza. Kishibe was shown into a conference room on the eighth floor. Besides Miyamoto, four other men were present in the conference room: the head of the sales department and his deputy, the head of development, and the project chief. The presence of this executive team made it painfully clear to Kishibe that developing paper for a dictionary was a major undertaking that Akebono took seriously. She greeted them in a flurry, afraid they were thinking, "What? This kid is the only one who came?" She cursed Majime for his lack of consideration.

Her fears notwithstanding, the faces in the room were friendly, if a bit tense, as they returned her greeting. Lying on the table in the center of the room was a sheaf of paper.

"This must be the paper for *The Great Passage*," she said, taking a step toward the table. Immediately the men fell back on either side, opening the way for her. She felt like Moses at the Red Sea.

"We devoted all our efforts to the creation of this paper." Miyamoto was the group spokesman. "We gave full consideration to waxiness."

The others were nodding. She sensed how hard this team must have worked, night and day, to satisfy Majime's demand.

Cautiously she slid her hand across what Miyamoto had called "the ultimate paper." It was thin and smooth, pleasant to the touch. It felt cool against her skin, and yet it had a warm yellowish tinge. She held a sheet up to the light and saw it had a touch of red. This was the coloration that Miyamoto was so proud of, that only Akebono could produce.

"We did a test run," he said cautiously. "It takes the ink very well with no show-through." Everyone nodded vigorously to back him up.

After Majime had forced Akebono back to the drawing board, Miyamoto had brought four other samples, produced by trial and error, visiting the office time and again to get a fix on their wishes. Each time, Kishibe had received him, and together they had exchanged opinions and contemplated the whys and wherefores of dictionary paper.

Kishibe was an employee of Gembu Books, but at the same time she and Miyamoto had become colleagues. She had no intention of toning down any criticism she might have on his behalf, and yet for his sake she hoped with all her heart that this was indeed the ultimate paper.

To help Miyamoto if she could, and to create the finest paper possible for *The Great Passage*, she had spent the last year and eight months exploring a variety of dictionaries. Before, she had never noticed, but it was definitely true that depending on the dictionary and the publisher, the paper differed in color, feel, and texture. Again and again she had turned the pages of the office dictionaries, getting to know them through her fingertips. In the end, she could touch a dictionary with her eyes closed and guess its publisher and title. She was hardly ever wrong. Mrs. Sasaki marveled that if there were a test for such ability, Kishibe would surely qualify at the highest level.

The paper in front of her was impeccable in color, thickness, and feel. The big question was its waxiness—the quality Majime valued over all else. How would that be?

Silently she swallowed and slowly turned a page. As if leafing through a dictionary, she went on, page after page.

Painfully loud silence enveloped the room. Finally the project chief, his nerves apparently stretched to the limit, spoke up. He was a thin, bespectacled man in his midthirties. "Well?" He looked at Kishibe with mingled confidence and anxiety.

It's wonderful, she meant to say, but her voice caught with emotion. She coughed once before she could get the word out. "Wonderful."

Cheers erupted. The project chief raised both arms in triumph, and the head of development shook hands with the head of sales. Miyamoto and the deputy manager of sales were hugging, overcome with emotion. Kishibe had never seen grown men behave like this.

"I'm really glad." Miyamoto let go of the sales division manager and gave his face, moist with perspiration or tears, a wipe with his sleeve. "We thought this would do the trick, but it's so good to hear you give the thumbs-up."

He trusts me. Even though I'm a total amateur where paper is concerned. The thought made Kishibe happy. She reflected back on all the times they had met to discuss paper. Now this "ultimate" paper had been created, and everyone in Akebono Paper Company was full of joy. She, too, was overcome, on the edge of tears.

She looked down at the sample before her. This paper was truly superb. When she turned the page, it clung naturally to the ball of her thumb, but never more than a page at a time. Nor did she feel any static electricity. It left her hand with the ease of dry sand slipping through the fingers. Majime was sure to be pleased.

"What a relief!" said the head of sales. "After all, how paper feels is something sensuous. Urabe here was very concerned about how to convey your wishes to the development team. Isn't that right, Urabe?"

"Um, yes," the man called Urabe answered with a weak smile. Compared to the dynamic, open-hearted head of sales, he seemed much quieter.

"So I told them flat out," said the head of sales. "I said, 'Make a paper that's like a beautiful woman you love but have to leave.' What do you think? Doesn't that sum it up perfectly?"

Not really, thought Kishibe, but she let it go with a smile. A comparison so hard to make heads or tails of must have caused the workers even more trouble.

"Well," he said, "as soon as you know the exact size of the first printing and the number of pages, let us know."

Miyamoto came over, perhaps worried that the man's previous remark could be construed as sexual harassment. He sent Kishibe a glance that said, "Sorry about that."

"We should be working on the fourth proofs of the second half by the rainy season, so when that happens I'll be sure to let you know." At the same time her eyes signaled to Miyamoto, "It's okay, no problem."

"Our papermaking machine is standing by, ready to go," the head of development said with enthusiasm.

The project chief smiled and gave her a sample of the "ultimate" paper to take with her. There were about a hundred sheets, cut to dictionary size. She was glad to have them, just in case her judgment was off somehow. She could show these sheets to Majime and get his final approval.

Carrying the paper in a bag, Kishibe decided it was time to leave Akebono Paper Company. Everyone trooped out to the elevator to see her off.

"Is it heavy?" asked Miyamoto worriedly, eyeing the paper bag.

"No, it's fine, thanks to the lightness of the paper you all made."

He scratched the tip of his nose in embarrassed pleasure. "I'll see her down," he told the others, and got into the elevator with her.

"Good idea," said the division head. "Well, thank you very much, Miss Kishibe. It's been a pleasure."

"Likewise. Thank you all very much." She bowed her head politely, and the elevator doors closed. No one was in the elevator but the two of them. She was acutely conscious of being alone with Miyamoto in an enclosed space.

"I'm so relieved, I hardly know what to do with myself." Miyamoto moved his shoulders up and down.

"Thank you for all you've done," she said. "Now it's up to us at Gembu to make the content as good as we possibly can, to match the quality of the paper you've given us."

"Miss Kishibe." The elevator reached the first floor, and they walked toward the entrance. "Would you have dinner with me tonight? To celebrate."

"Just us?"

He nodded. "Is that a bad idea?"

"Oh, no. But please let it be on me."

There was some back-and-forth, but in the end he yielded. "I'll go get my coat and things. Wait here. I'll be right back." He turned and ran up the stairs, as if he couldn't be bothered to wait for the elevator.

While he was gone, Kishibe called the office.

"Mr. Majime? This is Kishibe. The paper couldn't be better."

"That's good. One less headache."

"They gave me a sample, but . . ." She paused. "Would it be all right if I went straight home tonight?"

"Absolutely. If you think the paper will do, I don't even need to see the sample."

"Oh, no, I'll bring it in tomorrow. And one more thing . . ." She hesitated, then plunged on. "May I take Miyamoto to dinner and charge it to the company?"

"Of course. I was just leaving for Seven Treasures Garden with Professor Matsumoto. Shall we meet there?"

Majime could on occasion be considerate after all, but this time his consideration was wasted. Kishibe wanted to dine with Miyamoto alone. She politely declined the offer and telephoned a restaurant she had in mind to make a reservation.

The darkness of night around Kagurazaka always had a kind of moist radiance.

Making her way down a cobblestone lane, Kishibe led Miyamoto to Back of the Moon and slid open the lattice door. From behind the counter Kaguya called out a welcome. She seemed to be making an effort to exude warmth, but her smooth cheeks barely moved as she spoke. Though she could wield a knife with amazing dexterity, she was clumsy at such ordinary things.

Miyamoto looked around with apparent interest at the restaurant's interior, a remodeled traditional house. Kaguya seated them at the counter and handed them towelettes. The young man who worked for her was home with a cold, she said.

Perhaps because it was still early, they were the only customers. They had an appetizer of monkfish liver with ponzu sauce garnished with grated radish and red pepper. Before eating, they clinked glasses of cold beer. When they tried the monkfish liver, it melted in their mouths.

Kaguya continued working behind the counter, scowling with concentration. She served them a selection of sashimi, prepared with evident attention to temperature and thickness, followed by dishes such as deep-fried tofu stuffed with fermented soybeans and lightly oven toasted. The timing of the presentation was excellent.

"This is really good," said Miyamoto, eating with gusto. "Nice place. I have deep-fried tofu and *natto* at home, but it never comes out crisp and delicious like this."

Finishing her beer and switching to distilled *shochu*, Kishibe agreed. Kaguya bowed her head slightly, shyly pleased. Again tonight she was cool, like a female version of actor Ken Takakura.

"I came here once before, for the welcome party the department gave me." She glanced at Kaguya, but as Kaguya gave no sign of wanting her to keep it secret, she went on. "Kaguya here is married to Mr. Majime."

Miyamoto choked on his drink and quickly wiped his mouth with the towelette. He looked back and forth at the two women, and seemed to grasp that Kishibe was not pulling his leg. "He's married! That's a surprise."

He seemed less surprised that Majime's wife was Kaguya than that the man had a wife at all.

"Tell me, how did you two, uh . . .?" Before he had finished saying the words, he apparently decided it was an ill-mannered question and let it dangle, unfinished.

Kaguya, unconcerned, answered, "We lived in the same building."

Kishibe was feeling elated. The paper for *The Great Passage* had been selected, and she was here having dinner with Miyamoto. The alcohol was taking effect a little more rapidly than usual; her cheeks were already warm and flushed. She decided to take advantage of the opportunity to sound out Kaguya a little more.

"What attracted you to him?" This sounded vaguely rude, so she hastened to add, "I'm sure there were lots of things . . ."

"It was his total commitment to the dictionary." Kaguya kept a watchful eye on the grilling chicken as she replied. She swiftly took it off the fire and served it with *yuzukosho*, a fermented condiment made from chili peppers, citrus peel, and salt. The chicken skin was crisp and savory, the meat juicy, dissolving on the tongue like a precious fruit.

They exclaimed in delight and had her refill their glasses.

Smiling, Kaguya said, "The customer's appreciation of food doesn't require fancy words. All anyone needs to say is, 'It's good.' That and the look on someone's face is all the reward a chef needs. But we do need words when we're in training."

Kishibe had never heard Kaguya be so talkative. She rested her chopsticks and listened.

"I started learning to cook when I was in my teens, but only after meeting Majime did the importance of words strike me. He says that memories are words. A fragrance or a flavor or a sound can summon up an old memory, but what's really happening is that a memory that had been slumbering and nebulous becomes accessible in words."

Washing up as she spoke, Kaguya went on. "So the question for a chef is, when you eat something delicious, how do you capture the flavor in words? That's an important ability for a chef to have. Watching my husband's fascination with dictionaries made me realize that."

The Majime who wrote that off-the-wall love letter was now a husband who gave his wife advice on her job and whispered sweet words of love in her ear? Struck by this unexpected thought, Kishibe asked, "Is he very talkative at home?"

"No, he's quiet and always has his nose in a book."

Just as she had thought.

Beside her, Miyamoto nodded thoughtfully. "I think I understand what you were saying just now. I work for a company that makes paper, and verbalizing a color or texture to the person in charge of development is a huge challenge. But talking it over, coming to a shared understanding, and then seeing exactly the kind of paper I'd visualized come into being is a great source of pleasure. Nothing beats it."

Words were necessary for creation. Kishibe imagined the primordial ocean that covered the surface of the earth long ago—a soupy, swirling liquid in a state of chaos. Inside every person there was a similar ocean. Only when that ocean was struck by the lightning of words could all come into being. Love, the human heart . . . Words gave things form so they could rise out of the dark sea.

"How do you like working in the Dictionary Editorial Department?" Unusually for her, Kaguya posed a question.

Kishibe smiled. "At first I felt lost, but I really enjoy the work now. I find it rewarding." When she had first transferred there, she never dreamed the day would come when she could say those words with such warmth.

Two more groups of customers came in, so from then on Kaguya had her hands full. Even so, timing it just right, she ended their meal with hot green tea poured over cooked white rice with savory toppings, followed by a jellied dessert, followed finally by dishes of homemade vanilla ice cream. Miyamoto and Kishibe ate it all, chatting with pleasure.

"What's it like working with Mr. Majime?" In deference to Kaguya, Miyamoto asked this in a low voice. "He seems a little inaccessible, perhaps? A bit eccentric, I think."

"Well, let's see," Kishibe said, sensing that he wasn't looking to gossip but sincerely wanted to know. "For one thing, we're having it out now about man and woman." Seeing his look of surprise, she said hastily, "I mean, the *words* 'man' and 'woman.'"

He nodded. "When I was in junior high school, I remember looking up 'woman' in the dictionary."

"Whatever for?"

"Well, you know—kids that age have all sorts of ideas." He sounded embarrassed and apologetic. "All it said was, 'The sex that is not male.' What a disappointment!"

"That's just it!" she said excitedly. "When you look up 'man' in *Wide Garden of Words*, it says, 'one of the human sexes; the one not female.' Then if you look up 'woman,' it says, 'one of the human sexes; the one with childbearing organs.' For 'man,' *Great Forest of Words* has 'the sex possessing the organs and physiology for the purpose of impregnating a woman,' and for 'woman' it has 'the sex with the organs and physiology for the purpose of childbearing.'

Catching her dissatisfaction, Miyamoto fell to thinking. "Are you saying the definition should include transgendered people?"

"I'm saying that explaining human gender as a male-female dichotomy is a bit dated, even from the standpoint of physiology, isn't it? Dictionaries often do define a word by putting it in opposition to another one and saying, 'Not this.' But with 'left' and 'right,' they come up with some ingenious definitions."

"Like what?"

"Look it up sometime."

Kishibe finished her ice cream and sipped a cup of hot tea. "Maybe there's no way around it, but I don't think either men or women appreciate being defined in terms of pregnancy. There are such people as hermaphrodites, and I just think there should be a little more leeway in the definition. Something like, 'The gender that is not male. Also, those who so identify themselves.' But Mr. Majime is hesitant. He told me that would be precipitous."

"He said that, 'precipitous'? Not your everyday word." Miyamoto was momentarily distracted. "But you're absolutely right. If only for the sake of all the junior high school boys and girls looking up words with high expectations, a freer, more in-depth definition is better."

"An excess of caution makes dictionaries a bit conservative." Kishibe sighed. "Sometimes it seems like we're dealing with a stubborn old man."

"Who, Majime?" Miyamoto teased.

"No, the dictionary!"

He laughed. "Stubbornness makes a dictionary reliable and also gives it a certain charm. Working on a dictionary for the first time taught me that."

Dinner was over, but they didn't feel like calling it a night, so they went to a nearby bar. This time Miyamoto paid.

Afterward they went out to the street to hail a taxi, and Miyamoto said, "Miss Kishibe, may I have your number and e-mail address?"

She happily took out her phone, and they exchanged numbers by infrared data communication. They looked like two grown adults playing with radio-controlled model cars, she thought. They had never so much as held hands, but their phones were practically kissing. This struck her as funny, and she giggled. She might have been a bit drunk. Miyamoto laughed, too.

He hailed a taxi for her and waved goodnight. She waved back. The taxi sped off, leaving him there in the street.

The cell phone in her hand vibrated to inform her of incoming mail.

Subject: Thanks for dinner

Message: I had a great time. I'll do all I can to help bring *The Great Passage* to completion. Would you have dinner with me again sometime?

She quickly texted him back and then looked out the taxi window at the night scenery. As always, words flew invisibly to and fro through the air.

Happiness made her break into a smile. The driver might think she was batty. She lightly bit the inside of her cheek and tried hard to maintain her composure.

CHAPTER 5

Lately, Miss Kishibe was noticeably more enthusiastic about her work. This thought came to Majime as, out of the corner of his eye, he watched her talking to someone on the telephone. Despite suffering from the fall pollen, she was speaking cheerfully and politely into the receiver. The bottom half of her face was covered by a white hay-fever mask, but her skin and hair were lustrous and beautiful.

Uh-oh, better watch it. Did thoughts like these constitute sexual harassment? He dropped his eyes back on the fourth-proof galleys spread out on his desk, while his ears went on following Miss Kishibe's voice. It wasn't that he was attracted to her. It was that the person she was talking to was insufferable.

The Dictionary Editorial Department received all sorts of calls from dictionary users. They had found an error, or they wanted to know why such-and-such a word wasn't included, or something else along those lines. In order to keep on producing better and better dictionaries, the office paid careful attention to user opinions and kept them on file.

Yet some callers were a pain. Like the one Miss Kishibe was talking to right now—Mr. Particle, they called him. When the seasons changed—in the spring and fall—he called almost daily. Whether he was talking to someone or reading the newspaper, usage of grammatical particles seemed to bother him—particularly usage of the particle *e*, one of the most common in the Japanese language. If you obsessed over a thing like that, interesting examples popped up everywhere. Every time a new one came to his attention, Mr. Particle would call to inquire exactly which shade of meaning was intended, with reference to the explanations in *Gembu Student's Dictionary of Japanese.* "How do I know?" would have seemed a choice reply, but Miss Kishibe never failed to respond patiently. Since she'd started going out with Miyamoto, she seemed to take her work more seriously than ever before.

"Well," she was saying now, "in the phrase *tsuki he mukau roketto*"—a rocket heading toward the moon—"the particle *he* is clearly directional, so it would correspond to the first sense. Pardon? What about *Jikka e tsuitara, haha ni okorareta*?" (When I got home, I was scolded by my mother.) "Well, let's see." She paused. "That would be number four, *expressing imminence.*"

She sounded positive, but Majime wasn't so sure. An example of usage expressing imminence would be more like this: *Jikka ni tsuita tokoro he, takkyubin ga kita* (Just as I got home, the package arrived). The caller's example fit rather with number two, *indicating resolution of an action or effect.*

The caller deserved to know the correct answer. Majime started to get up, but just then Professor Matsumoto returned from the restroom. Glancing quickly around, he seemed to grasp the situation and motioned to Majime to sit back down.

"Let Miss Kishibe handle it."

"But she's giving him the wrong answer."

"Our friend is satisfied as long as someone here joins him in thinking about particle usage. If you took over the phone and gave him a different answer, you'd only confuse him more."

Majime lowered himself back onto his chair cushion. Professor Matsumoto sat down beside him and resumed work on the fourth proof. Stealing a glance at the professor's profile, Majime became worried. The professor's color wasn't good, and he had lost weight. Since he'd always been thin as a rail, the difference was slight, but there it was.

"Aren't you getting tired, sir?" He glanced at his watch. Past six already. The professor had been in the office all day and had hardly eaten any lunch. "What do you say we call it a day and go grab a bite to eat?"

At that, the professor laid down his red pencil and looked up. "Thank you," he said. "But aren't you going to work on the galley proofs any more today?"

"It's all right." He did intend to work late and take the last train home, as a matter of fact, but in any case, they had to eat. He picked up his suit coat from the back of the chair and felt the pocket to make sure his wallet was inside. "What kind of food are you in the mood for?" he asked, helping the professor gather up his things.

Slowly the professor put his pencils and eraser away in a well-worn leather pen case. "I spent all day sitting down, so I'm not very hungry. How about soba noodles?"

"Fine with me. Let's go."

Majime carried the professor's briefcase and informed the part-timers that they were going out to eat. They left to a chorus of see-you-laters. Kishibe, still on the phone, nodded and waved. Mr. Particle's curiosity was apparently still not sated.

The professor slowly descended the poorly lit staircase.

Damn, he's old. Following close behind the professor, Majime was struck by this thought. But of course he was old. He'd been an old man when they first met, fifteen years ago. How old would that make him now?

Majime was anxious to bring *The Great Passage* to completion. Perhaps because they were so close now, he was feeling intense impatience. *If we don't hurry, it'll be too late.* He dismissed the thought. Too late for what? Mustn't be morbid.

As always, the professor's briefcase was heavy, stuffed with papers and books. If he could lug it to the office every day, he had to be in pretty good health, Majime told himself. Yet in the old days, the professor would definitely have suggested dinner at Seven Treasures Garden. Perhaps, knowing that Majime would be heading back to the office afterward, he had deliberately chosen a quick, light meal. Or perhaps he wasn't feeling quite himself.

As if he could sense Majime's probing gaze on his back, the professor paused on the landing to catch his breath and said with a deprecatory laugh, "Age will tell. Lately the least bit of walking gets me out of breath."

"Shall we send out for dinner?"

"Oh, no. I'll be going home after this, and I wouldn't want to get in the way of people hard at work. I could use some fresh air, anyway." He started down the next flight of stairs. "This summer was so hot, I feel lethargic. But now that the temperature's cooled off, I'm sure I'll bounce back."

They left the building and headed for the Jimbocho intersection. The professor was right; there wasn't a trace of summer in the evening breeze. Night came on earlier now.

In the noodle joint, several men in suits, probably company workers, were swiftly fortifying themselves. The owner knew Majime and the professor and led them to seats with a clear view of the television. She even turned up the volume, out of consideration for the professor. During meals he never was without his file cards, and always kept an ear cocked to the flow of words emanating from the television.

They both knew the shop's menu by heart and didn't have to look at it.

"Will you have a glass of something?" Majime asked.

"No, not today."

Maybe he was feeling ill after all. Ordinarily he enjoyed a large carafe of hot sake.

"I already had drinks with dinner at home this week."

He justified his abstention in this way, but now Majime's worry turned to fear.

Majime ordered "stamina udon," a bowl of noodles and vegetables in hot broth topped with toasted rice cake. The professor ordered a plate of *tororo* soba, buckwheat noodles topped with creamy grated yam.

After ordering, the professor turned to Majime. "What a fine man you've grown into. I certainly appreciate all the trouble you take on my behalf."

I was an adult when we first met, Majime thought, until he remembered, *That's right, I couldn't even pour his beer properly.* When he had first transferred to the Dictionary Editorial Department, he hadn't known how to proceed with work or get along with his coworkers. He'd felt as if he'd been blindfolded and sent to grope his way through a labyrinth.

And now all aspects of *The Great Passage* were under his command. He issued instructions to over fifty college students working on the dictionary part time and finessed almost daily meetings with the advertising and sales staff while busily correcting proofs. He had shown young Miss Kishibe the ropes, as if he were a past master at dictionary editing.

"I still have a lot to learn," Majime said awkwardly and took a sip of the steaming tea that had just arrived.

Professor Matsumoto was writing on a sample card. He added a question mark. On TV they were doing a special report on "Unexpected Sweating: Exploring the Mysteries of the Autonomic Nervous System." Among the street interviews with men and women of all ages was an exchange between two high-school girls.

"Sweating all of a sudden, like for no reason?" said one. "Yeah, yeah!"

"It's like, *bamyuru!*"

"Yeah, *bamyuda!*"

Catching this conversation, the professor had lost no time in making a note of the words. He added a question mark as if unsure of what he had heard.

No, thought Majime, *the girls weren't talking about the autonomic nervous system.* More likely they randomly made Bermuda into a verb, *bamyuru,* to express how hot they felt—and this was probably a word they'd made up, used only by them and their friends. No real reason to take note of it. He felt like telling the professor all this, but seeing the look of intense concentration on his face, he let it pass.

"Are we on schedule?" the professor asked, turning to his noodles.

"Yes. *The Great Passage* should come out right on time next spring."

"It's been a long time coming." The professor scooped up some grated yam with a wooden spoon and smiled. "But you know, the real work starts after a dictionary comes out. To improve its accuracy and precision, we have to keep collecting samples for the revised and expanded edition."

The biggest Japanese dictionary of all time was the *Great Dictionary of Japanese.* Twenty-four years after its first publication, a second edition had come out, increasing the number of entry words from 450,000 to half a million—testimony to the editors' and contributors' determination to respond to changes in a living language by ceaselessly collecting words and nurturing the growth of the dictionary.

"I'll keep that in mind." Majime had just bitten off a piece of rice cake, but he nodded as he spoke. The hot, softened rice cake dangling from his lower lip swung like a white tongue and brushed against his chin, burning a little.

Even while the professor was busy eating, his thoughts remained on dictionaries. With a far-off look in his eyes, he said, "Majime, just look at the *Oxford English Dictionary* or China's *Kangxi Dictionary.* Overseas, a university founded by royal charter or some other ruling authority often takes the lead in compiling a dictionary of the national language. In other words, public funds go into the project."

"And here we are, perpetually underfunded. It's enough to make you weep."

"Right. So why do you suppose they use public funds to make dictionaries?"

Majime left off winding his noodles. "I suppose it's because they see a dictionary as a way to enhance national prestige. Language helps form a sense of national identity, and, to a certain degree, unification and control of language are necessary to bring a nation together."

"Exactly. Yet look at Japan. We have zero dictionaries compiled under the patronage of any public institution." The professor rested his chopsticks, leaving half of his soba noodles untouched. "Take the first modern Japanese dictionary, Fumihiko Otsuki's *Sea of Words*. Not even that had financial support from the government. Otsuki worked on it his whole life and published it with funds from his own pocket. To this day, every publishing company puts out its own dictionary, and no official bodies are involved."

Majime wondered if this was the professor's way of saying, "Apply for government funding. What have you got to lose?" Cautiously, he said, "Government agencies can be somewhat obtuse in their attitude to culture."

"When I was young, I used to wish we had more generous funding." The professor folded his hands on the tabletop. "Now I think it was all for the best."

"What do you mean?"

"If government money were involved, there's a strong chance they would interfere with the content. And just because national prestige would be on the line, language could well be made a tool of domination, a way of bolstering state legitimacy."

Until now, caught up in the grind of dictionary compilation, Majime had never stopped to think about the political influence dictionaries might have. "I guess words, and dictionaries, must always exist in the narrow, perilous space between individual and authority, internal freedom and public governance."

"Yes," said Professor Matsumoto. "Which is why even if we lack funding, we should take pride in the fact that dictionaries are compiled not by the government but by publishing companies. By private citizens like you and me, plugging away at our jobs. After devoting more than half my life to lexicography, that's one thing I'm sure of."

"Professor . . ." Majime was moved by this declaration.

"Words and the human heart that creates them are absolutely free, with no connection to the powers that be. And that's as it should be. A ship to enable all people to travel freely across the sea of words—we must continue our efforts to make sure *The Great Passage* is just that."

The professor spoke simply and quietly, but the passion in his words washed over Majime with the force of breaking waves.

When they had finished their meal and gone back outside, Majime hailed a taxi and all but forced the professor and his briefcase inside. The professor had shown little appetite, and under the circumstances Majime couldn't allow him to take the train home. He pressed a taxi voucher from the company into the professor's reluctant hand.

"Good night, sir. Till next time."

Inside the taxicab, the professor bowed his head apologetically.

Majime watched the taxi speed off and then went back to the office, on fire with new determination.

Three days later, the sky was a deep blue. Even inside the office, where bookshelves hid the windows, Majime felt somehow refreshed.

As usual, he spent the day at his desk. Then all at once Araki came rushing in. "Majime, we've got trouble!" he cried. In his hand was a large sheet of paper, part of the fourth proofs they were currently going over.

Despite himself, Majime started up, but before he could get to his feet Araki spread the sheet of paper on Majime's desk.

"Look at this."

The page contained words starting with *chi*.

"*Chishio* is missing!" The word for "blood."

"What?" Majime's glasses had slid down his nose. He pushed them back up and bent over the page, where the words were lined up in order.

Chishi idenshi (lethal gene), *chishio* (repeated soaking in dye), *chishiki* (knowledge). But no sign of the compound written in different characters but also pronounced *chishio*.

"Well, this is a bloodcurdling state of affairs."

"Majime, this is no time for levity!"

Majime had spoken from the heart, but Araki scolded him. He felt the blood drain from his face but managed to get hold of himself and think about what needed to be done.

"This is already the fourth proof," he said, "but we'll have to squeeze out enough space to insert 'blood.' We have no choice."

Araki nodded, grim-faced. "You're right. The question is, how did a mistake of this magnitude get by until the fourth proof without anybody noticing?"

"We'll have to be especially meticulous checking the fourth proofs. We'll start over from the beginning. Everyone will have to pitch in, including the students." It made Majime's head spin to think how far off schedule this would put them, but any delay was better than letting other possible omissions go unnoticed. "We also need to get to the bottom of this and find out how the word went missing."

The others had picked up on the tension in the air. Miss Kishibe, Mrs. Sasaki, and the few part-time workers still in the office began to drift toward his desk.

"Mrs. Sasaki, you check the usage sample cards, will you please?"

She nodded and promptly scurried to the reference room where the cards were stored. After a bit she returned and reported that the card for *blood* was there. She held out all the materials relating to the word and gave them to Majime. "It's marked as an entry word. You wrote the definition yourself."

Maybe so, but somehow or other the word and its definition hadn't been properly inserted. The first, second, and third proofs which Mrs. Sasaki had brought showed that the entry was missing in all previous proofs.

Majime stood up. "Everyone, I'm sorry, but this is an emergency. I need you to drop everything and help us check every last word in the fourth proof."

The air crackled. Silently they gathered around as Majime explained the procedure. "All we can do is go through and make sure that the data on every sample card marked 'use' is actually there. Recruit as many more people as you can. We'll divvy up the pages. Everyone, check the pages you are assigned with utmost care. However long it takes, let's dig in and get it done." He looked around at the faces surrounding him and added, "We mustn't let *The Great Passage* spring a leak!"

Although now, in the final stage of making the dictionary, a major problem had arisen, no one appeared downcast. Araki, Mrs. Sasaki, and Miss Kishibe, as well as the students, all looked determined to weather this crisis.

"Before we begin I'd like you all to go home and bring back a change of clothes and whatever else you may need," said Majime. "Starting tonight, we camp here."

No shoulders slumped at this announcement. Miss Kishibe returned to her computer and started typing an e-mail. Probably letting Miyamoto know she wouldn't be available for a while, Majime thought. The students varied in their reactions, some firing themselves up—"Okay, let's go! Let's do this!"—and others deciding to return to campus and see who else they could recruit. All were cheerful and positive. A state of emergency could induce temporary euphoria, he had heard. This might be something similar.

As he looked around at the eager, determined faces of his reliable crew, Majime couldn't help but bow his head in gratitude and humility. From the time Nishioka had left until Miss Kishibe arrived, he had toiled alone for years in the Dictionary Editorial Department, the lone full-time employee, working on *The Great Passage* whenever he could. He had often grown discouraged and wondered if the dictionary would ever see the light of day. His labors had not been misplaced, he thought now, looking at the crowd of people willing to roll up their sleeves and pitch in to save *The Great Passage* from foundering.

As people started coming and going, the phone rang. Miss Kishibe swiftly picked up the receiver. Thinking it was probably Mr. Particle yet again, Majime paid scant attention. After a few words, however, her face grew solemn.

"Mr. Majime." Having finished her conversation, Miss Kishibe drew near with a note in hand. "That was Mrs. Matsumoto. The professor is in the hospital."

The note she handed him bore the name of one of the larger hospitals in Tokyo. The symptoms weren't clear, but Majime felt a sense of foreboding. For a moment he couldn't move.

The subsequent verification process would long be remembered by dictionary editors at other companies as "Gembu Books Hell Camp."

Of course, in the midst of the turmoil Majime had no way of knowing this. All he could do was try his best to deal with events as they arose.

First, he and Araki went to see Professor Matsumoto in the hospital. The professor had just finished a round of morning tests. When they walked in, he was sitting up in bed watching television, scribbling on a file card.

What a man. Even in the hospital, he still gave the dictionary top priority. The professor's color was better than Majime had expected, and this cheered him as well.

"Thanks for coming," said the professor. He seemed embarrassed by the situation. "I'm sorry to drag you all the way here. My wife blew things out of proportion, I'm afraid. I'll be here a week or so for routine tests, that's all. Age has a way of catching up with you. I've started falling apart, and that's just how it is."

His wife bowed over and over to them. Majime had always assumed that the professor's total commitment to the dictionary must have meant he was a failure as a family man, but no, the couple seemed devoted to each other. At the moment she was carefully arranging a cardigan over her husband's shoulders.

"Sir, you mustn't overdo it," said Araki in a tone of concern. "This is a good chance for you to get some rest."

"I'm so disappointed in myself for creating a distraction at such a busy time." The professor seemed unable to reconcile himself to the exigencies of old age. "How is *The Great Passage* coming along?"

Exchanging glances, Majime and Araki said simultaneously, "Fine." It wouldn't do to cause the professor any worry. Wild horses couldn't have dragged the word *blood* from them.

After the visit, Majime said good-bye to Araki and went home to pick up a change of clothes. Ten or so years before, his landlady Také had died, ushering in a new chapter in the history of the two-story wooden structure. Ownership had passed to Kaguya, Také's granddaughter. She and Majime were already married by then, and they had continued to live there, carrying out occasional repairs as needed.

Také had always treated Majime like one of the family. As his library grew, gradually taking over the entire downstairs, she never uttered a word of complaint. He was clumsy at work and romance alike, but she always watched over and supported him. When he and Kaguya got married, she'd been overjoyed. Recalling the early days of their marriage, spent in that house with Také, always filled him with pleasant warmth.

One winter morning, Také had failed to wake up. They found her on her futon, dead of what the doctor called heart failure. Plainly speaking, it was old age. In her later years she ate little and spent almost all her time in her room on the second floor; going up and down stairs was hard labor, she used to say. The night before she died, she said she thought she might be coming down with a cold. She had seemed so full of life that the sudden farewell had been most upsetting. She hadn't suffered; that was their only comfort.

They held the funeral in a daze and returned to a house empty of Také. Only then did they realize that they hadn't seen any sign of their cat, Tora. They searched the neighborhood and even contacted the public health center. They waited for days and days, but never did find out what had become of Tora. Perhaps, sensing his owner's death, he had set out on a journey of his own. When they accepted that Tora wasn't ever coming back, then and only then were Majime and Kaguya able to cry over Také's death. They held hands and wept aloud with rasping sobs, as if trying to force air into lungs crushed by grief.

Now Majime slid open the lattice front door and called, "I'm home."

In response, out came their current pet cat, Torao, who had been with them for a number of years. He was a splendid tabby, very similar in appearance to his predecessor. Majime liked to think he was Tora's son or grandson.

He started up the creaking stairs, with Torao winding around his legs. The entire downstairs—except for the kitchen, bath, and toilet—was still taken up by his books, so he and Kaguya lived upstairs.

"Oh, you're back!" Still half-asleep, Kaguya poked her head out of the room at the end of the hall. "What are you doing back so early? Feeling okay?"

"That's not it."

He went into the middle room, the one that was his, and started to pull clean clothes out of the dresser. "A little glitch came up. I'll be sleeping at the office for a while."

Kaguya looked worried, but she didn't press him for details. She understood his passion for dictionaries and always tried to keep out of his way. Majime, too, tried to avoid being a burden on Kaguya, who was equally committed to her career.

She seemed about to get up and join him, so he hastily said, "It's okay. Go back to bed."

Having finished stocking food and making her preparations for the evening, Kaguya was undoubtedly trying to get a bit of needed sleep.

"Mitsu, did you have lunch?"

No, he realized, he hadn't eaten anything. Unable to come up with an excuse off the top of his head, he stammered. She slipped a cardigan over her pajamas.

"Let me make you something."

"Yeah, but—"

"You have time to eat, don't you? I'm hungry, too."

Torao followed her expectantly down the stairs.

The room at the top of the stairs, their living room, looked exactly as it had when Také was alive. They still hadn't gotten out the *kotatsu* table heater for the cold weather. Instead, there was a small, low table. Against the wall was an old wooden dresser. The window looked out on the clothes-drying platform and the autumn sky.

The one thing different from before was a small Buddhist shrine containing the memorial tablets and photographs of Také and her husband, Kaguya's grandfather, who had died years earlier. Kaguya had never met him. The photograph showed him as a fine-looking man. Majime was of the opinion that Kaguya had his eyes.

He stuffed some clothes and his shaver in a travel bag and, after a short breather, offered incense at the shrine, placing his palms together in respect. Kaguya came in carrying a tray, with Torao right behind her.

"Here you are."

"Thanks. It looks good."

"Let's eat."

They sat down at the small table and picked up their chopsticks. She had made grilled fish, an omelet, boiled spinach with soy sauce, and miso soup with onion, fried tofu, and silken tofu.

"This is more like breakfast than lunch, I'm afraid," she said.

"It tastes wonderful. As usual."

He said this with such feeling that she lowered her head, embarrassed, and ate a little more quickly. Torao mewed softly, his eyes fixed on the salmon.

"Torao, you have food in your dish and you know it!"

Reprimanded by Kaguya, Torao turned away reluctantly and put his face in the dish of cat food in the corner.

"I went to the hospital just now to look in on Professor Matsumoto."

"You what?" Kaguya set down her chopsticks and swallowed. "What happened?"

"He's going to be in the hospital for a week of routine tests, he says."

"Oh. Still, that's scary." The memory of Také's sudden death cast a shadow. "Let me know if there's anything special he'd like to eat. I could make it and take it to him. Please ask when you get a chance."

"Sure."

"He's getting on now, so make sure he takes his time recovering."

"That's just what's been bothering me."

"What?"

Majime stopped chewing and sat up straighter. "How old is he? Do you know?"

"No."

They looked at each other, then laughed.

"I've known him going on fifteen years, and he hasn't changed a bit in all that time," he said. "He could be in his nineties for all I know, or he could be sixty-eight. Either way, I'd believe it."

"Lexicographers are a bit otherworldly." Seeing Majime nod absently, she added, "I mean you, too, Mitsu. But you know, the professor may actually be surprisingly young. You wait and see, he'll be better in no time."

"Let's hope so."

After eating, Majime set off with his travel bag. After he had walked a short way, he turned around. Kaguya was standing in front of the house, waving. Torao, cradled in her arms, gave a big yawn.

"I forgot to tell you. Miss Kishibe is going out with Miyamoto from Akebono Paper Company."

"I'm not surprised. I told you when they came to the restaurant, I had a feeling about them, remember?"

"You're so observant. It always amazes me."

Majime and Kaguya smiled and waved to each other.

Gembu Books Hell Camp lasted a full month. Majime and Kishibe slept in the office practically every night. On rare occasions, they went home for fresh clothes but then came right back. For days on end he had no real conversations with Kaguya, nor did she with Miyamoto.

Majime saw to it that the students and Mrs. Sasaki periodically went home, urging them constantly not to wear themselves out. None of them were eager to leave. They slept at the office for days on end, sometimes for a whole week, and thought nothing of it. Everyone worked hard in near silence.

Araki's wife was long dead. "I'll see to the rest of this," he would say. "Go on home, everybody!" He took on more than his share of the work and never went home once for the space of a month.

The problem was the air in the office, which grew fetid. The staff had increased, and the room was now crowded. With windows inaccessible behind bookshelves, the air was increasingly stale—stuffy and dusty and smelling of ink. When they were in the office together, they didn't notice it so much, but coming back from a meal, they would grimace. Somebody would groan, "The air in here's so thick you could cut it with a knife!"

The main building had a small shower, but complaints started to roll in: "The dictionary staff is in the shower morning, noon, and night!" They decided to use the one remaining public bath in Jimbocho. The owner looked delighted at this unexpected boon.

"But we can't wash our clothes." Kishibe sighed after returning from the bath with her wet hair in a towel turban, wearing no makeup. Jimbocho, a center of used bookstores and publishing houses, was supposed to be a students' quarter, but for some reason there was no coin laundry. She and Mrs. Sasaki talked it over.

"There are lots of colleges around here, but you know, not that many students actually live in Jimbocho."

"I know. And how many people would come here to browse used books and decide to wash their clothes while they're at it?"

"People who go for used books are like potted plants anyway. I bet they don't do much laundry to begin with."

Majime protested inwardly. *I go for used books, but I'm no potted plant. I'm an omnivore! And yes, when I go to a used bookstore I think about books. What else! Anybody who thought about their laundry while looking at books—anybody that incapable of concentrating on what was in front of them—could never qualify as a true used book lover.* He gave his cuff a furtive sniff. He didn't think it smelled too bad, but he couldn't really judge.

Eventually, they designated someone to be in charge of laundry. They threw all the soiled clothes in one big bag, and every few days someone would take it to a coin laundry in Kasuga or Hongo. Those taking advantage of this service split the cost among themselves. Underwear was separate; they made do by buying new ones or washing the old ones out in restroom sinks. The ladies' room in the annex was newly furnished with a drying rack. Men's shorts hung on poles between the bookshelves. Needless to say, the women lodged protests about the sight of men's underwear dangling like the flags of all nations.

"This is an emergency situation. Please bear up." Majime went around with his head bowed and smoothed over the situation as best he could by extracting promises that the offending garments would be taken down as soon as they were dry.

While overseeing the final check of the fourth proofs, Majime had to visit the printing company frequently, accompanied by Miyamoto and his technicians. Dictionaries had large numbers of pages and high initial print runs, using that ultrathin paper, so the printing required meticulous care and expertise. Numerous test runs were made with Akebono's "ultimate" paper.

Subtle changes in the ink affected the color and shading of the characters. Which ink was best suited to this paper? How should the presses be adjusted for maximum readability? Representatives of the paper company and the printing company met with Majime to hash it out. Sometimes he went to the factory for consultations with experienced printers.

When he had made the necessary decisions about the printing, he was next summoned by the in-house designer, a man in his midforties whose nickname was "Redshirt," as he always wore a red T-shirt regardless of the season. Unlike the character of that name in Natsume Soseki's novel *Botchan*, however, he was, although eccentric, frank and cheerful.

Thanks in part to Nishioka's efforts, the publicity campaign for *The Great Passage* was unusually extensive. An advertising agency had contributed, helping to work out a strategy to unify the image of the dictionary in prepublication train station posters and bookstore pamphlets. Redshirt had been put in charge of production, the most crucial aspect of presentation, and was full of enthusiasm.

No sooner did Majime set foot in the design department office than Redshirt would come running up.

"Mr. Majimeee! It's ready! Come see the final mock-up!" He dragged Majime over to his desk, where the final design plan had been laid out with the help of a high-power printer: there before them was the box, the wraparound band for the box, the dust jacket, the cover, the inside cover, and even a sample of the cloth for *hanagire*, the flower-patterned material used to bind the ends of the spine.

"When people start to use a dictionary, they usually throw away the box and the wraparound band and the dust jacket. It's a shame. Anyway, I went all-out in the design."

Only half-listening to Redshirt's proud declaration, Majime was drawn to the design package spread out before him. The box, dust jacket, and cover were all a deep ultramarine blue, the color of the sea at night. The band was a pale cream, the color of moonlight. The inside cover was the same cream color, and the *hanagire* was the silver of the moon itself, shining in a dark sky. The title lettering was also silver, standing out boldly against the cover's dark blue. Closer examination showed a narrow, wavelike pattern in silver along the base of the box and dust cover. On the spine was the outline of an ancient sailing ship, just cresting a swell. The front and back covers were marked unobtrusively with a crescent moon and ship.

Redshirt had perfectly captured the intentions of *The Great Passage*. Filled with gratitude, Majime stood and studied the design package a long time in silence.

"Well?" Redshirt blurted out anxiously, unable to wait any longer.

Majime organized his thoughts. "It has both sharpness and warmth. I think it's terrific. What did the sales staff say?"

"I haven't shown it to them yet. I wanted you to be the first to see it."

"Thank you. One thing—is this die-stamped with silver leaf?"

"Don't worry. Printing technology is advancing all the time. It's only going to *look* as if it's die-stamped with silver leaf. Of course, the front cover will be real silver leaf, but I'll keep it well within budget."

"I should have known." Majime was embarrassed. "Go ahead with your plan, then. If Sales raises any issues, I'll do all I can to fend them off."

Now the packaging was settled. That was one burden off his shoulders. He returned to the office with a lighter step. On his desk lay the checked fourth proof. This would go back to the printers, and then they would send the fifth proof.

Peak after peak to climb.

Majime squared his shoulders and picked up his red pencil. Next he would go through the page proofs and make sure none of the changes affected the number of lines.

After the monthlong, all-hands-on-deck, round-the-clock proofreading marathon, it became clear that apart from *blood*, no other entry words were missing. Of course, through the extracareful check they did uncover typographical errors no one had caught before, as well as a few questionable definitions, so it hadn't been a total loss.

"A hue and cry about trifles," said Araki.

The deflated, exhausted expressions in the room echoed the sentiment.

"Everyone, I am sorry to have put you to so much extra effort for nothing. My apologies." Majime was sincerely contrite.

"No, no," said a student. "You know what they say: 'Make assurance doubly sure.'"

"Right," said another. "I can finally relax, knowing we left no stone unturned."

Despite their exhaustion, they seemed to have a great sense of accomplishment.

The Great Passage was blessed to have a devoted crew. Majime stood to one side in the office doorway and formally saw the students off as they filed out.

The camp may have been hell, but it greatly increased Majime's confidence in the dictionary. Dozens of pairs of eyes had checked the proofs from stem to stern and only uncovered a typographical error or two. The omission of *blood* had been a painful mistake, but they had escaped the awful fate of publishing *The Great Passage* with that glaring omission. All the other entry words were accounted for, and Majime was reassured that the definitions were meticulous. The dictionary would be balanced and precise, a pleasure to use or to browse through.

He saw that Kishibe was still there. "Thanks so much for all you've done, Miss Kishibe. Now go home and get a good night's sleep."

"Thank you. What about you?"

"Araki and I are going to go call on the professor."

Supposedly the week in the hospital had been for the purpose of a routine checkup, yet even after his release, not once during their "hell camp" had Professor Matsumoto come by. His wife had called once to say apologetically that he wasn't quite himself yet—that was all. The professor's health was worrisome, but during the past month their hands had been tied. Now that the proofreading was back on track, he and Araki had decided to pay the professor a visit at home. Kishibe looked as if she would like to join them, but she was clearly exhausted. He told her he and Araki would have a look first. They discussed what time to show up the next day and parted with her in front of the annex.

The professor lived in Kashiwa City, Chiba Prefecture. Neither Majime nor Araki had ever been there before. They got on the subway and headed east, taking adjoining seats. They were ahead of the evening rush hour. Besides his briefcase, Majime held a box of éclairs on his lap. The professor was fond of the éclairs from a bakery near the office.

While Majime had bought them, Araki had been silent, but now he began to talk.

"When I called before to say we were coming over, the professor answered the phone."

"How did he sound?"

"Fine, I thought. But I'm concerned that he never came by the office last month."

They were unsure how to get to his house, so they took a taxi from the station. A five-minute ride brought them to the door of a snug-looking wooden home.

They rang the doorbell, and Mrs. Matsumoto quickly welcomed them and showed them into the parlor. As they might have expected, the little house was overflowing with books. Bookshelves lined every wall, and the floor in front of them was piled high with more books. The hallways and stairs had so many books there was barely room to get by.

Did Mrs. Matsumoto and the children put up with this hodgepodge uncomplainingly? Even Majime was taken aback. But perhaps all the paper in the room absorbed sound; the atmosphere was peaceful and quiet.

Mrs. Matsumoto brought out tea and éclairs for three. "Thank you for this lovely gift. You'll have to excuse me for turning around and offering you what you brought us."

The door opened, and the professor came in.

"Thank you both for coming."

At the sight of the professor, Majime was dumbstruck. Always thin, the professor had lost considerable weight. He was wearing a suit and bolo tie as usual, but his shirt collar, though buttoned, hung loose. Apparently he had gotten out of bed and dressed himself just to come out and see them.

Araki nudged Majime, who recovered his wits and apologized for the sudden visit.

The professor's wife left the three men to themselves, and the professor sat down on the sofa across from his visitors. When he saw the éclairs, he broke into a smile. "Thank you for the lovely gift."

Majime couldn't help noticing that he and his wife used the same words to express their appreciation. They were clearly in perfect harmony.

"It turns out," the professor went on, "I have cancer of the esophagus."

What had he said? Majime heard the words without registering their significance. He felt Araki gasp beside him and sensed that something serious had happened, but he was unable to respond.

Araki asked discreet questions, and the professor answered them. He was taking anticancer drugs now and undergoing radiation therapy. The tumor had shrunk a bit, but side effects made it hard for him to get out of bed most days. His doctor was monitoring his progress, and he might possibly be readmitted to the hospital.

Majime and Araki were resolute and daring with words, but when it came to sickness, they were at a complete loss. Even words failed them. *You'll be fine. Hang in there.* Unable to bring themselves to utter such platitudes, they fell silent.

Seeing their stifled anxiety and concern, the professor adopted a determinedly cheerful tone and inquired about the dictionary's progress. Without touching on the hell camp, Majime reported that everything was proceeding in good order. He had brought the mock-up and took it out to show to the professor.

"It's perfect for our ship," he said.

The professor spread out the samples on his knees, tracing the silver waves with a finger. "I can't wait for it to be finished. As soon as I feel able, I'll drop by the office again. In the meantime, if you have any questions or problems, don't hesitate to call me."

"We will always seek your judgment." *The Great Passage* was the professor's alter ego. Forcing the professor to maintain distance from the final editing process would be like forcibly separating him from a part of himself.

Majime and Araki decided to walk back to the station, and left the professor's house before sundown. The professor and his wife came out to the front gate and waved them off. When they reached the corner and turned to look back, he was still standing there, his frail silhouette waving lightly good-bye.

The three éclairs sat untouched on the parlor table.

When the fifth proofs arrived, fear of not finishing in time drove Majime.

What if something happened to the professor before he could see *The Great Passage* completed? *Don't be morbid, don't think negative thoughts,* Majime reminded himself, but the outlook was hardly positive. Shortly after they had visited him, the professor had been hospitalized again. He was released at the end of the year and spent New Year's at home with his wife, but no sooner were the decorations put away than he was back in the hospital. Araki visited him there frequently and received valuable advice on various problems that arose during the check of the fifth proof.

At this rate, they wouldn't make the March deadline. This very real and pressing possibility also sent Majime into panic. At year's end, students went home for the winter break, and there were not nearly as many as in the summertime. Finding enough people to carry on the work was difficult. To make up for time lost during the monthlong work camp, Majime, Araki, Kishibe, and Mrs. Sasaki had taken work home on New Year's Eve and worked there the first three days of the New Year.

Now it was mid-January. The students were all back, and they were proceeding with the final check fully staffed. The dictionary had so many pages and the initial print run was so huge that printing would take time. As each page was approved, they had to send it off so the printing process could get underway. If the printing press didn't start up by the end of January, there was no hope of finishing on time.

Night after night Majime got home around midnight, just as Kaguya was arriving home after closing the restaurant. She would make a midnight meal for the two of them. Normally Majime made supper and put Kaguya's share in the refrigerator for her, covered in plastic wrap. After she ate she would wash the dishes and make the next day's breakfast. This was the relay system they had worked out to knit their lives together, since they kept such different hours.

They rarely had dinner together at home, and so Majime was happy to share the time with her, but their conversation lagged. He was exhausted, for one thing, and for another the state of Professor Matsumoto's health weighed on his mind. Concerned, Kaguya made dishes to give him energy: grilled eel on rice or cubed steak with plenty of garlic. He was sorry to put her to the extra trouble, knowing her work kept her busy, too. She sat across from him, silent and reliable, as he gratefully polished off every bit of the food.

Eating these rich foods in the middle of the night was giving him a bit of a paunch, he thought. If he kept this up, he shuddered to think what he would look like in a few years. Her loving midnight meals gave him renewed determination to finish *The Great Passage* with all possible speed.

While Majime was tied down at the office, Kaguya paid the professor occasional visits. From the time she had worked at Umenomi, he had always appreciated her cooking and sometimes used to visit her restaurant on his own, so it was only natural that she, too, should worry about him. She began making his favorite dishes and taking them with her. When Majime asked whether he ate them or how he seemed during her visits, however, she was vague. "He always sounds apologetic for making you shoulder the main burden," she would say. "We can't have that," he would reply. "Be sure to tell him the dictionary's coming along fine, so he can just relax and concentrate on getting well." Countless variations on this dialogue took place.

Heavy gray clouds hung low in the sky, as if it were midwinter. *The Great Passage* crawled toward completion, and the professor's health showed no sign of improving as January drew to an end.

As long as progress continues, eventually the end comes in sight. Xuanzang, the seventh-century Chinese monk and scholar, accomplished the amazing feat of journeying to India, bringing back sacred Buddhist texts, and translating them into Chinese. The priest Zenkai devoted the final thirty years of his life to chiseling through rock to create a cliff-side tunnel for worshipers. A dictionary is a repository of human wisdom not because it contains an accumulation of words but because it embodies true hope, wrought over time by indomitable spirits.

Finally the printing press began turning out pages of *The Great Passage*, with Majime standing by alongside Araki and Kishibe. Majime picked up a packet of freshly printed pages and held it reverently.

The pages were on giant uncut sheets of thin paper. They came in signatures of sixteen, with text printed on both sides, so thirty-two pages in all. The pages as seen on the sheets seemed to be out of order. But when the sheets were folded in half four times, the thirty-two pages lay sorted out in the proper size and order. Each such batch was called a "gathering." Each group of thirty-two pages equaled one gathering. *The Great Passage* would have nearly three thousand pages, enough for over ninety gatherings bound together.

The large, still-uncut sheets of paper gave off a faint warmth. Majime knew this was because they had just come through the printer, yet he couldn't help believing that the heat was the condensed passion of all those who had worked on this dictionary—Araki and Professor Matsumoto, Miss Kishibe and Mrs. Sasaki, the scholars and students, the staffs at the paper company and printing press, and himself.

Against the slightly golden tinge of the paper, the lettering stood out clearly with the darkness of a summer's night. Realizing that the page he was looking at included the word *akari*—light—Majime had to blink back sudden tears. The word referred not only to sunlight and lamplight, but also to testimony or evidence. Here before him was clear evidence that the past fifteen years of struggles had not been in vain.

"It's so beautiful." Kishibe looked at the printed page as if it were a precious gem and wiped her eyes with a handkerchief.

Beside her, Miyamoto was nodding with emotion.

Araki reached out and touched a page in trembling awe. Having apparently reassured himself that this was no dream, he said, "Majime, we have to deliver this right away."

"Yes," Majime agreed. "Let's take it to the professor."

The staff was still checking the fifth proofs for the final section of the dictionary, containing words starting with the series *ya-yu-yo*. They left Kishibe in charge and set out for the hospital in Tsukiji with a gathering rolled in a tube.

Professor Matsumoto was hooked up to an IV and had an oxygen tube in his nose to assist his breathing. The bed was raised and he was sitting up, leaning against pillows and writing something on a file card. When he caught sight of them, he smiled and laid his pencil on the bedside stand. "Well, well, Mr. Majime! It's been a long time."

Mrs. Matsumoto had temporarily gone home. Encouraged by the professor, whose voice sounded a bit raspy, Majime and Araki sat down in folding chairs by the bed.

He was no fatter or thinner than a year ago. His color looked slightly better, Majime thought as he studied the professor discreetly, looking for hopeful signs. Nudged by Araki once again, he caught himself. Mustn't linger, mustn't tire the professor out.

"We're here because there's something we couldn't wait to show you." He spread out the paper and laid it on the professor's lap.

"Oh!" the professor murmured. It was an expression of delight, wrung from his innermost depths. "Finally, finally, *The Great Passage* has come this far!" His frail finger traced the characters.

Yes, finally a part of our dictionary is here before us, in print. Impulsively, Majime wanted to reach out and grasp the professor's hand and say these words. Yet he couldn't bring himself to do anything so improper.

"Professor Matsumoto," said Araki, "*The Great Passage* will be published on schedule in March. As soon as a sample copy is available, we'll bring it to you. Or better yet, let's have a celebration in the office."

"I'll look forward to that." The professor wore a look of pure joy, like the expression on the face of a boy who has captured a beautiful butterfly. "Thank you both so much."

Professor Matsumoto died in mid-February, without waiting for the completion of *The Great Passage*.

After Araki called from the hospital to tell him the sad news, Majime opened his locker at work in a daze. He was checking to make sure he had a black tie. He knew it was strange to be checking for such a thing at such a time. His emotions and actions were at odds in a way he couldn't control.

The Dictionary Editorial Department handled the wake and funeral arrangements, while helping Mrs. Matsumoto as well. Majime learned that the professor had been seventy-eight years old. He had left his post at the university well before retirement age and devoted himself from then on to lexicography. He had no students who kept in touch with him and distanced himself from the academic world, giving his life solely to words.

Araki had worked with the professor on dictionaries for many years, going back to when the professor still taught at the university. Araki had been a faithful partner, supporting him, encouraging him, and bringing various dictionaries into existence by the professor's side. Now Araki was ushering mourners to their seats, dry-eyed. Perhaps silent wails were echoing inside him; his cheeks were sunken, the color of chalk.

That evening after the funeral Majime went home. He had brought purifying salt with him to scatter at the doorstep, following custom, but inwardly he cursed the idea. If the professor should choose to come back and watch over them, he would be only too glad.

Kaguya had arrived home just before him and was no longer wearing her mourning clothes. Apparently worried about him, she would be opening her restaurant a little later than usual that evening. They went up silently to the living room and drank hot tea that she'd prepared.

"I was too late," Majime murmured. He hadn't been able to show *The Great Passage* to Professor Matsumoto. If someone else had been assigned as editor, it might have been finished sooner. *Because of my fecklessness, he died without ever seeing the realization of his lifelong dream.*

Before he knew it, Majime was sobbing. In front of Kaguya, no less. Despite himself, tears and groans that sounded like animal cries kept coming and coming without end.

Kaguya came around the *kotatsu* and sat down beside him. Without saying a word, she gently caressed his shaking shoulders.

The launch party for *The Great Passage* took place in the banquet hall of a venerable hotel in Kudanshita just at the end of March, when the cherry buds were just about to bloom.

Scholars who had contributed to the dictionary were invited, along with representatives of the paper and printing companies. There were over one hundred guests in all. The festivities began with a welcome speech by the CEO of Gembu Books.

In the rear of the hall was a waist-high table bearing a copy of *The Great Passage* and a photograph of Professor Matsumoto, surrounded by flowers, with a large carafe of sake and a cup. The arrangement looked like a small altar. Mrs. Matsumoto paused in front of the table and looked at the display with moist eyes.

Too bad they couldn't have invited all the student workers, thought Majime as he made the rounds of the buffet-style party, greeting guests. Management had feared that if the fifty-odd students came, they would descend on the food like a swarm of locusts and devour every scrap. Gembu's budget couldn't accommodate such extravagance, so they decided to take them all out to a bar on another day.

This evening, representatives of major bookstores and university libraries were also in attendance. Reviews of *The Great Passage*, which had been published two weeks earlier, were favorable, and sales were exceeding expectations. The party was an excellent chance to get even more orders, and the marketing department had gone all-out. The sales, promotion, and advertising staffs were on hand, too, busily pouring drinks, chatting, and otherwise attending to guests.

"Majime!"

Hearing his name, Majime turned to see Nishioka separate himself from a group and come toward him. He was wearing a narrowly cut suit with a red handkerchief poking out of the breast pocket. Majime couldn't help staring at the handkerchief.

"My name is listed in the acknowledgments!" Nishioka sounded excited and deeply moved.

"Yep."

"I bet that was your doing."

"Professor Matsumoto was in the hospital, so I wrote it for him. Of course, I talked it over with him first."

Since Nishioka used to work in the Dictionary Editorial Department and had exerted himself on behalf of *The Great Passage*, it was only natural that his name should be included. Majime couldn't understand why he would bring it up. "Don't tell me we got your name wrong or something."

"No, that's not it. It's just that I wasn't—I never—" He broke off, smiled wryly, and clapped Majime on the shoulder. "You son of a gun." Then he disappeared back into the crowd.

Majime thought he had caught a faint "Thank you," but he wasn't sure.

Nishioka's eagle eyes spotted someone from an advertising agency, and he greeted him with a smooth, "Hey, Mr. Ogiwara! Thanks so much for coming! We owe you big-time." Mr. Ogiwara, or whatever his name was, smiled benignly.

After he, too, had made the rounds and greeted people, Majime went over to the little table in the back of the room, where Mrs. Matsumoto had picked up the copy of *The Great Passage* and was examining it lovingly.

"You know," she said quietly to Majime, "I think my husband was prepared for the worst from the day he first went into the hospital. He was never one to give up, but to the very end, even when he was delirious, all he talked about was this dictionary."

"I'm so sorry I couldn't show it to him while he was alive." Majime bowed his head in contrition.

"Good heavens!" said Mrs. Matsumoto, shaking her head. "He died happy—I know he did. I'm happy, too. *The Great Passage* meant the world to him, and you made his dream a reality. I can never thank you enough."

Gently, she laid the dictionary back on the table in front of her husband's photograph. Then, with a faint smile, she walked away.

Majime watched her go and then turned toward the photograph and placed his palms together in reverence.

"Well done."

Thinking the professor had said the words, he looked up in surprise. Araki had come up beside him without his realizing it. *He's gotten old, too,* Majime realized. *Well, of course he has. Fifteen years slipped away while we all worked on this dictionary.*

"You're a bit down, aren't you?" said Araki. "I went to Back of the Moon the other day. Kaguya was worried."

"I feel so bad for the professor. It's all my fault, my second-rate skills got in the way." Feeling it was immature of him, Majime still couldn't stop the words from pouring out.

"I was afraid you might be brooding over something like that. I brought something that should help." He took out a white envelope from an inner pocket. "This is a letter the professor sent to me."

His eyes urged Majime to take it. Majime drew out a sheet of stationery and unfolded it. The letter was in the professor's handwriting, so familiar from all those file cards.

> *I apologize for not being able to fulfill my responsibility as editor-in-chief to the very end. On the occasion of* The Great Passage*'s launching, I most likely will no longer be on this earth. But I feel neither anxiety nor regret. That's because, as clear as day, I can visualize* The Great Passage *setting out on the sea, its hold filled with the treasure of words.*
>
> *Araki, allow me to correct one thing I said. I told you I would never encounter another dictionary editor like you. I was wrong. Thanks to Mr. Majime, whom you brought into the department, I was able to press forward on the path of lexicography. I cannot tell you how fortunate I've been to encounter editors like you and him. Thanks to the two of you, my life has been extraordinarily fulfilled. In the next world I will keep on collecting word samples in search of words surpassing the only ones I know to say now: Thank you.*
>
> *Editing* The Great Passage *has been a great pleasure. I wish everyone a long and happy voyage aboard her.*

Majime carefully refolded the letter and inserted it in the envelope.

He looked around in turn at the professor's photograph, the copy of *The Great Passage* inscribed with the professor's name, and the many faces of the attendees.

Sometimes words were useless. No matter how they called out to him, Araki and Mrs. Matsumoto had been unable to tether the professor's life to this earth. And yet the professor wasn't completely gone, either. Because of words, the most important part of him was lodged in their hearts.

The memories of the professor were proof that even after life functions cease and the body turns to ash, beyond physical death, the soul lives on. In order to speak of the professor's aura, his speech and behavior, in order to share their memories and pass them on, words were indispensable.

All at once, in the palm of his hand, Majime felt the professor's touch—a touch he had never felt before. That last day in the hospital room, he had failed to take the professor's hand in his, but he knew this was how it would have felt, cool and dry and smooth.

Human beings had created words to communicate with the dead, and with those yet unborn.

Miss Kishibe was eating cake with Miyamoto. The other staff members were busy attending to guests, joining them in eating and drinking although they had explicit orders not to do so. The two lovebirds were jabbing at each other's pieces of cake with evident pleasure. Mrs. Sasaki was over by the wall, drinking a glass of white wine, and Nishioka was going around tossing off his usual stock of pleasantries. Everyone was all smiles, rejoicing at the completion of *The Great Passage*.

They had made a ship. A ship bearing the souls of people traveling from ancient times toward the future, across the ocean rich with words.

"Majime," said Araki, drawing Majime back to the center of the room, "tomorrow we start work on the revised edition."

Majime thought that the intensity of his emotions overflowed in a streak down his cheek, but it might have been his imagination. On this jubilant evening, Araki's thoughts were of the future of *The Great Passage*, the evolving dictionary still to come. How like him that was! He was Professor Matsumoto's true soul mate and fellow traveler.

Dictionary making knew no end. The voyage of the ship bearing hope as it crossed the bosom of the deep was everlasting.

Majime laughed and nodded. "Tonight, then, let's drink!"

Taking care not to let the foam spill over, he poured beer in Araki's glass.

A Love Letter from Majime to Kaguya (The Complete Edition)

Greetings
Cold winds are blowing, a reminder of the swift approach of winter's frosty skies. I trust that you are well.

I am writing because I have a confession to make. My emotions are at full tide, and I know with certainty that this tide, unlike those of the ocean, will never ebb. The suddenness of this letter may surprise you, but I beg you to read it to the end.

Until now I have lived immersed in the world of books. My closest friends, therefore, are to be found not in the real world but in the pages of books.

> Snow envelops the mountain house, tree shadows darken.
> Eave-bells are still, night deepens.
> Quietly arrange scattered books, ponder difficult things.
> In the lamp's blue flame, ten thousand ancient minds.[1]

Nishioka: Okay, let's check out Majime's love letter.

Kishibe: This is exciting! But it starts off in an awfully roundabout way. Doesn't make much of an impression.

Nishioka: Yikes! A Chinese poem, right off the bat![1]

Kishibe: I brought some notes by Professor Matsumoto. He says this is a seven-character quatrain by the Edo-period Confucian scholar Kan Chazan called "Reading a Book on a Winter's Night." Here's his paraphrase: "Falling snow piles on the mountain cabin, tree shadows turn black./Bells hang silent from the eaves as the night quietly deepens./I put away my scattered books, think back on passages that bothered me./Blue lamplight in my room sways as I see into the minds of the ancients."

This poem expresses exactly how I have lived. And yet now I understand.

My eyes discern writing of East and West,
My mind embraces regrets old and new.[2]

All this time I have merely been amusing myself with books while understanding nothing of the anguished truth, the deep emotions, that lie behind the lines penned by the ancients. Finally, even my books, which I have counted as my only friends, have lost patience and ceased speaking to me.

Though surrounded by a mountain of books, I am alone. This is my reward for having failed for so long to take action, yielding to my fear that I might not be able to communicate my feelings. At this rate I will end my days without ever having had a heart-to-heart conversation with anyone, without ever engaging deeply with them, without learning their thoughts and sharing mine. And in the end I am incapable even of truly savoring the joy that books can bring. This is how I have belatedly come to perceive my

Nishioka: That's pretty cool. Is the next one in Chinese, too?[2]

Kishibe: Yes. It's from a poem by Natsume Soseki. The professor's version is "My eyes take in writing of East and West,/My heart embraces regrets old and new." In other words, "I have learned to read books written in the writing systems of the East and the West, yet my mind is now filled with a melancholy surpassing time and space."

Nishioka: He's regretting that he hung back, afraid to convey his feelings for fear she might not understand, yet here he is firing off Chinese poetry. That's Majime for you.

Kishibe: He might at least have provided some kind of annotation.

Nishioka: Don't look now, here comes another one![3]

plight. Yet something within me cries out vehemently,
"No! This must not be."

I shall pluck up my courage.

In the world there is nothing to fret over.
White clouds only float and drift.[3]

Whether I can attain that state of mind, I do not know. It all depends on my efforts and your response.[4] If you respond to me, I swear that for the rest of my life I will devote all my strength to engaging in sincere good faith and honesty with the hearts and minds of others, especially you.
Since knowing of your existence, I feel that for the first time I have truly come to life. Until now I have been as good as dead. Though my eyes perused letters of the alphabet and Chinese characters, their meaning eluded me; though I breathed in and out, I was not alive.

Kishibe: This is from the end of that same Soseki poem. "People get nowhere by worrying. White clouds naturally fluff up and float."

Nishioka: You're kidding, right?

Kishibe: Sorry. That was my own free translation. Anyway, I think he's saying, "Let's relax and take things slow and easy."

Nishioka: That's up to Kaguya. Whoa. Isn't he getting a little intimidating here? "It all depends on your response."[4]

Kishibe: It's all right, I think. With all that Chinese poetry flying around, she couldn't read between the lines, so any tone of intimidation must have gone right by her.

There is the example in the ancient tale of a radiant princess named Kaguya (Shining Night) who descended to Earth from the moon, and indeed from the night I first encountered you I have felt such pain in my chest and found breathing so difficult that it is as if I myself were living on the moon. And yet, I can say that I am truly alive! How strange, how marvelous. You have given me life.

If I had a poetic turn of mind, here I would offer you a poem of my own making, but in the sadness of mediocrity I can only gaze sighing at the radiant moon. Let me instead borrow the celebrated words of an ancient poet.

In the sea of heaven,
cloud waves rise
and the moon boat rows
into the star forest
to be seen no more.[5]

Does this poem not seem as if it were written just for you?

Nishioka: This really is one hell of a love letter.

Kishibe: Next is an eighth-century Japanese poem from the *Collection of Ten Thousand Leaves*, by Kakinomoto Hitomaro, the great poet of that era.[5]

Nishioka: This one I can get, even without a paraphrase. It's kind of like a scene from a science-fiction movie. Notice the way every character she uses to write her name occurs in the text. Way to go, Majime.

Kishibe: You're right! He's giving it all he's got now, isn't he?

I like this poem. It has a beautiful grandeur and imparts a sense of calm majesty. At the same time it strikes me as lonely, filled with intense yearning for the unobtainable and a keen, penetrating awareness of the trifling nature of one's own existence. Did people of old live burdened with the same sense of loneliness that I feel? I am enticed into such imaginings. It is a poem overflowing with beauty and power, using the sense of aloneness to tie our hearts to the universe and beyond; to the human heart, surpassing time and space.

As you know, I am engaged in the work of lexicography. I am editing a dictionary to be called The Great Passage.

[omission][6]

And so the path of lexicography is extremely steep, and I often feel discouraged. I hasten to add that I am not asking for your cooperation or dedication in the least. I seek no such thing. All I ask would be to walk my path sensing your gaze upon me. And if I might be allowed to do so, I would want nothing more than to watch over you from

Nishioka: Hey, what's with the omission?[6]I thought this was going to be the whole thing!

Kishibe: The letter's just too darn long. Really. In the part that got left out, he goes on about how he feels about lexicography and kind of sums up his resume. You really want to read it?

Nishioka: Um, no, come to think of it.

the shadows [7] *as you pursue the steep path of cuisine.*

The spring silkworm dies;
only then does its thread end.
The candle turns to ash; only
then do its tears dry.[8]

Both lexicography and cuisine are disciplines with no end. Nor is there any end to my longing. I am a silkworm who will continue producing the silken thread of yearning till I die. I will show you that from my candle's melted wax, fire will rise anew. Have no fear. My feelings are a perpetual motion machine. I am applying for a patent![9]

And yet, you may say, I must need some sort of fuel. Do not worry. Since I am a perpetual motion machine, even without fuel my heart is continually on fire. I guarantee that I will spin on and on until my cocoon of silk grows enormous, bigger than Tokyo Dome. And I speak not only of the fire within my soul but of physical combustion, for I believe that I can survive well on the simplest of diets. I of course am happy to eat fine food when it is available, but I could go for a week eating Nupporo Ichiban

Nishioka: Now he's getting scary.[7]

Kishibe: Kind of stalker-ish, yes, or like some kind of guiding spirit. The next Chinese poem is part of a seven-character quatrain by the Tang-dynasty poet Li Shangyin.[8] "Spring silkworms die and only then cease spinning their strands./ The candle turns to ash and for the first time ceases shedding tears of love." It's a declaration of love that only death can end.

Nishioka: Pretty intense. Whoa. Calm down, Majime.[9]

ramen noodles morning, noon, and night without any grumbling from either my stomach or my taste buds. I would do my utmost not to impose any burden on you.

Forgive me. What I just wrote was posturing. I made it sound as if I ask nothing whatsoever. That is not true. Sensing your presence, every night I toss and turn. How could I have known that living under the same roof could bring such sweet despair!

Times to see each other are
hard, parting, too, is hard.[10]

*How true this is! Since we live our lives in such different stretches of time, it is difficult to meet, and on those occasions when you have the night shift and can enjoy a relaxed morning, I am in danger of developing a phobia about leaving for work myself. Yet I cannot give in to such temptation but must remind myself the dictionary is waiting for me and drag myself from the doorstep in tears. On such days my thoughts scatter far and wide, and the order of the kana syllabary changes from "*a ka sa ta na ha ma ya ra wa*" to "*a ka sa ta na ha ri ma o ya.*"[11] *I cannot help feeling anxious about whether*

Kishibe: The next one is by the same poet.[10] It's the first line of the silkworm poem.

"It is hard to meet, yet harder still to part." Wait, doesn't that sound as if it's referring to two people already in a relationship?"

Nishioka: Never mind, let it go. What's this got to do with silkworms and candles, though?

Kishibe: Chinese poetry is dynamic.

Kishibe: Uh-oh, now he wrote something off-the-wall again.[11]

the entries in The Great Passage *will appear in the correct order.*[12]

If I were to write my present feelings in plain terms, I would sum them up this way: "Kaguya Kaguya, what shall I do with you?" Or perhaps I should say this:

Chang'e regrets having stolen the elixir.
Jade sea blue sky night after night in her heart.[13]

Chang'e is the Chinese moon goddess, a woman who drank a magic potion and flew off to live on the moon, much like Princess Kaguya in the Japanese folktale. Some say the poet had in mind a woman who had abandoned him and disappeared, that he was likening her to that remote moon goddess and wrote these lines in bitterness and longing. I concur. These lines are exactly expressive of my state of mind.

If only she had not drunk the forbidden potion, she would not have had to spend her nights picturing the same human face in fierce yearning!

I yearn. The expression "to want something so much a hand reaches from the throat to grasp it"

Nishioka: Really, this is getting to be . . .

Kishibe: Hang in there, Nishioka.

12

Kishibe: This is the last Chinese poem.[13]Another seven-character quatrain by Li Shangyin, called "Chang'e." I guess Majime really likes his poetry. It means "Chang'e must regret stealing the elixir of life and drinking it/as night after night she casts her gaze from the lonely moon world onto the cold azure seas." It describes extreme loneliness in the void.

must surely refer to what I feel as I burn with great intensity. I yearn for radiance. For beautiful beams of light. And yet for so many years, I never even knew that I lived in total darkness.

This is all I have to say. Or no, this is not all I want to say, but if I tried to say it all, even if I lived 150 years it wouldn't be enough, and I would use up so much paper they would need to cut down every tree in the rain forest, so I will rest my pen here.

I would be very grateful if after reading this you would let me know what you think. Whatever your response, I am prepared. I will take it solemnly to heart.

Do take care of yourself.

To Kaguya Hayashi
from Mitsuya Majime
November 20xx

Nishioka: You know, I have to say, on rereading this thing, it seems to me that Majime is actually being pretty straightforward with his declaration of love. No real curveballs.

Kishibe: You think so? I think it's pretty hard to follow. Plus his calligraphy is just too good. It takes away something, makes this seem like a letter from an old man.

Nishioka: Ouch. Poor Majime.

Kishibe: But in the end he and Kaguya got together, so all's well that ends well.

Nishioka: True. Damn it. Majime, you sly fox! All right, we're through here!

BIBLIOGRAPHY

Dictionaries Cited

Kojien (Wide Garden of Words) and *Iwanami kokugo jiten (Iwanami Japanese Dictionary),* Iwanami Shoten.

Nihonkokugo daijiten (Great Dictionary of the Japanese Language), Shogakukan.

Daijirin (Great Forest of Words) and *Shin meikai kokugo jiten (The New Clear Dictionary of Japanese),* Sanseido.

Daigenkai (Great Sea of Words), Fuzanbo.

References

Kurashima, Tokihisa. *Jisho to Nihongo: Kokugo jiten o kaibou suru (Dictionaries and Japanese: Dissecting Japanese Dictionaries).* Kobunsha Shinsho, 2002.

Matsui, Eiichi. *Deatta Nihongo 50mango: Jishozukuri sandai no kiseki (Encounters with 500,000 Words: Three Generations of Dictionary Making).* Sanseido, 2002.

Ishiyama, Morio. *Urayomi fukayomi kokugo jisho (Reading Between the Lines, Reading Too Much into Things: Japanese Dictionaries).* Soshisha, 2001.

Shibata, Takeshi and Yasushi Muto, eds. *Meikai monogatari (The Story of Meikai Dictionaries).* Sanseido, 2001.

Matsui, Eiichi. *Kokugo jiten wa koshite tsukuru: Riso no jisho o mezashite (This Is How Japanese Dictionaries Are Made: Seeking the Ideal Dictionary).* Minato No Hito, 2005.

Yamada, Toshio. *Nihongo to jisho (Japanese and Dictionaries).* Chuko Shinsho, 1978.

Okimori, Takuya, ed. *Zusetsu Nihon no jisho (Dictionaries of Japan: Illustrated).* Ohfu, 2008.

ACKNOWLEDGMENTS

The author gratefully acknowledges the assistance of the following in the writing of this book. Any deviation from fact in the book, intentional or otherwise, is the author's sole responsibility.

Iwanami Shoten, Dictionary Editorial Department
Shogakukan, Inc., Japanese Dictionary Editing Department
Oji F-Tex Co., Ltd.
Yasunari Hiraki, Yuriko Moriwaki
Hiroshi Sato, Kenichi Matsunaka, Yoshiko Kagawa, Junko Kusumoto, Hisayo Kobayashi
Taro Soma, Satoshi Kusuzawa
Haruko Kumota, Nobuko Okubo
Toru Kato, Hiroo Ito, Hideo Takahashi
Hiroshi Suzuki, Maki Mitsufusa, Kaori Okawa, Tetsuo Fujino

ABOUT THE AUTHOR

Photo © Hiroyuki Matsukage

Shion Miura, the daughter of a well-known Japanese classics scholar, started an online book-review column before she graduated from Waseda University. In 2000, she made her fiction debut with *Kakuto suru mono ni mar* (*A Passing Grade for Those Who Fight*), a novel based in part on her own experiences during her job hunt. In 2006, she won the Naoki Prize for her linked-story collection *Mahoro ekimae Tada Benriken* (*The Handymen in Mahoro Town*). Her other prominent novels include *Kaze ga tsuyoku fuiteiru* (*The Wind Blows Hard*), *Kogure-so monogatari* (*The Kogure Apartments*), and *Ano ie ni kurasu yonin no onna* (*The Four Women Living in That House*). *Fune o amu* (*The Great Passage*) received the Booksellers Award in Japan in 2012 and was developed into a major motion picture. She has also published more than fifteen collections of essays and is a manga aficionado.

ABOUT THE AUTHOR

Photo © [illegible]

Shion Miura, the daughter of a well-known Japanese classics scholar, started an online book-review column before she graduated from Waseda University. In 2000, she made her fiction debut with *Kakuto suru mono ni maru* (*Passing Grade for Those Who Fight*), a novel based in part on her own experience during her job hunt. In 2006, she won the Naoki Prize for her linked-story collection *Mahoro ekimae Tada Benriken* (*The Handymen of Mahoro Station*). Her other prominent novels include *Kaze ga tsuyoku fuiteiru* (*The Wind Blows Hard*), *Kamusari nānā nichijō* (*The Nature of Kamusari*), and *Ano ie ni kurasu yonin no onna* (*The Four Women Living in That House*). *Fune o amu* (*The Great Passage*) received the Booksellers Award in Japan in 2012 and was developed into a major motion picture. She has also published more than fifteen collections of essays and is a manga aficionado.

ABOUT THE TRANSLATOR

Photo © 2014 Toyota Horiguchi

Juliet Winters Carpenter attended the Inter-University Center for Japanese Language Studies in Tokyo. Her first translated book, Kobo Abe's *Mikkai* (*Secret Rendezvous*), received the Japan-US Friendship Commission Prize for the Translation of Japanese Literature. In 2014, more than three decades later, *Honkaku shosetsu* (*A True Novel*), by Minae Mizumura, received the same award, as well as the Lewis Galantière Prize of the American Translators Association. Carpenter's other translations—more than fifty—include nearly every genre of fiction and nonfiction, as well as film subtitles and song lyrics. A professor at Doshisha Women's College of Liberal Arts in Kyoto, Carpenter has lived in Japan since 1975. She's licensed to teach the Japanese instruments koto and shamisen and sings alto in the Kyoto City Philharmonic Chorus. She and her husband divide their time between Kyoto and Whidbey Island, Washington.